The Ripple

A FREEDOM BEND NOVEL

KATHY NEIGHBORS

TIKA
PRESS

"I have experienced God working miracles that you would not believe, and I have also experienced profound grace and peace when the miracles I prayed for did not occur.
Life is this way, and so is our road to Heaven."

Chapter One

WITH EACH TWIST and turn of the road, Margaret felt more desperate. Desperate to get away from the never-ending obligations, the late nights, the interviews, and even her adoring husband. She drove in a daze, clueless that her destination was less about writing a novel and more about saving her life.

With her hands clutching the steering wheel, she breathed a heavy sigh. Her eyes, which had been vacantly staring straight ahead, began to tear up as she considered the enormous burden she was bringing with her. *It wasn't supposed to be this way,* she thought.

Margaret had begun dreaming about this opportunity many years ago. She would often picture herself snuggled up in a cozy cabin with rushing water nearby. Her body and mind would rest in blissful satisfaction as she created a work of literary art with words that could penetrate the soul of every reader.

When Margaret first began writing, it was as if Heaven was dropping each story from the sky. The words flowed, the experience was spiritual and beautiful, and she was indeed changing lives and making a positive impact.

Now, 25 years later, she felt lost and unsure about every aspect of her life. Her dreams had quickly evaporated as she was pulled into the fast-paced life of being a well-known author, mother, and wife. Her joy had been stolen, replaced with fame. She would gladly become a ghostwriter at this point and disappear in the shadows, but it was too late for that.

Her phone rang for the tenth time since she'd left home. She looked at the screen and considered throwing it out of the window, but tossed it in the back seat instead. She took another deep breath and drove a little faster.

I have to get away ...

After almost three hours on the road, the picturesque North Georgia town appeared in the distance like a mirage. The short, narrow main street housed various local businesses that seemed to be frozen in time.

There was an old-fashioned barber shop with a traditional barber pole twisting in the afternoon sun and a florist with window boxes full of bright yellow flowers. The open door of a bakery filled the air with the wonderful aroma of fresh bread while travelers passing through enjoyed lunch at a charming café with single sunflowers adorning each pansy purple outdoor table.

Margaret slowed her vehicle to a complete stop, allowing a young mother and two little boys to cross the street. The youngest boy locked eyes with Margaret. He waved and gave her a tender smile. Margaret smiled back. "This place doesn't even seem real," she whispered, shaking her head as she thought of her urban hometown, complete with traffic jams and sirens that wailed day and night.

Margaret exhaled long and slow and began scanning for her next turn. Her hands became clammy, and her heart quickened as she turned off Main Street.

I am almost there ...

Her anxiety grew at the thought of being alone with her shame and guilt. Several months ago, she would have been over-joyed to spend the summer writing in the mountains, but that was before she betrayed her family, her readers, and God.

After a couple of miles, the road narrowed, and the pavement ended.

"You have arrived at your destination," the navigation system reported. Margaret spotted the mailbox that read 924 Willow Springs Drive. Tall river birch trees lined both sides of the driveway and seemed to be welcoming her as sunlight illuminated the well-worn path. She pulled into the driveway and stopped. With her foot still on the brake, she began to weep.

Margaret sat at the top of the driveway.

Hands still clutching the steering wheel.

Head throbbing.

Unsure of what lay ahead.

Her mind was racing as she considered every reason not to continue down the driveway.

I should have told Mitch everything before I left.

I wonder if I can get out of the contract.

Will my boys understand why I lied to them?

She felt the darkness close in. She looked out of the windshield, taking shallow breaths.

"I don't deserve to be here. I'm sick of living a lie." Margaret's words faded to nothing in the sticky, southern heat.

Quitting now would be exactly what the world would expect. Perhaps her life imploding would finally give her critics something exciting to report.

With her hands shaking, she shifted into reverse to head home, giving in to the voices in her head. *You are a failure and a fake.*

Margaret released the brake, and a gentle breeze began blowing through the open windows. The soft wind calmed her senses, and her mind became quiet for a moment.

The breeze intensified and surrounded her from all sides. She looked around for suspicious weather and saw only a blue sky.

Then she heard a tiny whisper within her soul.

Keep going.

She sat motionless for a couple of minutes, listening again for that still, small voice.

Keep going.

Keep going.

With faith as her accelerator, Margaret slowly shifted into drive. As much as she wanted to give up, that gentle nudge within her soul was just enough to keep her moving forward.

The tall trees created a perfect canopy and ushered her deeper into the property. Her eyes, still wet with tears, could not believe the beauty she encountered when the meandering driveway ended.

A quaint cabin was perfectly positioned in the middle of what she imagined the Garden of Eden would have looked like. Everything her eyes beheld was beautiful. She parked, got out, and began stretching her tired body while breathing fresh air into her lungs.

She unloaded her belongings, quickly realizing she had over-packed, but even with her life falling apart, Margaret was the consummate organizer; it was both a blessing and a curse. Once inside the cabin, her first thought was to get settled, but that felt too daunting. She decided to take a walk outside instead. A rock pathway led through the forest and down to a bubbling creek. She kicked off her flip-flops and tiptoed into the cold water.

Her phone began to ring in her back pocket; it was her new literary agent. She ignored the call and looked up, watching the sun flicker through the trees. She walked through the shallow water and sat on a large rock. She began replaying the last several months over and over in her mind.

"I never should have signed that contract," she told herself while watching the shadows of the trees dance upon the water. Margaret closed her eyes, remembering her family's concern when they discussed the newest publishing proposal.

If only I had listened.

She pulled her knees to her chest and allowed the tears to

escape. The memories began spinning like a fast-moving carousel. Margaret's mind returned to a year ago when she sat at a long, cold boardroom table with her agent, Tom. She could almost hear his devious voice as he persuaded her to sign the new contract.

She could picture her husband, Mitch, standing in the doorway when she got home that night and the ensuing fight. She could hear the words she had yelled that still haunted her to this day, "I don't need you telling me how to handle my career."

She recalled the look on Mitch's face and how it felt to watch him walk away.

I should have told him the truth, echoed in her soul.

The betrayal never left her—the lies she told her husband, the lies she told her boys; the lies she told herself were perhaps the hardest part of all because she could no longer trust herself.

Several minutes passed as the anguish continued to flow. The images of Mitch and her boys faded when her phone began ringing again. "Of course, I can't get one minute of peace," she yelled in frustration, fumbling to push the off button. A glance showed her it was her husband. She ignored the call.

Twenty seconds later, the voicemail alert chimed. Hesitantly, she listened to Mitch's short but impactful message. "Margaret, please call me. I just got a message from Tom. You need to explain what is going on."

Oh no. He knows. The guilt fell on her like a boulder.

Margaret stared at the screen, unsure what to do. Before she could decide, her phone rang again, and this time it was Tom. Almost a full minute later, his voicemail arrived.

"Hi, love. I wanted to let you know that the announcement about the series and book tour went live today! Hooray for us! Congratulations on stepping out of your old, tired writing style. I sent Mitch a congratulations, too. Call me as soon as possible. The path to success is wide open for you!"

Margaret hung her head. *I am such a fool.*

She made her way back to the cabin and found the nearest

bed. She swallowed a sleeping pill and then buried herself under the thick quilt. She fell into a deep sleep, not hearing the ceaseless ringing of her phone.

Chapter Two

MARGARET WOKE the next morning feeling groggy and unsure of her surroundings. She looked around the bedroom, rubbing her eyes as the previous day's reality flooded her mind.

In the distance, she heard her phone ringing. Her heart began to thump against her chest.

That's probably Mitch.

Ring. Ring. Ring.

She shimmed back under the quilt, noticing how every muscle in her body ached. Her head felt as if it was going to explode, and her stomach rumbled deep within.

Several minutes passed before Margaret emerged from the warmth of the bed and walked to the bathroom. She stepped into the shower and turned the water as hot as it would go. The water ran down her tired body until it eventually went lukewarm and then cold. It was as if she were trying to wash away her burdens. One by one, she ran each problem around in her mind.

I wonder if this is the final straw for Mitch?

I wonder if our boys know that I lied to them?

I wonder if my fans will like the new book?

Margaret began to shake, and her eyes became blurry.

"My family deserves so much better than me ..." Her words bounced off the hard tiles as she reached for the shower handle.

With chill bumps from head to toe, Margaret stepped out of the large glass enclosure and grabbed the nearby robe. She made her way to the family room and positioned herself in the corner of the sectional sofa. She wrapped herself in a blanket and stared out of the windows, feeling utterly empty.

Birds fluttered about and a chipmunk scurried across the deck, but she sat motionless, her mind racing and her body tense.

Her phone, which she had thrown onto the couch the evening before, lay only inches from where she sat. With a heavy sigh, she reached for it. Her heart dropped when she looked at the screen. Twelve missed calls and four voicemails.

The first voicemail was from Mitch. "Call me! We need to talk."

Margaret held the phone in her trembling hand and felt the blood rush to her belly. Sweat gathered on her forehead.

The next voicemail was from her agent. "Hi, love! I wanted to let you know that we have to take a quick trip to Tampa. I realize this will cut into your little retreat, but I'm sure you understand. I'm finalizing the arrangements now. I have also sent over an email regarding an issue with your contract that we need to take care of. Let's chat soon."

Margaret closed her eyes, feeling nauseous at the sound of Tom's cheery voice.

The third message tore at Margaret's heartstrings the most. It was from her older son, Matthew. "Mom, please answer your phone. We are worried about you." She shook her head, absorbing the full weight of what felt like a lifetime of bad decisions.

Margaret held her breath as the last voicemail from Mitch sounded in her ear, "I can't believe you don't even have the decency to call and let us know that you are okay. I am heading to the cabin if I don't hear from you by 9 a.m."

Margaret looked at her phone. The time read 8:51 a.m.

With her hands quivering, she pulled up Mitch's number.

He answered on the first ring in a stern voice, "Hello?"

"Mitch, honey, I'm sorry ... I was just so tired. I fell asleep and I didn't hear my phone. I didn't mean to worry you and the boys."

"Okay."

She listened for more.

Words of forgiveness, affirmations that it would be okay.

Something.

Anything.

"Mitch, I know you didn't want me to sign the contract, but is it really that big of a deal?" Margaret squeezed her eyes tight, unsure why she'd even spoken those words.

"Are you serious? You would think after the thousands of dollars we have spent in counseling, you would understand why it's a big deal."

"I'm sorry, I shouldn't have said it like that." She lowered her head, feeling the tension in her neck muscles pull tight.

"When Ernie retired, that was the perfect opportunity for you to slow down. The boys only have a couple of years left before they're completely out on their own. Their entire lives have revolved around a deadline or a book tour. You promised us things would change."

"I know," she said, her voice just above a whisper.

"But instead of you slowing down, you started working with Tom, which none of us thought was a good idea. And then, you go and sign a four-book contract and you step away from the Christian content you've always written. It just doesn't make sense to me."

Margaret paused, searching for the right words. "The boys are so busy with college, and you've got so much going on, I didn't think it would matter."

"Really? Is that what you really think?"

Margaret began rubbing her left temple. "I don't even know what I think at this point."

"Even when Ernie was your agent, you had a hard time balancing work and our family life, but now that you have signed with Tom, it's like you have forgotten you even have a family. You are a completely different person."

"How can you say that?" Her pulse quickened as heat rose into her face.

"I suggest you look back over your calendar to see where you have spent your time these last several months and go ahead and check your screen time while you're at it."

"What? Why are you being so mean?" Tears began rolling down Margaret's face.

"I am not trying to be mean, but you spend more time in front of your computer and on the phone than you do with us. And if I thought you were happy, it might be worth it, but from what I can tell, you are far from happy."

Margaret swallowed hard, feeling his words penetrate the façade she had created.

"We always manage to get through these difficult times, God knows we've had enough of them, but after this contract is complete, you're going to look back and realize you missed a part of our family life that you'll never get back. I'm honestly exhausted with your career and all the chaos it brings."

Silence.

"I just don't understand why the life we built isn't enough," Mitch added.

Margaret felt desperation close in. "It is enough. I want you to try and understand that I did this for us. This opportunity is the most lucrative of my career. We will be set for retirement," she pleaded.

As she spoke the words, her soul whispered, *Oh Margaret, you know it's not about the money.*

"Okay, whatever you say," Mitch responded, sounding sarcastic. "You know what? I'm glad that I surprised you with the cabin rental for the summer. Wasn't that always your dream? A summer writing in the mountains by a creek."

The guilt felt as if it would strangle her. "Yes," she murmured.

Mitch shook his head. "Well, I hope and pray that you are able to use this time to figure out what really matters in your life."

Both lapsed into silence, listening to the other breathe.

"Margaret, I love you, but it feels like you have been bought. And ... I never realized you were for sale."

She shifted on the sofa, "I don't know what to say."

He exhaled forcefully, "Enjoy your time away."

He ended the call. It was the first time in 25 years that Mitch had hung up without telling his wife goodbye.

The full weight of her deception and selfishness pressed hard into her soul. She slumped into the pillows. *No amount of money is worth this feeling,* she thought.

Margaret spent the rest of the morning disgusted with herself. She paced the cabin back and forth, hoping to summon the courage to call her son back. The courage never surfaced. She took her phone and stared through the tears, scanning for his number. His photo popped up when she hit his contact information. The picture was from his recent high-school graduation that she'd missed because of a delayed flight.

A tear fell to the screen. She typed three simple words.

- I am sorry.

His immediate response shattered her already broken heart.

- I thought you decided against signing the new contract with Tom.

Her heart sank. *Why don't they understand? I just wanted to help our family.*

She paused. *That is a lie, and you know it. You did this for yourself and your pride.*

Surprised by these thoughts, she crumbled to the floor. *I didn't mean to hurt them, but I knew I would.*

Margaret felt every ounce of hope leave her body. "Oh God, what have I done?"

She typed a reply through her tears.

- I will do my best to be there for you guys. I promise.

Margaret leaned against the wall in the kitchen, steadying herself.

Matthew responded with a simple one-word text.

- Okay.

She sat on the wood floor, feeling the hardness of the planks as the beveled edge of the cabinet pressed into her sore back. She began coughing. Acid rose in her throat and chill bumps covered her entire body. "I can't believe how awful I feel."

She looked up, desperately wanting the emotional and physical pain to subside. She swallowed hard, jumping when her phone began to ring. She fervently hoped it was Mitch or Matthew, calling back with a peace offering.

She glanced at the screen and saw Tom's name. She silenced her phone and walked to the refrigerator. She opened the door. Cold air began spilling onto her face. She surveyed the food she had thrown onto the shelves from her cooler, none of which looked the least bit appetizing. She stared vacantly until the refrigerator door alarm jolted her back to the present. She shook her head, got dressed, and grabbed her leather satchel, slamming the door on her way out of the cabin.

MARGARET REACHED THE BLUEBIRD CAFE BETWEEN the breakfast and lunch crowds. The bright lights and unfamiliar staring faces made her want to turn around, walk out, and never look back, but the hunger gnawing in her gut urged her to stay. She settled into a corner booth with her back against the wall, head down.

A young lady, who looked to be just a bit older than Margaret's boys, approached with a mason jar full of ice water, a patriotic napkin, and spotless silverware. The pretty waitress carefully laid down each item in the perfect position.

"Hi, I'm Sally. I haven't seen you in here before. Are you just passing through, maybe headed somewhere fun?"

Margaret exhaled with frustration, not wanting to engage. The waitress didn't break her gaze or her smile and stood patiently waiting for a response. Margaret shifted in the booth, speaking just above a whisper. "Actually, I will be in town for a few weeks, if I can get some things settled at home."

"Oh, that's great. We are open seven to seven, so feel free to join us anytime. And, just so you know, the apple pie is a local favorite."

Margaret placed her order and buried her head in her journal, silently pleading for direction. Her hand hovered over the creamy beige page with her expensive writing pen gripped tightly. With glassy eyes, she stared down as the smell of bacon and coffee filled the air. A nearby speaker softly played a local Christian radio station while an older woman sang along two booths over.

Several minutes later, Sally reappeared with a plate full of southern breakfast fare. She didn't seem to notice Margaret's bleak emotional state. "What brings you to our little town, if you don't mind me asking?"

Margaret swallowed hard, feeling a lump in her throat. "I'm here to work on a book. I write Christian novels." She paused, looking down at her journal. "At least I used to ... I am in a bit of a transitional period."

"Oh, wow. It must be so cool to be a writer. I used to love to write ... of course, that was a few years ago," Sally's smile faded as she poured Margaret's coffee and waved goodbye to the last of the locals shuffling out of the cafe.

Margaret had planned on saying as little as possible while at the cafe, but Sally was so kind and curious that Margaret dismissed her depressive thoughts and embraced the childlike wonder of the young waitress.

The quiet, empty space gave way to an hour-long conversation about writing and small-town living. As Margaret walked toward the door on her way out, she felt a gentle nudge within her soul. *Give that sweet girl your journal.*

Margaret reached for the door and then hesitated. She turned around and walked back to Sally. "I know this may seem strange, but I have this journal that I haven't written in yet, and I thought perhaps you might enjoy it."

"Oh my, it's beautiful," Sally rubbed the soft leather cover with her hand. "Thank you so much. I don't think anyone has ever given me a gift for no reason."

"I know we've just met, but I can tell you have so much to offer the world. Maybe this will inspire you to begin writing again."

"Thank you, Mrs. Margaret. I don't know what to say," Sally blushed.

"You don't need to say anything. Enjoy."

Sally pulled the journal to her chest. "I really love it." She leaned forward and hugged Margaret, who smiled, knowing that the gentle nudge was right once again.

Neither of the ladies knew what a glorious encounter had just taken place, but God knew, and He began working.

Chapter Three

MARGARET COULDN'T STAND the thought of how much she had hurt her family. She tossed and turned all night, replaying the loop of her betrayal over and over in her mind. At daybreak, she decided to call Mitch. She reached onto the nightstand and picked up her phone.

She paused, feeling nervous and unsure. She inhaled a deep breath and scanned for his name. She hit dial and said a silent prayer that he would answer.

No answer.

She hit end and tried again. This time, he answered on the first ring.

"Yes, Margaret, what do you want?"

"Mitch, I am just sick over all of this. I don't know what I was thinking. Ernie never put me in these situations, and I guess for some reason, I believed Tom. I feel so stupid and selfish. I should have listened to you and the boys."

She sat silent, unsure of what to say next.

His voice was strong and direct. "Listen to me. The enemy has you by the throat. I could feel it before you left. You just weren't yourself. I was hoping I was wrong and that you wouldn't get coerced into signing up for three or four years of obligations that aren't even in line with who you are, but I must admit I wasn't surprised when I got Tom's text."

"Oh, Mitch, I am so sorry," Margaret began wringing her hands as she paced in the kitchen.

"I know you never intend to get into these situations, but time after time, you do. I wish I could just forget the whole thing and move on, but we have a long history of you making careless decisions that hurt yourself and our family."

"I know, I don't know what is wrong with me." She stared straight ahead, thinking *there is nothing I can say to fix this.*

"I've had a rough morning already, let's talk sometime next week. You have a book to write, and I have an organization to run. What's done is done." He ended the call.

Margaret walked to the family room in what felt like a trance. She looked around the cabin, which was supposed to be home for the next three months, and felt more alone than she had ever felt. She desperately wanted to call Mitch back, but she knew that would only make matters worse.

Deep in her soul, she recalled the words her grandmother spoke when she first met Mitch and she was unsure of his feelings toward her. *"Give him time, honey."*

Margaret looked out of the large windows and watched the clouds roll by. "Oh, Grammy, I wish you were still here. I could use some front porch time to hash things out. I really screwed up this time."

Margaret closed her eyes and thought back to her childhood and the long, slow summers on her grandparents' farm.

The tall pasture grass blowing in the wind.

The brilliant sun's rays filling the sky with hues of red and orange each morning and evening.

Grammy standing in the kitchen for hours, whipping up delicious, fresh food from the garden.

And then there was Margaret, the only girl in a family full of boys and men.

Dancing in muddy rain puddles, chasing butterflies, and dreaming about life beyond the county line ...

Tears began to gently roll down Margaret's face. She stood and began walking around the cabin to try and rid her mind of any remaining thoughts about those she once held so near to her heart.

She walked through the main entryway, stumbling over a pile of her belongings that she had not moved since she arrived.

"What a mess I've made of this beautiful place."

She stepped around the piles and rummaged through the cosmetic bag that was full of meaningless items. She found her bottle of ibuprofen and grabbed two, along with several antacids. She gulped them down with a glass of water, feeling her stomach rumble from emptiness. Her heart felt as if it was going to break into a thousand pieces or burn to ash.

"The biggest mess I have created is what I have done to myself." Margaret's words seemed lost in the stillness of the moment. She leaned into the pain, feeling her light grow dimmer and dimmer. She stood still for several moments hoping to feel some type of reassurance stir within. The silence was more than she could bear. She picked up her satchel and headed for town. Perhaps another visit to the cafe would nourish her body and spirit once again.

THE JINGLE BELL RANG AGAINST THE CAFE DOOR AND Margaret was greeted by Sally, who was, once again, all smiles. Margaret ordered the same items as the previous day and quickly drank her first cup of coffee. She sat quietly and watched Sally interact with the locals and the other waitresses. She found herself envious of Sally's simple life and her simple job in such a simple town. It had been decades since Margaret's life had been simple.

Margaret's gaze was broken when Sally walked to the table

and laid down her hearty breakfast. "How are you enjoying our little town?"

"It seems nice. Although, I haven't been anywhere but here and the cabin."

"Oh, are you staying in a cabin?"

"Yes, my husband leased a cabin only a couple of miles from here. I guess someone recently bought and renovated it. I am the first person to stay there since the work was completed, at least that's what the leasing agent said. My husband set it all up as a surprise for me." Margaret diverted her eyes when she mentioned Mitch.

"If you don't mind me asking, are you talking about the cabin at the end of Willow Springs Drive?"

"That's the one. Are you familiar with it?"

"Yes! That was Joseph's cabin. He was the nicest man in the whole town. He was like a grandfather to me. I heard some lady from the city bought it. I haven't been there since Joseph passed away."

"It does feel like a very special place. Let me know if you want to drop by sometime and see the updated version," Margaret suggested.

"Oh, my goodness, I would love that."

"I obviously don't know what is new and what was already there, but it is certainly lovely."

"Thank you. I really appreciate you offering to let me come over," Sally beamed with excitement.

After eating, Margaret paid her bill and walked to the door, looking back at Sally who was already clearing the table. They exchanged a smile.

Margaret stepped onto the sidewalk, noticing the warmth of the sunshine and the sound of the train whistle on the other side of town. She looked straight ahead watching a couple walk hand in hand. The young woman squeezed the young man's hand, and they stopped for a moment. He leaned down and gave her a soft kiss. The world seemed to stop for them as they held each other tight.

Margaret's heart sank in her chest as she witnessed what would have normally been inspiration for a future story. *Young woman and young man find love in a small town in the mountains.* Instead, she felt a surge of guilt and loneliness, combined with the feeling that her career as she knew it was over.

WHEN MARGARET ARRIVED BACK AT THE CABIN SHE reluctantly decided to deal with Tom. She pulled up his number, hit dial, and held her breath, hoping he wouldn't answer. She heard his familiar, yet sharp voice on the first ring.

"Margaret, dear, finally we connect! How have you been, love?"

"Uh, I'm doing okay. Just busy. I know that you have been wanting me to call. What do you need?"

"First, we must finalize your trip to Tampa for the writing conference. Some of the higher-ups want you there and they will not take no for an answer. I sent you the itinerary. Did you see that email?"

"No. I haven't read through my emails in a while. What are the dates?"

"June 13 through 16, and two weeks later, we need you to be available for a couple of days to do some interviews. I'll know those exact dates soon. How's the cabin? Do you love it?"

She rolled her eyes and clenched her jaw. "Those first dates won't work. It's my son's 21st birthday and we made plans to be together weeks ago. I can't back out on my family. I have missed too many birthdays over the last several years and right now is definitely not a good time to skip out on them."

"I understand, love. I'm sorry, but we don't really have a choice. The contract you signed is pretty clear about this sort of thing. We have already purchased the airline tickets and we got you a suite at that hotel you like. Cheer up, it will be great fun. I'm sure your son will understand."

And so, it begins. Mitch was right. I have been bought.

She closed her eyes, feeling the room spin. "I have to go, Tom."

"But wait, I need to tell you about ..."

She hit end and scrolled until she found her attorney's number. *There must be a way to get out of this contract.*

Margaret kicked off her shoes, chewed four antacids, and waited for the beep to sound before leaving a message for John, her attorney and long-time friend.

"John, I need your help. I'm going to send you a quick email with details about the mess I've gotten myself in. Please call me back at your earliest convenience."

She took her laptop to the back deck overlooking the creek and began typing.

John,

I am sorry to bother you, but I have a real problem. As you know, my long-time literary agent, Ernie, retired last year. When I signed with the new agent, Tom, he positioned me with a new publisher. It's a long story, but essentially, it's not a good fit. I hate everything about the new arrangement, but I already signed the contract. What can I do?

Margaret

She laid her laptop on a nearby table and stood. Her mind raced as she considered all that was at stake if she terminated the contract, but, more importantly, she considered the full impact of seeing it through.

She was aware that, although John was a great attorney, the publishing company had more legal power behind them. She also didn't want to commit professional suicide by not honoring her word.

It's a lose-lose at this point, she thought as a squirrel hopped onto the deck railing.

"Maybe I should just write the stupid books," she said out

loud as if she was speaking to her fluffy-tailed friend that was squeaking a message back to her.

She watched the squirrel take one giant leap between two tall trees. Leaves rustled and floated to the ground. *If only I could be so carefree.*

The squirrel scurried out of sight, leaving Margaret alone with her thoughts.

"Yes, that's what I should do. I'll just write the books, and when the money is rolling in, Mitch and the boys will eventually come around," she proclaimed with false pride.

She picked up her laptop, closed out her emails, and switched into her writing program. Her fingers tapped on the keyboard without a single letter being typed.

The blinking cursor flashed on the blank screen. Her headache and nausea intensified. Inspiration was nowhere to be found.

She typed five words: *You are such an idiot.*

MARGARET SPENT THE ENTIRE DAY WAITING FOR JOHN to return her call. At 4:58 p.m., her phone rang, and by 5:00, the call had ended. John's words felt like daggers in her ears.

"I'm really sorry, Margaret, but if you have already signed the contract and accepted the first installment of the advance, I am afraid your best option is to honor your commitment."

Margaret stood in the kitchen and briefly considered calling Mitch. For years, he had been her safe place and best friend. He was the reassuring voice she needed when doubts pressed hard. But not anymore. She had ruined all of that. She thought back to the last time they talked. His parting words tore through her soul. "What's done is done ..."

Chapter Four

MARGARET ENDURED ANOTHER SLEEPLESS NIGHT. Stress and endless mind-chatter were consuming her from the inside out. Words for the novel she was supposed to be working on continued to elude her. The obligation to create a story that would please Tom and the new publishing team seemed like an insurmountable task.

Her mind wandered back to the brainstorming session she had had with Tom when they first became acquainted. 'You are such a great writer, Margaret, but I need to be honest with you, your writing is a bit old-fashioned. I'm afraid your age is showing through your storytelling. You don't want to appear old and outdated, do you, Margaret?'

She felt a chill go up her spine. *How could I have been so gullible?*

She threw back the quilt and made her way to the kitchen to drown her emotions with strong coffee and sugar. She took her espresso and a pastry to the back deck. She pondered calling John once again to beg him to find a way out of the contract. With her finger resting above his name, her phone lit up. It was Matthew, and as much as she wanted to hear her son's voice, she found she couldn't answer.

She held the phone close to her chest and felt her heart thumping against the hard case.

She closed her eyes as the phone vibrated with an incoming voicemail. "Hey, Mom, maybe you should call Dad. He seems really mad about the contract."

Margaret stared at her phone. Sweet Matthew was often the glue that held her heart together. She rubbed her left temple, which was pulsing against her forehead. She wanted to call her son and apologize and beg for forgiveness. She stared into the screen. Hesitation pressed in. She paused, then laid down her phone and walked away. *Call him*, her soul begged.

"I can't," she whispered into the desolate forest.

After several minutes, she walked back to her phone, feeling her heart rate increase with each step. She pulled up his name and began typing.

- I promise I will try and make this right. I hope classes are going well. I love you.

MARGARET'S TEXT LIT UP MATTHEW'S SMALL DORM room. He sat at his desk and turned on the lamp. He sighed as he read the words.

"Oh Mom, how do you get yourself into these situations?" he said, frowning. He laid his phone back on his desk and began working on his assignments. His fingers raced across the keyboard. He typed a few paragraphs and then stopped. He glanced back at his phone. He reread his mom's text and began typing a reply.

- I tried to talk to Luke today about the contract. He didn't want to talk about it. I hope this all smooths out before we come to the cabin for his birthday.

- I'm working on it. I'm so sorry, buddy. I love you.

- Okay, Mom. I know this is hard for you. Love you too.

MARGARET SIGHED, GRABBING HER HAIR WITH BOTH hands. Her head was throbbing. Things were getting more complicated by the hour. She had to figure out a way to be available for Luke's birthday. Mitch would never forgive her if she were in Tampa instead of with her family.

Thoughts swirled through her mind. *I can't be in two places at the same time, but maybe I can make it work. Maybe I can be in and out of Tampa in a day or two.*

Margaret opened her laptop and was surprised to see an email from Mitch. Her heart sank when she read his short message.

I thought you might find these early reviews of your most recent book interesting. I am praying you find your way back.

Mitch

Attached were several reviews from readers who were part of the early promotional period of her first novel in the new market.

- What a huge disappointment. Did Margaret Taylor really write this?

- I have spent the last two decades counting on Margaret to inspire me with her beautiful stories, this one missed the mark. Read more like a soap opera.

- I usually buy several copies of Margaret's books for my ladies' book club. We love a story that inspires. I'm not sure what happened. Sadly, this is a pass for us.

Margaret gasped. She reread the reviews several times. She screamed in anguish, but there were no tears this time. The crushing weight of the denial of her God-given gift consumed her. The enemy had won this battle, but the war was far from over.

Margaret grabbed her phone and found John's number. It was nothing short of a miracle when he answered his cell phone on the third ring.

"Hello."

"I'm sorry to call again, but I can't do this. I cannot and will not stay committed to writing this series as I promised. You have to help me get out of this contract. What can we do?'

"Margaret, are you okay?"

"No, John, I am not okay! I have been trying to pretend I can do this, but I can't. God called me to write, not just write, but write for Him. I sold out. I have destroyed my reputation. My family no longer trusts me, and worst of all, I have denied God and who He created me to be. John, you know me, I am not some perfect Christian, but writing is my calling, it is my gift. I can't do what they want me to do," Margaret began to sob.

"Please, calm down. We will figure out something. For now, just stay the course and let me work behind the scenes and see what I can do."

Through the tears, she whispered, "Okay,"

"Margaret, I have to tell you, getting you out of this contract may cost you a lot financially."

"The decision to sign that contract has already cost me too much, John. I don't care about the money. I just want out."

Margaret felt miserable both physically and mentally. John had promised that he would do his best to help her, but he was working on a case that required his full attention. So, she quietly and patiently waited for instructions on how to proceed.

Still wearing yesterday's clothes, Margaret grabbed her keys and headed out as the sun continued rising above the tall trees. With no motivation to prepare her own food, the cafe was her saving grace.

MARGARET WAS MET AT THE CORNER BOOTH BY SALLY, who was grinning from ear to ear.

"Guess what?"

"What?" Margaret said, envious of Sally's obvious joy.

"Mrs. Betty, the owner of the cafe, just told me that she is going to give me tomorrow off with pay."

"That's great. I guess all your hard work is paying off."

"Actually, tomorrow is my ten-year anniversary working for Mrs. Betty, so this is her way of thanking me."

"Wow, ten years; that's a really long time."

"I know, I never thought I would be here this long. I guess I kinda got stuck." Sally filled the sugar dispenser and shifted her eyes.

Margaret noticed the change in Sally's demeanor. "I am sure you have been a tremendous blessing to the cafe during those ten years. I know you are the best server I've ever had."

"Thanks, that really means a lot," Sally's face brightened as she poured Margaret a fresh cup of coffee.

"What are you going to do with your special day off?"

"Gosh, I don't know."

"I wouldn't mind some company at the cabin, if you want to come check it out."

"That would be amazing! Are you sure you don't mind? I know you have a lot going on, and I don't want to interfere with your book."

"I am in the process of waiting some things out, so it would be nice to have company and forget about the book for a few hours."

"Oh my goodness, thank you so much." Sally grabbed a napkin and jotted down her number. "Just text me and let me know what time is good for you. Other than helping my parents on the farm early in the morning, I will be free all day."

Margaret took Sally's number and smiled at the thought of how God continued to work, even in her darkest hours.

By the time Margaret got back to the cabin, she felt exhausted. She looked around and thought about cleaning up in preparation for Sally's visit, but decided to lie down instead. *How can I be this tired? It's not even 9 a.m.*

She shook her head, disgusted with herself, and kicked off her shoes. She threw her things on the kitchen counter and made her way to the sofa, burying herself in the pillows and blankets.

Her heavy eyes watched a cardinal hop around on the outdoor table, while its mate flitted about. They seemed so content and happy. She thought of Mitch and how he had always been by her side, even when she was flitting about. Her heart ached from loneliness. She lay there watching the birds until she couldn't fight the exhaustion any longer.

An hour later, Margaret's phone startled her awake. She squinted at the screen and saw that it was John. Her heart quickened. She sat up and answered with a scratchy, "Hello."

"Hi Margaret, I'm sorry if I woke you."

"It's okay. I'm glad you called. I hope you have good news for me."

"Actually, I need to review the actual contract you signed before I can give you any real feedback. I have time to do that later today, and then we will know what we are dealing with."

Margaret's heart sank when she realized John had not even begun the process of terminating her obligations.

"I don't even know where my copy is. I probably filed it in my home office, but I'm not sure. I'm sorry, it has been a rough few months."

"Okay, check and then get back with me. I really need the contract to be able to go forward."

They both fell into silence. Her mind raced, trying to recall the details of signing the lengthy document.

She remembered feeling horrible when she met Tom and the publishing team without Mitch's knowledge. They were very persuasive, and if she was being honest, she knew Mitch wouldn't agree to the terms. So, she decided to ask for his forgiveness instead of his blessing.

The days that followed that meeting never seemed to lend themselves to Margaret owning her mistake. Her courage failed as she realized she had signed away her purpose and passion in life, along with the freedom to be fully available to her family.

The guilt suffocated her words, and she became increasingly disengaged. When Mitch surprised her with the lease of the cabin for the summer, the truth was on the tip of her tongue, but she couldn't bring herself to tell him.

Margaret inhaled a deep breath, trying to bring herself back to the present moment. Her heart pounded against her chest as she tried to recall where she would have placed the contract. "I just thought of something. I know they emailed the contract for me to review before I signed it. I probably still have that old email that I can forward you." Margaret felt her face flush, knowing that she hadn't thoroughly read either copy.

"That's definitely a good start. I will still need you to find the original and get it to me in the event they made any changes. In the meantime, I will look at what you've got."

"I will forward that as soon as we hang up. I'm sorry to have brought you into this mess. I should've had you look at the contract before I signed it, or, better yet, I should have never even considered it. I am really sorry."

"It's okay. Different seasons of life bring about different opportunities and setbacks. I will do everything I can. Let's touch base tomorrow."

Margaret hung up and began searching her old emails. She found the email he needed, forwarded it, and fell back to sleep.

Margaret slept for another restless hour then was once again awakened by her phone, this time, it was Tom. She ignored the call and shuffled to the shower instead. As the hot water relaxed her tense muscles, she began thinking through her decision-making over the years.

Margaret began recalling every mistake that had led her to this place of isolation and desperation. The broken promises, the missed experiences, and the half-hearted way that she lived when things got hard.

I always screw things up.

She leaned against the wall of the shower. Her body felt heavy, and her mind raced with negative thoughts. The water ran cold as her hope washed down the drain.

She got out of the shower and bundled up in the cozy robe

that had been left for her and a pair of Mitch's thick hiking socks that she had claimed years ago. She longed to tell Mitch that she was trying to get out of the contract, but it all felt too uncertain at this point.

She sat on the edge of the bed with her laptop and begrudgingly logged into her social media accounts. Her mouth dropped and her eyes widened when she began to read more feedback from her previously joyful community of readers. Her devoted audience was not shy about sharing their feelings of the advance copies, which they had received in exchange for an honest review.

- *Another Christian author sells out.*

- *I guess Margaret lost her faith somewhere along the way.*

- *This was the most disheartening book I have read in a long time.*

Margaret had been accustomed to less than favorable reviews throughout her career, but these comments dismantled the alter ego she had tried to create.

She closed her laptop, shuffled into the kitchen, and took two more ibuprofen while refilling her coffee mug. Her phone lit up with an incoming email from Tom. She swiped out of the notification and began rummaging through one of her bags that was still sitting in the middle of the kitchen floor. Her hand felt around until it brushed against the soft leather cover of a new journal. She made her way to the back deck and began doing the only thing she knew to do: pour her soul out on paper.

~

~Margaret's Journal~

I wanted to be more relevant as an author. I wanted my writing to be seen by more people. I wanted to please the new publishing team. I wanted to feel young and alive again.

In an act of desperation and confusion, I have squandered and sold my gift of writing. I dishonored my readers by selling out and stepping away from the stories they loved and expected. I dishonored my body, my mind, and my spirit by avoiding the very things I need to do to care for myself. I dishonored Mitch and my boys by being dishonest as I chased my selfish ambitions. But most of all, I dishonored God by turning my back on His plan for my life. Trying to become someone I am not has ripped me apart at the seams and everything I once held dear is gone.

Chapter Five

THE NEXT MORNING, thunder boomed in the distance as Margaret paced around the cabin waiting for a call from John. At 10 a.m., her phone rang, and it was John's office number.

"Hey, John, so how does it look?" she answered with panic in her voice.

"Hello, Margaret. This is Jenna, John's assistant. John had a bit of a business emergency come up, but he wanted to let you know that he sent you an email a few minutes ago. He will be available later in the day if you would like to discuss his findings."

"Oh ... okay. Thank you."

Margaret rushed to her laptop, held her breath, and began to read.

Margaret,

I am sorry to inform you that the contract you signed is going to be very difficult for you to terminate. I am not saying it's impossible, but I believe it would do you more harm than good to pursue termination. I understand your desire to sever ties with the publishing team and your agent, but you did sign a legal contract that binds you to continue with the three remaining books and the promotional obligations.

The only loopholes would be if the contract you signed is

different from the unsigned copy you sent me, although it most likely isn't. Another viable option for termination would be if you had refused the advance. I am truly sorry; I know this isn't the news you were hoping for. Feel free to call me this evening or tomorrow.

John

Margaret stared at the screen, unsure what to think. John was a good friend and a great attorney, so if he didn't advise moving forward with termination of the contract, she had no choice but to trust him.

As her gaze deepened, her phone began to ring. It was Tom. She ignored the call and closed her laptop. She sat down at the kitchen bar and leaned forward, resting her head on her folded arms. She jumped when the voicemail chimed in the quiet cabin. She played the message.

"Hi, love! I'm sure you are busy working your magic with book two. I can't wait to hear all about it. I hope you are packing your bags and getting ready for sunny Tampa. I will arrive the day before, so I will have everything perfect for you. Call me."

Margaret had never felt so burdened as a writer. She only had 1,100 words written for the second novel she had promised, and those words were superficial at best.

I guess I have been bought after all.

Margaret read John's email three more times. Her mind and body went into pure survival mode. Her depression shifted into anger and false confidence as she tried to convince herself that she could handle the chaotic mess she had created.

"Mitch and the boys need to get over it. I did this for them." Her face hardened, and her breathing became quick and shallow with each forced word she said aloud. In the deepest part of who she was, she knew she had shifted into the fake version of her self.

She stood up and spotted Sally's number.

"Oh my gosh, I completely forgot about Sally." She grabbed her phone and glanced at the clock, which read 12:07 p.m., and began typing.

- Hi! I am so sorry I forgot to text you earlier. I am free the rest of the day.

Sally replied in less than a minute.

- Are you sure? I don't want to be a bother.

Margaret smiled.

- Yes, I am sure.

- That's great! I'm so excited! I will be there around 2.

Margaret pulled herself together preparing to begin her performance as happy-go-lucky Margaret.

Sally arrived at exactly 2 p.m. Margaret greeted her on the front porch with a smile and a light hug.

"Oh my gosh, Margaret, it's all just as beautiful as when Joseph lived here." Sally was grinning from ear to ear as she scanned every detail of the property.

"It really is beautiful. I have loved my stay here." *Liar,* Margaret thought to herself.

"I really appreciate you inviting me."

"I'm glad you're here. I know this place is special to you."

Sally followed Margaret into the cabin. "This makes we want to cry. I love how the new owners brought fresh life to the cabin while keeping the heart of Joseph here."

"I wasn't sure what was original and what's new."

"Gosh, I sure miss him." Sally laid her things down and walked slowly through the main living area. A deep smile emerged on her face. "See that cross hanging above the front door?"

"Hmm, I actually never noticed that."

"Joseph carved that from one of the trees that was cut down to build the cabin. He used to talk all the time about the early years of building the cabin and living here with his wife."

Margaret grinned, feeling warmed by Sally's presence.

"And, see those small antlers above the back door?" Sally asked as she ran her hand over the smooth wooden banister that led to the loft.

"Hmm, I hadn't noticed those either." Margaret's face turned red, realizing just how little she had paid attention to since arriving.

"An injured buck showed up on Joseph's doorstep, and he nursed it back to health. The next spring, Joseph found those antlers right behind the cabin and felt sure they were Bucky's, which was what he named the buck. Did you know deer actually shed their antlers each year, isn't that amazing?"

"God is quite the Creator." Margaret listened to Sally overflow with excitement. It was really good to have someone else in the cabin. For the first time in a long time, Margaret felt a spark of joy.

They moved their conversation to the back deck with tall glasses of lemonade and slices of apple pie, which Sally had brought from the cafe.

"So, are you from here originally?" Margaret asked.

Sally smiled and chuckled. "Oh yeah, you could say that. My family on both my mom's and dad's sides are from this area. Honestly, I know it probably sounds silly, but I don't know where else we are from."

"I don't think that sounds silly at all. I think it actually sounds wonderful. You have deep roots, which isn't common nowadays."

Sally shrugged. "Hmm. That's a great way to look at it. Sounds a little less boring that way. What about you? Have you moved around a lot?"

Margaret leaned back in the patio glider and began to glide. "Well, I am originally from South Georgia, but I left as soon as I graduated high school. I met my husband, Mitch, at a small college a couple of hours from here. We moved around quite a bit before settling in Tennessee. I am not proud to say that I couldn't wait to pull my roots up." Margaret looked down, watching the ice swirl in her glass.

"Do you get to see your parents very often?" Sally asked.

"Sadly, my parents have both already passed away. I didn't go back as often as I would have liked. Being an author and having a family has kept my plate a little too full, I am afraid."

"Oh, I'm sorry to hear that. I'm sure they were so proud of you."

Margaret briefly closed her eyes. "I think so, but mostly they just loved me for me. I think that's what was so hard about losing them. They loved me, not for how famous I became or how much money I made. They knew my beginning and my flaws and loved me anyway."

"They sound sweet. My parents are a lot like that. What about your kids, are they still at home?"

Margaret's whole face lit up when she thought of her sons. "Oh, my boys. They are really something. Luke was our first, he is about to turn 21. Matthew is our baby and he is almost 19. They are great guys. Both are away at the same college where Mitch and I met."

Sally looked at Margaret, who was beaming with love over her sons. "What about your husband, what's he like?"

Margaret felt a lump form in her throat and her heart ache.

"Mitch. Mitch is everything that I'm not. He's strong. He's reliable. Dependable. He holds our family together. I really don't know why he has put up with me all of these years."

Sally watched Margaret's face change when she talked about Mitch. "He sounds wonderful, but it seems like you are being hard on yourself."

Margaret shrugged her shoulders and sighed. "You don't know me very well."

"Maybe not, but from what I know, I would say Mitch is just as blessed to have you."

The rest of the evening could best be described as a divine appointment between two soul sisters. A delightful, but simple dinner, lots of laughter, and a few tears as each woman shared more than they had planned.

~

~SALLY'S JOURNAL~

No one, and I do mean no one, has ever understood me like Margaret. Our time together has been such a blessing to me. Before I met her, there were days I wanted to get in my car and drive and never look back. It's not like I hate my life or anyone in it, I just feel so different than everyone else I know. According to Margaret, God isn't done writing my story. She thinks He will use me in a mighty way. I really don't see how that is possible, but I want to believe her.

Chapter Six

As the time grew closer for Margaret's trip to Tampa, her anxiety heightened. She had given Mitch the space he requested, but she now had to face the situation.

She felt her hands grow clammy as the phone began ringing. *I wonder if he will even answer,* she thought.

After several rings, Mitch answered with a stern "Hello."

"Um, hello honey. I'm sorry to bother you, but I wasn't sure what our plans are for Luke's birthday."

"We will be there this weekend, like we talked about before you left. The boys don't need to suffer because of your lies."

Margaret's eyes widened, unable to process his anger.

She waited for him to break the tension, for his reassurance.

He didn't speak for what felt like an eternity. The silence felt heavy.

Margaret closed her eyes, feeling the wall of division between herself and the man she vowed to honor and love until the day she took her last breath.

"Do you need something else? I'm busy trying to get things wrapped up before we leave," Mitch said, the sound of papers being shuffled in the background.

"Um, I have been wanting to call you, but you said not to call.

There is a conference in Tampa that I have to attend. I am one of the speakers. I will be back in just over 48 hours. It was supposed to be a longer trip, but I decided to do the bare minimum to satisfy the agreement I made to Tom and the publishing team."

"Okay."

Silence.

"Mitch, I want you to know that I tried to get out of the contract. I called John and had him look it over. He said it's not really an option. I promise I will do everything I can to be there for you and the boys."

"Okay."

Silence.

"Um, okay. Well, I guess I'll let you go. I'll text you the codes for the cabin. I love you, Mitch."

"Okay."

The line went dead.

Margaret made her way to the bedroom and began packing her bags.

I can't believe Luke will be 21 in two days. But, most of all, I can't believe I will be in Tampa instead of here with them like I promised.

Even though she tried to convince herself that she was noble to shorten the duration of the trip, she knew the truth: she shouldn't go at all.

Margaret packed her final few items and glanced at her boarding pass one last time.

Tampa Flight 7889.

She did a last-minute calculation for timing and headed to bed with what felt like the weight of the world on her shoulders.

Margaret tossed and turned for hours until she finally gave up the fight at 3:33 a.m. As she swung her legs over the edge of the bed and sat up, she felt a wave of nausea surge through her body. She rushed to the bathroom, hoping that perhaps she had a virus, which would be a viable excuse for not going on the trip. But she knew better. Her anxiety was winning, and her nerves were shot. She lay on the cold, hard floor, shivering and sobbing.

"Please God, help me... I am so sorry. Show me the way back to You."

Margaret got on her knees and wailed.

She bent forward, gasping for air.

As the tears flowed, she caught a glimpse of herself in the mirror. At first, she was startled, as if a stranger had broken into the cabin. Her eyes locked in on her reflection and she stopped crying. She stood and leaned in to take a closer look.

"What have I done to myself?"

The reflection staring back was, indeed, a stranger. Hollow eyes with dark circles, bright red from crying. Full face with deep creases between her eyes, which prominently displayed the extra weight that she had gained and the stress she was carrying. And most noticeable was the look of deep sadness and the absence of light.

Margaret stood for several moments. She felt as if she had not truly looked at herself in years. She gazed at the shell of the woman God had created her to be.

And then, like a gentle breeze, she felt her heart calm, and she began to pray.

"Help me to see myself the way You see me."

With her eyes closed, she sat still and quiet. Belief began to fill her body.

"Help me to lay it all down. All of it. My need for control. My desire to be someone I'm not. My fears. My doubts. Please, take it all."

She knelt on the floor once again, this time bowing to her Savior, and there, on the floor of Joseph's cabin, which had been built with love and faith, Margaret begged God for a new beginning.

Margaret began to think of her boys and of Mitch. She thought of the morning she had walked to the altar of that little country church and accepted Jesus into her heart.

Happy images of her life began to replay in her mind. Her family, friends, church, and readers. Joy-filled moments stirred within her heart. She managed a smile, knowing that the Holy Spirit was at work. She began to pray and proclaim who she really was.

"I am loved and highly favored."

"I am redeemed and forgiven."

Margaret stood and headed for the family room, grabbing her Bible and journal on the way. Verse by verse, she began reading aloud,

"Therefore, if anyone is in Christ, the new creation has come: The old has gone, the new is here."

As she continued to flip through the worn pages, she read each scribbled note that she had written over the years. As the words penetrated her soul, she began to feel something she had not felt in a long time: peace.

To the side of one of her favorite verses, she had written,

He makes all things new.

He will make a way.

And then, she knew. She looked at the clock and wondered if it was too early. She dismissed her hesitation and dialed Mitch's number. He answered on the third ring with a gruff, "Hello."

"Mitch, honey, I really need to talk."

"Okay ..."

"I don't want to go to Tampa, and I don't want to honor the contract."

He sat up in bed and turned on the lamp.

"What do you mean?"

"I don't really know. I don't know what will happen if I skip the trip to Tampa or if I terminate the contract. I just know that since the day I signed that contract, I have felt nothing but shame and regret. I want our life back. I want you back."

Margaret began to cry, "Mitch, honey, you have to believe me. I love you, and I never want to hurt you again."

He hesitated, closing his eyes as he felt his heart thump against his chest. "Margaret, I love you, and I want our life back, too."

"Oh, my gosh, Mitch. Do you really mean it? Are you willing to give me another chance?"

"You and I have a covenant with God, and I don't ever intend to break that covenant. I am deeply hurt by how you handled this situation, but I am committed to you and this marriage."

"I love you so much." Margaret felt the grace and mercy of Mitch and her Heavenly Father wash over her. "Mitch, pulling out of this contract could significantly impact us financially and me professionally."

He took a deep breath and exhaled months' worth of tension. "It will work out as it should. I'm not worried, and you shouldn't be either."

"Thank you, Mitch."

He smiled as he pushed back the covers and ran his hand across the top of a picture frame that held a photo of Margaret on their wedding day. "Welcome back, Margaret. I have missed you."

Margaret slid to the floor, her phone soaked with tears and her body relaxing for the first time in over a year. If it took her the rest of her life, she would prove to her family how much she loved them and that she had, indeed, changed through the grace of God.

Chapter Seven

WITH THE WEIGHT of the trip off her shoulders, Margaret typed a quick text to Tom.

 - I have decided against the trip to Tampa. As I previously mentioned, I have a prior family commitment. I will be honoring that commitment. I apologize for the late notice. Please be aware that I will not be available to discuss this until next week.

Margaret hit send, blocked Tom's number, and breathed a sigh of relief. Her family would be arriving in about 24 hours, so with a newfound hope rising within her, she began making a list of preparation details.

Tidy up the cabin
Visit Sally
Get groceries
Prep favorite foods

She placed the list in her purse and walked onto the back deck. She took a deep, cleansing breath and stood tall, feeling the air fill her lungs. *What a gift*, she thought.

A brightly-colored butterfly dipped into a nearby fuchsia azalea bloom and fluttered within inches of where Margaret was standing.

"Look at you. Once, you were crawling on the ground, and here you are, flying all about. I have a feeling I am about to do the same."

Margaret watched the butterfly until it flew out of sight and then reached into her pocket and pulled out her phone. She found John's number and waited until she heard the voicemail prompt.

"Hi, John. I know you may think I am crazy, but I have decided to terminate the contract. I am aware we may have significant backlash, but I no longer care. I feel at complete peace with my decision. I sent a quick text to my agent to let him know that I will not be attending the writers' conference this weekend. I also blocked his number. My family will be here tomorrow morning to stay throughout the weekend. I honestly don't want to deal with any of this until next week. I just wanted to let you know. Thanks, I'll be in touch."

Margaret ended the call, shaking her head at the turn of events.

"Wow, what a difference a few hours can make."

She walked back into the cabin, grabbed her purse, and made the short drive to the cafe.

～

The flashing "OPEN" sign seemed more noticeable this time as Margaret walked through the cafe doors. *Thank You for opening my eyes and my heart,* she thought as she sat at the counter instead of her usual corner booth.

Sally looked up from the dishes she was drying. "Hey, Margaret, aren't you supposed to be out of town?"

"Yes, but ... God had other plans for my day."

"Well, okay, that sounds interesting. Let me grab your coffee and put in your order and you can tell me all about it."

"Actually, Sally, I think I will pass on my usual. It's time for me to start taking care of myself again and I don't think my usual is the best option right now."

"Okay, now I know something big happened, because it's not easy to pass on Mrs. Betty's French toast." They both laughed.

"I am about to go on a break if you want to join me out back. There is a really nice sitting area." Sally said.

"That would be great."

Margaret and Sally moved their conversation to the wooden picnic table behind the cafe. Vegetable plants and flowers surrounded the table. A small birdbath was nestled among ivy that sprawled up the back of the building.

They sat across from each other, enjoying hot mugs of tea.

"So, what's this all about?'

Margaret leaned in and began telling Sally all about the sweet moment of surrender she'd had just hours before.

Sally listened intently and began to tear up as Margaret moved through the many emotions she was feeling. When Sally's break was over, they held hands and prayed together, both women marveling at the fact that God is indeed the God of New Beginnings.

MARGARET ARRIVED BACK AT THE CABIN AND BEGAN preparing one of her family's favorite desserts: banana pudding. She smiled as she placed each ingredient in the bowl, recalling her boys arguing over a chance to lick the spoon. Her finger traced the outer edge of the bowl as the rich, smooth pudding began to thicken. She licked her finger, savoring the familiar taste.

Margaret noticed a small vintage radio nestled in the corner of the cabinets. She leaned over and turned the dial, wondering if it still worked. One of her favorite worship songs rang out through the cabin. She grinned, grateful for her own miracle. She began to sing along, hands raised and heart full. As the song ended, the DJ began praying. Margaret listened as she continued to whisk the pudding.

"Father God, times like this we don't understand why there has to be so much pain in the world, so help us have peace among the heartache. I pray, Lord, for those precious souls on the plane that crashed early this morning out of Atlanta. I pray they knew You. Please be with the loved ones who are left behind and the recovery team that is on the scene. In Jesus' name we pray. Amen."

"Oh my gosh. Did a plane crash?" Margaret laid down the spoon and grabbed her phone. She began searching for plane crashes. Several recent posts appeared.

Margaret gasped when she read the headlines.

Flight 7889 headed to Tampa from Atlanta crashes upon take-off.

"Oh my ..."

Margaret quickly found her boarding pass and read the details.

Flight 7889

She held her breath and continued reading the reports.

There doesn't appear to be any survivors.

Most likely, all aboard have perished.

Rescue efforts are futile as deaths are confirmed.

Margaret flipped on the TV and scanned a couple of local channels until she found more evidence of the horrific tragedy. Video footage of the wreckage played as Margaret paced back and forth.

Sirens bellowed, flashing amid flames and smoke. Then, the story shifted to inside the airport where families and friends were in total despair, crumbling under the weight of the unimaginable.

"I should have been on that plane. Oh my gosh, I should have been on that plane. This can't really be happening."

Margaret stepped onto the back deck to get some fresh air and call Mitch.

"Hello."

"Mitch, have you seen the news?"

"No, you know I don't watch the news."

"Mitch, the plane I was supposed to be on this morning crashed and they don't think there are any survivors."

"WHAT? Honey, are you sure it was your flight?"

"Yes, I'm sure. I've checked my boarding pass several times. Mitch, I was supposed to be on that plane."

Mitch slammed his laptop shut and stood to his feet. "Honey, I am going to quickly pack up and head that way. I don't want you to be alone and I don't want to wait until tomorrow to see you."

"Mitch, as much as I would love to see you, I think you should wait and drive the boys. I don't want you driving upset or them driving alone tomorrow."

"Are you sure? I hate the thought of you being by yourself."

"I'm sure. If I change my mind, I promise I will call you. I'm honestly in shock right now and I could use the time to process what happened or better yet, what could have happened. Oh Mitch, all those poor people ..." Margaret began to cry as she thought about the lives that had been lost.

Mitch exhaled long and slow, shaking his head. "I can't believe how close you were to being on that plane. I love you and I am so grateful you changed your mind. I'm really sorry I have been so distant the last several months. I should have been there for you."

"I deserved your distance. I was wrong on so many levels."

"Right now, none of that matters. I'm just glad we get a second chance to make things right. I will tell the boys what happened after they get here this evening. We will leave first thing tomorrow morning, unless something changes, and you want us sooner."

"Okay. Please be gentle with the boys. I don't want them to be upset for Luke's birthday. I am going to go now if it's okay. I want to lie down for a while."

"Okay, I love you, Margaret, and I've really missed you."

They hung up, feeling closer than they had in months.

Margaret lay on the sofa as the news continued to replay the scenes over and over.

She stared out of the large windows that overlooked the creek and wondered, *Why me? Why was I spared?*

She turned off the television, closed her eyes, and thought of what could have been.

An hour later, Margaret woke from a nap in a cold sweat. The television was still on with a talk show now filling the screen, laughter from the audience blaring through the cabin.

Did I dream about the crash?

Her sleepy eyes scanned the room, spotting her boarding pass laying on the end table beside the couch. She picked it up, stared at the numbers 7889, and knew it wasn't a dream. It all came flooding back. She grabbed her journal and a bottle of water and moved to a rocking chair on the front porch.

~

~Margaret's Journal~

It feels as if I cheated death today. It's like I looked my very own mortality in the face and said, "Not yet." I am currently searching for some sense of reality. I don't want to seem overly dramatic, but this is literally the first obligation of my career that I have withdrawn from in 25 years. It's the first time I chose to listen to the Holy Spirit and put my family first. It's the first time I had a place like this cabin to sequester myself, which dismantled my routine and, ultimately, saved my life.

The ironic thing is part of me desperately longs to be in the presence of Jesus, so death does not scare me, but then, I think of my boys and my husband, and I can't imagine how they would have felt if I had gotten on that plane, especially considering the circumstances leading up to the flight.

Who would be there for my husband after a long day? Who would cheer on my boys as they lived their lives? What about my future grandchildren, who would cuddle them up and pour Jesus into their lives with the same love and passion that I know I will? What about the stories that are still in me that have yet to be written and the lives that have yet to be touched? What about Sally, who is just beginning to believe in herself?

Although everything within me is still wrestling with the question of why I am alive and why the other passengers are not, I feel certain that God will use this chapter of my life for His Glory.

Chapter Eight

THE NEXT DAY, Margaret woke with the sunrise. She lay in bed for several minutes as the morning light spilled through the windows, illuminating the cabin's beauty. She closed her eyes and felt the warmth of the heavy vintage quilt, heard the soft chirping of the birds outside, and smelled the lavender candle that sat on the bedside table.

She pushed back the quilt, inhaling a new day. The news of the crash still lingered in her mind and heart, but she moved through the cabin with a newfound spring in her step. The warm water of the shower cascaded over her achy muscles and a deep smile emerged from her once weary face.

After her shower and a few minutes of prayer, she made herself a cup of tea and walked onto the back deck. The outdoor space Joseph had created brought tears to her eyes. She stood overlooking the creek and held the hot mug as the world around her woke up.

Birds continued chirping a beautiful melody, a ladybug carefully walked along the railing, and two squirrels played chase in a nearby tree. The creek cascaded over the rocks as the morning dew made everything it lay upon glisten like diamonds.

Her phone, which she had placed in the pocket of her robe,

began to ring. Her eyes lit up when she saw Mitch's name on the screen.

"Hello."

Mitch smiled when he heard her voice. "Good morning, honey. How did you sleep?"

"Better than expected. I seem to go between being horrifically sad to overjoyed to still be alive."

"I'm sure. I was so worried about you. The boys are packing the truck now. We will be heading your way in just a few minutes. I can't wait to see you."

"I know, it feels like forever since we've been together." Margaret took a deep breath and let it out. "What did the boys say about the crash?"

"Well, as expected Luke didn't say a lot and he seemed very serious about the whole thing. Matthew was mainly concerned with how you must be feeling. They are both very eager to see you."

"Okay, well I am glad they know and I am longing to see them, and you. I have missed you so much."

"It won't be long. I love you."

"I love you." Margaret hit end, lay down her mug, and strolled to the creek. Her bare feet felt every blade of grass, each tiny pebble, and the soft moss as she got closer to the water's edge. Her senses were awakened, and her life had never felt more beautiful.

Margaret spent several minutes at the creek watching, listening, and experiencing life—fully present.

As she walked back toward the cabin, she began thinking about Sally. *I wonder if she knows about the crash.*

Margaret got dressed, grabbed her purse, and headed to the cafe, hoping to find it quiet, so that she could speak with Sally privately.

~

SALLY LOOKED UP FROM FILLING THE SALT SHAKERS. "Good morning, I'm surprised to see you today. I thought you would be at home waiting on pins and needles for your family."

"Very true, my guys are heading this way now, but I wanted to talk to you. I was wondering if you have a minute?"

"Oh, sure. Is everything okay?"

"Well, that is actually a complicated question."

"I have a few minutes, if you want to go out back."

"Sure, that would be great."

Sally led Margaret through the kitchen, with morning greetings being offered along the way from the rest of the cafe crew. A stray kitty scurried off as Margaret and Sally sat down at the picnic table.

"Did you hear about the plane crash that happened in Atlanta yesterday?" Margaret asked with her brows furrowed.

"Yes, it was just awful."

"I agree, it was awful ... that was the plane I was supposed to be on yesterday morning." Margaret closed her eyes, feeling the full weight of her narrow brush with death.

"Oh my gosh, my dad was watching the news last night and there was footage of the crash. I couldn't stand the sight of it all. I can't believe that's the plane you were supposed to be on."

"I know, I can't believe it either. I am honestly still in shock."

"Oh, Margaret, I am so glad you didn't go," Sally exclaimed, with tears filling her eyes.

"I know. Me too. I wanted to come tell you because I'm sure at some point, I will bring Mitch and the boys to the cafe, and I didn't want you to find out through anyone but me."

Margaret sat with her eyes closed, feeling the warm sunshine surrounding her. *Keep going,* was once again whispered into her soul and she became fully aware that her life had meaning beyond her understanding.

EXACTLY THREE HOURS AFTER MARGARET SPOKE TO Mitch, she heard his truck coming down the driveway. She kicked off her flip-flops and ran to her family.

Mitch was the first to get out. He ran to her, wrapped his strong arms around her, and they held each other as if they hadn't seen each other for years. Mitch took his calloused hands, cupped Margaret's face, and looked into her eyes. "I love you so much. I'm so sorry for how I treated you. If I weren't so stubborn, maybe it would have been easier for you to talk to me."

Margaret felt her body fully relax as her husband held her up, both physically and emotionally. She buried her head in his chest and began to weep.

She wept for the time they had lost and the hurt she had caused. She wept for just how fragile and short life can be and because she felt her love run deeper than she once thought was possible.

Margaret listened to the beat of his heart and wondered if she had ever felt more safe and secure in her entire life. He continued to hold her as the boys got out of the truck, giving their parents time to reconnect.

Several moments later, Matthew and Luke joined the embrace, their arms wrapped around Mitch and Margaret. Everyone sighed with relief.

Margret stood wrapped in the love of her husband, her sons, and God. It all made sense now. The shame, the regret, the pain... it all led to this feeling of complete gratitude and love. Without the challenges, the perfection of that moment would have never existed. Margaret smiled and took a deep breath, realizing God had never left her side. She felt His presence and thanked Him for this second chance at life.

Chapter Nine

THE NEXT MORNING, Mitch woke as the sun was just peeking over the tall trees. He reached his hand across the bed and found it empty. He got up and began his search for Margaret. He wound his way through the unfamiliar cabin and found her nestled into the couch, reading, with sunlight radiating through the windows spotlighting her face.

"Good morning, babe. I hate to bother you; do you want a little more alone time?" he asked.

Margaret began to smile. She stood and walked to Mitch, who already had his arms outstretched. He kissed her, and she wondered how she could have betrayed such a wonderful man.

Margaret and Mitch made their way to the back deck and found a warm breeze as the sun continued to climb above the trees.

Mitch gazed over the outdoor paradise. "This place really is spectacular."

"Honestly, I barely even noticed how great it was until you and I were on better terms. Mitch, I was so blind. I can't believe what a fool I was."

"Let's not talk about any of that this weekend. We will get it figured out in due time." He took her hand and held it tight.

They stood silent for several minutes, watching Creation wake up all around them.

Margaret didn't speak as gentle tears rolled down her cheeks.

He leaned down, brushing the tears from her cheek. "What's wrong? Why are you crying?"

"Those poor people. Why did God allow me to live and not them?"

"Oh, honey, I know this is all so hard."

"Mitch, I looked at my boarding pass twelve hours before the plane was scheduled to take off. Twelve hours. I packed my bags. I had my schedule all worked out. I should have been on that plane. Why did God save me?" Margaret buried her face in his chest.

He held the embrace. "I don't know, Margaret, but I fully believe there is a reason."

~

MITCH WAS FLIPPING PANCAKES WHEN MARGARET walked into the family room after her shower. Luke and Matthew were on the deck laughing about stories from college. They waved hello when they saw Margaret squeeze in behind Mitch so she could help him.

Within a few minutes, the meal was complete with everyone's favorites. They filled their plates and sat down at the table overlooking the creek.

Margaret spent several minutes trying to explain why she had signed the contract. Mitch and her boys sat and listened, never breaking eye contact. She paused to compose herself, and Mitch raised his hand and placed it on her shoulder.

"Honey, we forgive you. You don't have to keep explaining yourself."

"But —"

Matthew interrupted her, "Mom, you have always told us that you do better when you know better. You have forgiven us for every stupid thing we have ever done. Don't we owe you that same grace?"

Margaret nodded her head and leaned back in the chair, noticing the warm breeze.

Luke spoke up. "You and Dad have always taught us to own our mistakes and then move on. I think it's time to move on, Mom."

Mitch winked at his boys. "I couldn't have said it better myself."

Margaret exhaled and nodded her head a second time. "Thank you."

When the meal was over, Mitch and the boys began clearing the table. Margaret sat in silence, basking in the sunshine.

Matthew reached down to get Margaret's plate and noticed a trail on the other side of the creek. "After we get things cleaned up, we should check out that trail. Have you been on it, Mom?"

"I'm ashamed to say, I've barely even been down to the creek. Sally told me there are miles of trails behind the cabin."

Mitch softly ran his hand along her shoulders and said, "Well, I think it's time we changed that."

Within minutes, the family set out for a mountain adventure. The twists and turns of the dusty path kept them guessing what was around every next corner.

The half-mile ascent provided a scenic view of the valley below with distant wildflowers dancing in the soft-blowing wind. They spent several minutes at the top of the mountain, each watching their own unique part of Creation.

Mitch was scanning the area, looking for wildlife, settling in on a nearby hawk that was skillfully flying through the sky. Matthew was watching the soft, billowy clouds tiptoe across the horizon. Luke bent down to take a picture of a large centipede crossing the trail, one tiny leg at a time, and Margaret stood watching her family, one of the most magnificent parts of Creation she had ever witnessed.

After three hours of hiking, the family returned to the cabin hungry and tired.

"I can't wait for you guys to meet Sally," Margaret said as she hopped into Mitch's truck for the short ride to the cafe.

∾

TEN MINUTES LATER, MARGARET AND HER FAMILY WERE sitting in her favorite corner booth, sipping perfectly prepared lemonade while experiencing the best of small-town service and hospitality.

"I am telling you, Sally is a hidden treasure. She has been a great friend as I worked to get my life back in order."

Sally blushed. "Thanks, Margaret. It's me that should be thanking you."

"I think we can agree, we have both been good for each other."

Margaret leaned forward, thinking about the first time she'd shuffled into the cafe, exhausted and distraught.

Mitch and the boys smiled as they dug into the hearty lunch that Mrs. Betty, the owner of the cafe, had made special for them.

By the time the last plate was picked up, it was as if Sally had known the family for years instead of minutes. Upon leaving, Mitch reached into his wallet and pulled out a very generous tip. "Sally, it was so nice to meet you."

"It was so great to meet you all. Let me grab you some change,"Sally said, turning to walk away.

"No change is necessary," Mitch called out, wrapping his arm around Margaret. They both grinned at Sally, who was beaming with gratitude.

Luke spoke up, "Hey, Sally, if you don't have anything going on later, we are doing a cookout for my birthday, and you are welcome to join us. Right, Mom and Dad?"

"Of course," they said in unison.

Sally's face blushed once again, graciously accepting the tip and the dinner invitation.

~

SALLY ARRIVED AT THE CABIN A LITTLE AFTER FIVE with fresh tomatoes and a watermelon from her parents' garden. She was met outside by Matthew.

"Hey, Sally, I'm glad you could come. We are down at the creek. I was just coming up to get the fishing poles out of the truck. Do you need some help?"

"No, I've got it. Is it okay if I put these things in the kitchen before I head down?"

"Of course. And by the way, thanks again for being there for Mom. It's not like her to get herself in this big of a mess."

"I admire your mom so much. I know she isn't perfect, but none of us are."

"That's for sure."

They nodded in agreement.

Sally joined the family down by the creek and spent the next hour watching the guys try to catch the "big one." They never caught a fish, but they did create memories that would last a lifetime.

After dinner was served fireside, they went back into the cabin to enjoy birthday cake and homemade ice cream. As the family and Sally became better acquainted, Mitch began to notice every special detail of the cabin.

"So, not to brag or anything, but I think I did a pretty great job choosing this cabin for you, honey." He looked around the room, nudging Margaret.

Luke nodded his head in agreement. "I wonder who lived here before it became a rental?"

Margaret perked up at her family's interest. "Actually, Sally knows the entire history of the cabin, and she even knew the gentleman who built it. I would love to hear more about Joseph now that I am a little more clear-headed."

"Oh, I would be honored to tell y'all about Joseph," Sally said as she set down her empty plate and licked the last bit of ice cream off her spoon.

"Joseph and his wife retired to our little town almost 20 years ago. He and some of the locals built this cabin. Unfortunately, his wife got sick shortly after they moved in, so they never enjoyed their dream retirement, but Joseph made the best of it, just like he did with everything. He would care for his wife every day, and when she was resting or reading, he would work outside, which is why it seems like the Garden of Eden out there."

Margaret nodded her head. "That's funny, that is exactly what I thought the first time I saw the property."

"I know, right?" Sally continued. "Joseph said he felt closer to God when he was outside working with his hands. He was easily the most devoted Christian I ever knew. He seemed to know the Bible through and through, but not just in his head; also in his heart. Ya'll should have heard him pray—it was like he had a direct line to the Lord. He prayed with such boldness and humility."

"He sounds like a wonderful man." Margaret squeezed Mitch's thigh, which was pressed against hers on the couch. He responded by pulling her in even closer and giving her a soft kiss on her cheek.

Sally grinned. "Joseph really was a wonderful man. After his wife died, he would take fresh flowers to his bride's grave every week before church gathered. I asked him one time why he called her his bride and he said he did that to remind himself to honor and love her as if every day was their wedding day."

In unison, the family said, "Awwww," and then began to laugh.

"Wow, that is so wonderful. How long ago did Joseph pass?" Margaret scooted to the edge of the sofa, engaging with every word.

"He died about a year ago. The last Saturday that Joseph was seen, he was in the pasture between here and the cafe, picking wildflowers for his wife's grave. Several hours later, someone spotted him lying in the soft grass with the flowers still in his hand and a smile on his face. There was never an autopsy, but the coroner said it was probably a heart attack and that he didn't suffer. I hope he was right. A great man like Joseph didn't deserve one bit of suffering."

"Joseph certainly left a remarkable legacy." Mitch leaned up and whispered in Margaret's ear, "I am so thankful you didn't get on that plane."

Chapter Ten

MITCH WAS JUST WAKING up when Margaret eased the door open and made her way to the bed she had left two hours before. She pulled back the quilt and snuggled into his side. He held her tight, neither of them saying a word for several minutes. He was breathing heavily, totally relaxed and almost asleep when she broke the silence.

"I hate to even bring this up, but what are we going to do about the contract?"

He rubbed his eyes and cleared his throat, "Do you really want to talk about that right now?"

"Well, no, I have been trying to push it out of my mind while you and the boys are here, but it is really bothering me."

"I have already sent a text to John. I told him that we need to meet with him. Do you think you can come home for a couple of days sometime soon?"

"Well, considering what a mess I've made of things, maybe I should just come home and stay. I absolutely love this place, but it's certainly not been the retreat I dreamed of for the last decade. Of course, it's nobody's fault but my own."

Mitch scooted up in bed. His tone got more serious. "Margaret, you screwed up big time, no doubt, but we have been given a second chance, so can you please drop the victim mentality and focus on moving forward?"

Margaret sat up and pulled the quilt tight around her body. "Mitch, I am not trying to portray myself as a victim. I know it was my fault."

"I'm sorry, I guess that didn't come out quite right. What I mean is that going forward, we need to look at this situation as a challenge that we will conquer together. I don't want to spend the next several months or years or whatever it takes to get out of this contract placing blame on you alone. Does that make sense?"

"Yes," she whispered, feeling unworthy of his forgiveness.

"Today is our last day with the boys here in the cabin, so let's focus on today. I think you should stay for as long as you want to be here. Give yourself some time to process what has happened and pray about the next steps. Not to mention, I love it here. We should plan a couple more visits as a family before the lease is up."

Margaret leaned her body against his, resting her head on his chest.

Thump, thump, thump ... *what a marvelous sound*, she thought, as his heart beat against her cheek. He held her and closed his eyes.

Mitch gently pulled them both back under the quilt. "How does all that sound, bride of mine?"

"It sounds like a wonderful plan from a wonderful man. I really don't deserve you, Mitch."

"Neither of us deserves this life we have been given, so we'd better not waste it."

⁓

MARGARET AND MITCH LET THE BOYS SLEEP IN AND enjoyed breakfast down by the creek. After everyone had eaten and dressed for the day, the family went for a hike on a path they had seen the previous day.

The new trail was spectacular in every way. The sun was

shining brightly, yet somehow, the Georgia humidity was nice and low. The trail meandered by the creek, and then deeper into the forest, passing pockets of native ferns and playful wildlife scurrying about. Time with her family, out in Creation, was like medicine to Margaret's weary soul.

Margaret's family could see and hear the difference in her outlook and perspective on life. Her career felt like a distant part of who she was, not her main identity.

As the evening wound down, the boys built a fire down by the creek and sat immersed in conversation and the starry night. Margaret and Mitch lay in the oversized hammock a few feet away, holding onto the night and each other as they listened to their boys' endless chatter and the sound of crickets and tree frogs. Low-flying bats kept the insects at bay and provided a mesmerizing aerobatic show.

Margaret leaned into Mitch. "I really want to know what you think I should do about staying here."

"Honey, we already talked about it this morning. I think you should stay."

"I really want to head back home soon, but I keep getting this nagging feeling that I am supposed to stay. What do you really think I should do? I am done with trying to figure things out on my own."

Mitch laughed softly. "I would love for you to come home, but you have been talking about this opportunity for as long as you have been an author. Who knows, there may be a bestseller in you that can only come out if you stay and have this time to yourself."

Margaret grinned and began lightly rubbing his arm with her hand.

"I know I have always wanted this, but that was before this whole contract fiasco. I hardly deserve a three-month retreat. We don't even know how much money it will cost us to get out of that stupid contract."

Mitch turned and looked her in the eyes. "When you called and told me about the plane crash, I have never felt more grateful in my entire life. That gratitude was quickly replaced by shame for how cold and hateful I was with you. I should have been more willing to listen to you and be involved with the things that matter to you."

"Oh, Mitch, I can't even begin to tell you how much I appreciate you. I guess we both could have done things a little better."

He kissed her right cheek and then her left cheek. He rubbed his hand down her face and traced the outline of her lips. "I don't care about the money. I care about you."

She melted into his touch, with the sound of her boys conversing in the background and the crackling of the fire.

Mitch softly kissed her. "I am glad we get the chance to start fresh. Not everyone is so lucky."

"That is so true." Images of the plane crash flashed into Margaret's mind. She closed her eyes and felt her pulse quicken. As she lay in her husband's arms, she couldn't help but wonder, *why, God, why was my life spared?*

~

~MARGARET'S JOURNAL ~

I woke up this morning with Mitch by my side. His deep breathing reassured me in a profound way of the gift of the very air I breathe each day. I tiptoed out of the bedroom and quietly made my way down the hallway, past the open doors of our sleeping boys. I stood for a long time and just watched them, breathing in and out, resting and restoring their bodies. I am astonished that I grew these boys in my womb and now they are such amazing young men. It honestly feels like a miracle that I could do something as wonderful as helping to create the two of them.

As I eventually made my way through the cabin, it was as if I were seeing it for the first time. With my eyes wide open, I saw it all.

The cross, the antlers, the old stone fireplace, the perfectly matched chenille blankets amongst the incredibly cozy pillows. I can see clearly for the first time in years.

I was exhausted from trying to keep up with the chaos I had created and from trying to be someone I thought the world expected me to be. This is a freedom I have never known.

Chapter Eleven

MITCH and the boys headed back to the city as the fog mingled with the early morning sunrise. Margaret leaned against the front porch railing as she watched them drive away. A family of cardinals perched in a nearby tree, their melody of life singing out through the forest.

After several minutes, Margaret went back into the cabin. She picked up her Bible and her journal, determined to spend the next couple of hours in quiet reflection.

Around ten o'clock, Mitch called to let her know they had arrived home. With soothing music playing in the background, Margaret found her eyes feeling heavy as she relaxed into the couch. Within moments, she was dreaming ...

The dream began with Margaret standing on the runway at the airport. Flames were all around her and sirens were screaming as she surveyed her surroundings. Firemen were yelling and pulling hoses and cops were screaming orders in anguish. Out of the smoke, a young girl walked toward Margaret.

Margaret ran to her. "Oh my gosh, are you okay?"

The girl seemed unfazed by the chaos all around her. "I am doing great, how are you?"

"WHAT? What do you mean you are doing great? Obviously something really terrible has happened."

"Hmmm, maybe, but I am safe and happy. Will you tell everyone that I'm okay?"

"What? I don't understand."

In a flash the young girl vanished.

Margaret spun in circles, looking for her and screaming "Where are you? Are you okay?"

Margaret stood in disbelief at what had just happened. She then noticed an older gentleman standing several feet away. She ran to him.

"What is going on? I don't understand what is happening!"

The older man just stood smiling, looking up into the smoke-filled sky.

"Hello, can you hear me?" Margaret yelled in confusion.

"Well, hello, yes, I can hear you."

"What is going on?"

"I don't know, but I feel such peace. Do you feel it? It's like it is surrounding us from all sides and from within, do you feel it?"

"NO, I do NOT feel it! Obviously, something really bad has happened. Why are you so calm?"

"I'm not sure. My life flashed before my eyes before the light arrived."

Tears of joy ran down the man's wrinkled face. "I lived my life well. I am at peace. Will you tell them to live, will you please tell them to live?" And with his arms stretched to Heaven, he vanished.

Margaret stood in total shock. "WHERE ARE YOU? WHAT IS HAPPENING?" She yelled.

The scene went dark, everything and everyone disappeared. Margaret began running around, reaching out with her hands, hoping to find something or someone.

She was totally alone.

Margaret stood still, heart pounding, breathless from the adrenaline surging through her body.

Then, she heard the young girl's voice, "Tell everyone that I am okay."

"Where are you, who are you? Oh my God, what is happening?"

Then the older man's voice sounded over her. "I lived my life well, I am at peace. Tell them to live."

"Tell who? Who do I need to tell? Who are you? Please tell me. I can't see you, tell me what you want me to do. GOD, PLEASE HELP ME ..."

Complete silence surrounded her from every side and from within.

The darkness began to fade.

Margaret closed her eyes as the light got brighter and brighter, and then it came ... complete, all-consuming peace.

Every sense in her body that was heightened fully relaxed, as warmth embraced her.

She felt her body go limp as the young girl and the old man spoke over her.

"Tell them."

"Tell them."

"Please, tell them."

~

MARGARET WOKE AND LOOKED AROUND THE CABIN. Her eyes were damp with tears, her heart racing and full of hope. She lay on the couch for several moments, fully soaking in the love she felt.

"What now? What does this mean?"

She recounted the dream over and over in her mind. A smile covered her face. She reached for her phone and scrolled until she saw her previous literary agent Ernie's name. She hit send, feeling what felt like butterflies fluttering in her belly.

"Hello."

"Hi, Ernie. I know we haven't talked in a while. You got a minute?"

"Of course, Margaret. How the heck are you? I saw on the news that you just barely escaped death. I was going to call you, but I wanted to give you a little time."

"What do you mean you saw it on the news?"

"I guess your boy, Tom, felt it necessary to broadcast how grateful he was that he rearranged your travel plans, which ultimately saved your life."

"Are you kidding? He didn't rearrange my plans. I backed out of the trip because I can't stand him or anything that he stands for. Ernie, I am in quite a mess, and from what you just said, the mess is now even bigger."

"Wow, you canceled a work trip at the last minute? Things must be bad."

"You have no idea."

"Alright, young lady. Spill the beans."

Margaret and Ernie talked for the next hour and a half. She filled him in on the contract situation, her life with Mitch and the boys, and her cabin retreat.

He filled her in on his attempt at being retired, his lovely wife of 35 years, and a fishing trip he had taken to the Florida Keys. When they had finally gotten all caught up, Margaret brought up the main reason she'd called.

"Okay, Ernie, you may think I'm crazy, but I need to talk to you about a really weird dream I just had." Margaret told Ernie every detail of the dream.

Ernie rubbed his chin over and over. "Wow, that's heavy, what do you think it means?"

"I think my next writing project should somehow be a legacy book about the passengers on Flight 7889. You know, kinda like a memoir from the other side. I could interview family members of the deceased, interject my experiences at this second chance at life I've been given, and share how God is in it all. You know, turn some of the pain into something for His Glory. What do you think?"

"It is certainly a unique concept." He paused. "Actually, I think it's a pretty good idea."

"I am severing all ties with Tom and the new team. Can you help me start fresh, Ernie?"

"Well, actually, I have been talking with some folks at a smaller publishing house about some contract work, and they would probably be over the moon to snag you and this project. What does Mitch think about the idea?"

"I haven't told Mitch yet, so I will need his blessing first, but I think he will be on board. He is tied up most of the day, so I will run it by him tonight.He and I were just talking this weekend and we both agreed that I should beg you to come out of retirement and represent me again. We all miss you. You were more like family than my agent, although you were a great agent, too."

"Thank you, Margaret, I have missed you all too."

"I hate to say it, but I am glad that you were getting bored with retired life."

They both laughed and said their goodbyes.

Chapter Twelve

MARGARET BEGAN RESEARCHING the published information about Flight 7889. As she read through the list of passengers, her writer's mind began to formulate a book that would honor those who perished and inspire those left behind.

She gazed out of the windows toward the creek, hearing her phone ring in the distance. She ran to get it, a smile emerging when she saw it was Mitch, "Hello honey, what a nice surprise."

"Hey babe. I hate to bring this up because you sound so happy, but I just read the email that John sent over about the contract. He said he needs the original that you signed and the bank statement indicating the deposit of the advance. I looked through every account and I don't see any deposits. Did you open a new account?"

Margaret's gratitude faded as anxiety took its place.

"I think the original contract might be in the file cabinet in my office. As for the advance, I used that old account we opened when I first got started with writing, you know the one we barely use over at the Credit Union. I haven't checked it, but the advance should be in there."

"Yeah, I checked that account. Nothing new is there."

"Hmmm, that's strange. It should have been deposited weeks ago. Let me check through my emails and see if I can find anything. I have been ignoring Tom for a while, so maybe I missed something along the way."

"Okay, just let me know."

Margaret took a deep breath and let it out, trying to refocus her emotions. "By the way, I talked to Ernie earlier today. I have so much to tell you."

"Good ole Ernie, how's he doing?"

"He seems to be doing good. Oh, and have you heard that Tom reported that he rearranged my flight and was responsible for sparing my life?"

"Are you serious? What a jerk. I guess he was eager to get some notoriety from this tragedy."

"I know. It's such a shame that I got involved with him. I got online and as usual the press is all over the story. I guess our little secluded cabin retreat had us oblivious to what was happening in the real world."

"I guess so. Wasn't it great?" he said, smiling a deep smile.

"It was great indeed. Maybe God gifted us with such a wonderful weekend to help us get stronger for what is to come. I'll go through my emails and maybe we can discuss it all later this evening."

"That sounds perfect. Love you."

"Love you." She grabbed her laptop, headed to the loft, and sat at the quaint desk.

Margaret scanned through hundreds of emails that she had neglected. More than 50 emails were waiting on her from Tom. After several minutes, she found one that might hold the answers she was looking for.

Hi Margaret!

So, it seems that we neglected to get one little paper signed when we were doing the contract. It's no big deal, but the guys over in accounting won't release the advance until they are told everything is all squared away. Can you be a doll and come into town for a day? I will treat you to lunch and you can tell me all about Book Two!

Call me ... Tom

"What's going on?" Margaret said aloud.

She scanned the remaining emails and found one with the subject *Delayed Advance*.

With her hands shaking, she began to read.

Hey, you!

Since, you haven't gotten back to me, I will assume you are too busy writing to touch base with your loyal agent! You must have a bad connection with your phone down there in the mountains because I can't get a call to go through.

I will bring the paper we need signed with me to Tampa, so we can get you your hard-earned money. I arrive the day before you, so I will have your suite perfect and dinner reservations at your favorite cantina for the day you arrive.

See ya soon! Tom

"Does this mean what I hope and pray it means?"

Margaret's heart pounded against her chest. She quickly forwarded the emails to Mitch and Ernie, and then sent a text telling them to expect them. Mitch called her in less than a minute.

"Margaret, do you think this means your contract isn't valid? They haven't actually paid you and something appears to be missing from the contract? Is that how you are reading this email?"

"I don't know. I blocked Tom's number before the planned trip to Tampa because he was driving me crazy and I couldn't stand to hear his voice. It looks like he was emailing me for several weeks, but I wasn't checking my email. It does seem like the contract is waiting on me, which explains why the advance hasn't been deposited. Oh my gosh, Mitch, is this really happening? Has God just performed another miracle?"

"Hold tight. Let me call John and see what he thinks."

Margaret walked downstairs and paced back and forth on the back deck until she saw Mitch's number appear on her phone. She held her breath, anxiously preparing herself for what he might say.

"Hello."

"Margaret, you might want to sit down for this."

"Okay." She sat, her heart racing.

"When we hung up earlier, I went into your office and found the original contract. It was very lengthy, so it took me a few minutes, but it does look like a page is missing. I scanned what we had and sent it over to John along with the emails you forwarded me from Tom. John called me right away. Margaret you're never gonna believe this, but it appears the contract is not valid."

Margaret could not form words. She bent over, taking long, slow breaths.

"Margaret, darling, are you still with me? Margaret? Margaret, honey, please say something."

"Mitch, I don't know what to say. I don't know what to think. First, God spares my life, and now, this ..." she began to shake from the inside out.

"Margaret, I wish I could be there with you, but since I can't, I want you to make your way to the hammock by the creek. I want you to get in the hammock and imagine my arms around you. Can you do that, Margaret?"

"Yes." Margaret clutched her phone, eyes fixed on her destination, feeling the smooth, cool rocks beneath her feet.

She shimmied onto the hammock and lay her head back, resting her body on the soft, woven rope. "Okay, I'm here."

"Let's go to the Lord in a prayer of thanksgiving."

She closed her eyes, "That sounds wonderful."

"Father God, we come to You today in complete awe of who You are and how much You have blessed our lives. We see Your hand, we feel Your presence, and we are fully aware that Your favor is upon us. We thank You, Lord, for the way that You continue to work in our lives. We are thankful for the lessons and the hardships and the opportunity to begin anew. Please God, continue to use us as individuals, as a couple, and as a family to bring you all the glory You deserve. Amen."

Tears rolled down her face. "Amen."

Chapter Thirteen

SUNSHINE SPILLED through the large windows as Margaret finished her morning workout. She lay down on the floor, stretching her ever-changing body. She took long, deliberate breaths, breathing out the past and all its regrets, and breathing in possibility and a new day.

She lay quietly watching the trees sway in the morning breeze and began wondering how she had managed to live in the city for so many years. Somewhere along the way, she and Mitch had traded peace for convenience. Although her family's home in the city sat high atop a ridge with expansive views, it did not come close to the beauty she encountered at the cabin.

After stretching for several minutes, Margaret moved to the kitchen table with a cup of herbal tea. Although she was working hard to get her physical body back in shape, she felt tense and tight from the years of neglect. She began rolling her neck in slow circles to loosen the tension that pulled and tugged at her tight muscles.

The last few days had proven to be emotionally heavy. She worked tirelessly on gathering information about the passengers of Flight 7889. She took pages of notes, listened to interviews, and immersed herself in news story after news story regarding the tragic event.

Grief was a very difficult topic to delve into, but throughout Margaret's career, she had learned that her most inspirational work occurred when she leaned into pain and embraced human suffering instead of trying to avoid it.

After drafting a rough outline, Margaret stood and began walking around the cabin. She stepped onto the deck and watched life happening all around her.

She smiled as she saw the bumblebees buzz about and a hummingbird swoosh through the air on its pursuit of gathering nectar from the various flowers. She sat in one of the gliders and began moving back and forth. The gentle motion calmed her busy mind. She closed her eyes and enjoyed the warmth of the sun on her skin.

Several minutes had passed before her phone startled her from her peaceful state. She grabbed it from where it lay on the deck railing and looked at the screen. She was surprised to see Ernie's name.

"Hey, Ernie! How are you?"

"I am doing good, sweet lady. I am feeling better than I have in a long time. Being retired is completely overrated," he chuckled.

"I'm sure. I felt certain you wouldn't be able to stay on the sidelines for too long."

"I guess I just missed my craft. I mean, after all, I was a literary agent for 40 years. I didn't think I would miss it so much, but I sure did. And I think Michelle is ready for me to be out of the house."

Margaret smiled thinking of how kind and patient Michelle had always been with her husband. Ernie was the perfect blend of completely grounded and experienced, yet also spontaneous and brave. He would do just about anything if he thought it would benefit the authors he represented. He had been the backbone of Margaret's success.

"Well, I am glad that the one time you aren't good at something, it's being retired."

"I'm sorry you and your family went through so much hardship this past year. I knew I didn't get a good feeling about Tom when you were telling me about him. I should have spoken up or given you more notice to find someone who would be a better fit. I was so happy when you copied those emails to me about the contract."

"Ernie, don't think for one moment you are responsible for any of the chaos. There were so many factors that led to me signing with Tom and agreeing to the contract, none of which was your fault. And now that the contract isn't valid, John is busy severing all ties with Tom and the team. I lost my way for a bit, but thankfully, God's grace proved to be sufficient, like always."

"Young lady, I sure have missed your positive spin on every single thing you see and experience."

"Thanks, I've missed that about me, too. I have spent the last week really focusing on this next chapter of my life and I have to say, I'm really excited."

"Okay, now that we got all the sappy stuff out of the way, let's talk shop." Ernie laughed his usual hearty laugh.

Margaret and Ernie talked for almost an hour. When they hung up, she lifted her hand and attempted to rub out the knot in her upper back.

"Goodness, I need a break."

She walked back into the kitchen and sent a text to Sally.

- Hi there! I was thinking of hiking later today. Would you like to join me?

In less than 30 seconds, she got Sally's reply.

- YES!

Sally was a very eager hiking partner, arriving in less than an hour. She was ready and willing, although not very prepared in her worn tennis shoes that doubled as her work shoes. Margaret felt silly in her expensive hiking boots and wondered how many times she missed out on the joys of life by being overly prepared.

They hiked for almost two hours. The fresh mountain air and wide-open blue skies created the perfect backdrop for their blossoming friendship. When they arrived back at the creek, Sally kicked off her shoes and stepped into the water, being careful not to fall on the slippery rocks.

"Wow, this feels so good."

Margaret watched Sally and began unlacing her boots. She sat on the mossy edge of the creek bank and dangled her feet in the cool water.

Sally sat a few feet away on a large rock that protruded above the water's surface.

"Hey, I've been wondering—how is the book going?"

"I'm glad you asked. I have been trying to work through the details, and I would love your opinion."

"Sure, I'm happy to help."

"Okay ... so, Mitch set up a landing page for people to visit and find out more about what I am doing and why. We can receive inquiries there and there is a secure messaging option for people to leave a few simple words in honor of a passenger who perished. In essence, it will be a collection of short legacy stories."

Sally moved her feet back and forth in the cool water. "I think it sounds great. I have never heard of a book like this."

"That's partly why I'm nervous. I have never heard of a book like this, either. I worked on an outline today. I like the concept; it's certainly unique," Margaret said while reaching to push her leggings up a little higher on her legs.

"Well, there is a first time for everything, and it seems like the entire concept was divinely inspired, so I don't see how it couldn't be the right thing for you to do. I love the idea."

"Thank you. Your vote of confidence means a lot. Everyone seems to love the idea, including the new publishing team. I should feel a bit surer of my decision, but it's still a struggle some days."

Margaret stepped into the water and looked up into the blue sky, feeling the breeze blow through her long, wavy hair.

"I know what you mean. It seems like every time I even think about doing something different with my boring life, something gets in the way." Sally stood and waded into the deeper water.

"In time, I think you will find that it gets easier to push through fear of the unknown. I'm not saying you won't still feel afraid, because obviously I still do, but the 'What if I don't?' begins to override the comfort of not doing things we feel called to do."

"You make it sound so easy ..." Sally said with her head lowered.

"Well, as we know, I'm still prone to heading in the wrong direction. Thank goodness for God's grace."

Sally perked up when she was reminded of Margaret's short-comings. "Amen to that. So, when will you start the interviews?"

"Mitch is going to start scheduling them in the next couple of weeks. I am both excited and nervous about interviewing people who are grieving. Grief isn't really my favorite topic to write about."

I am actually more than nervous, Margaret thought.

"I can't imagine interviewing people you've never even met. You are so brave."

"I'm really not very brave, Sally. I've just spent a lot of my life trying to avoid pain and grief, and the more I do that, the worse I feel."

"Well, I think you are brave... I would love to be a fly on the wall at the interviews. I bet you will hear some amazing stories. Of course, I would probably cry the whole time," Sally smiled.

Hmmm. We will see about that, Margaret thought as she play-fully kicked water toward Sally, who kicked water back. Happy laughter filled the forest.

~

~Sally's Journal~

I can't even believe this is my life! I am so grateful for the last few weeks as I get to know Margaret. It seems like she is living in that sweet spot of being exactly who God has called her to be. I desperately want that for myself.

Margaret told me that every setback and moment of doubt that she has ever encountered helped shape her into who she is today. So none of the heartache was wasted. None of it. Maybe that means everything I have been through will someday make sense, too. I sure hope so.

Chapter Fourteen

AFTER A LONG MORNING OF WORKING, Margaret decided to spend time at the creek. As she arrived, a hummingbird swooped down as if to say hello. She took a moment to be fully present.

The smooth round pebbles that lay around the creek's basin were a reminder of a time in Margaret's life when she felt desperate for change. She fondly recalled that on her first day at the cabin, she had dropped a pebble into the creek. She had watched that pebble create a perfect ripple. The significance of that moment sat deep within her soul.

The pebble represented Margaret's journey back to God in many ways, and the purpose He had for her life. Today, she chose another pebble and, once again, watched it break through the water and create ripples that radiated out with beauty and precision.

If the pebble stayed on the surface, change would not occur, but when the pebble submerged into deeper water, the ripple formed. *Such is life*, thought Margaret.

She felt a little whisper in her soul, *Go deeper.*

She closed her eyes and felt the warm wind blow around her. She lay her things down and bowed her head.

"Thank You. I know I don't deserve Your mercy on my own,

but because I have put my trust in You, it is my birthright to live in this place of favor and love, so thank You. Thank You for this place, thank You for my life, and thank You for this new beginning and the opportunities You have laid before me. Thank You for never giving up on me. I pray for Your peace, strength, and confidence today and every day. Amen."

Margaret kneeled on the soft, moss-covered ground, overwhelmed with His goodness. As the sun broke through the trees, she made her way to the hammock and positioned herself so she could write in her journal. She spent several minutes watching the tall trees sway in the wind.

She scooted up in the hammock to begin writing. The words flowed, and she found herself crafting a plea to her readers instead of working on the new book.

I wonder if I should do a video for my readers.

Margaret sat with her feelings for a couple of minutes. She held her phone, looked into the screen, and prayed that her words would penetrate the hearts of those who needed to hear from her. She took a deep breath, exhaled long and slow and hit record.

"Hey, friends. I am joining you today from one of my favorite places on the planet. Welcome to my little mountain retreat." She scanned the property showing her audience the beauty of the creek and its surroundings.

Margaret switched the view back to her grateful face. "Someday, I will share in more detail how special this place really is, but today, I come to you in hopes of being of service to those who need to share their story. Allow me to explain."

She paused, swallowed hard, and continued.

"I was recently scheduled to be on Flight 7889 from Atlanta to Tampa. That morning, I chose to not go. It's a long story, but ultimately, that choice saved my life. Tragically, 172 individuals were not as fortunate, as the plane crashed upon takeoff, and no one survived. Since that day, the day my life was spared, I have tried to make sense of why I am still alive."

"I now question, when I do take my last breath, what my

legacy will be? Have I truly lived my life to its fullest potential? Have I served and loved to the best of my ability? Have I poured myself out as an offering often enough? In some ways I can answer yes to these things, but in many ways, I am certainly glad I got a second chance."

Margaret teared up. One lonely tear escaped from her right eye. Her voice became strained, fighting off the emotion; not to avoid it, rather so she could convey her message with better clarity. She paused, cleared her throat, and continued.

"My deepest desire is to take this second chance at life that I have been granted and do something meaningful. This brings me to why I am speaking to you today."

"Shortly after the plane crash, I was filled with an idea to create a book that would honor those who perished on Flight 7889. A compilation of sorts that will showcase the wonderful souls who are no longer here. An opportunity for family and friends to share tidbits of life about those they loved most. Voices in the darkness, hope in the tragedy, and inspiration amid devastation."

"I feel certain that God placed this idea in my heart, because I have never considered a project like this. Unlike my typical fictional storytelling, my desire is that I will be able to share the real-life stories of men, women, and children who lived a life worthy of knowing. After all, we all have a story to tell."

"My husband and I are creating a secure website, which will be a landing place for these incredible stories. I also plan to interview individuals who would like to give more details and who perhaps feel more comfortable face-to-face."

Margaret took another deep breath, noticing the rustling of the leaves through the trees. She exhaled, feeling the weight and glory of this calling.

"You may be asking why I would pursue such a unique project. I will be honest. Every single day since the crash, I have thought about how different life would be for my family if I had gotten on that plane."

Margaret paused as she visualized her family. She closed her eyes for a moment, feeling their love push through.

"Had I been on that plane, my notoriety would have given my family a platform to say lovely things about me and an opportunity to carry on where I left off, but not everyone has that unique chance. I hope I can bridge that gap."

Margaret's heart quickened, as the images of the young girl and the old man from her dream flashed in her mind.

She left a long pause.

Biting her lip, with tears slowly escaping her eyes, she spoke from her heart, "I also want to thank you for being patient with me the last couple of years as I went through the refining fire. I know I haven't been living up to the Lord's call on my life and that I dishonored God, my family, and you, my readers. For that I am truly sorry. I appreciate you all more than you will ever know," Margaret's voice cracked as a single sun ray lit her face.

"I guess that's enough for now. Please share this post if you happen to know someone affected by flight 7889. Thank you, my friends, for being a part of my life."

Margaret turned off the video. Tears broke loose like a dam. She lay in the hammock, allowing her body and mind to be fully at rest. Being in God's will was beautiful but tiring work.

MITCH WAS WORKING IN HIS HOME OFFICE AS THE SUN rose above the downtown buildings. He alternated his days between his home office and The Ranch, the organization he ran. More than a decade ago, Mitch and Margaret had bought an old ranch style home just outside the city. He had slowly built what had become known as Reality Ranch, a life coaching program for veterans.

He opened his computer and quickly scrolled through social media to check for any updates that might be pertinent to Margaret's book. After a couple of swipes, he saw Margaret's face light up his screen. He watched the video three times, his smile widening with each viewing. He reached for his phone and dialed her number.

Margaret was still dozing in the hammock when Mitch's call came in. The noise startled her, but she quickly answered when she saw that it was him.

"Hi, babe."

"Well, hello. I just watched the most beautiful woman give the most wonderful speech on my computer. You should have seen her; it was like watching an angel."

"Oh, really, well isn't that interesting," she responded flirtatiously.

"I am wondering if this woman would be up for a visitor later today?"

"What! Really? I thought you were slammed this week?"

"I am, but I've got the new guy pretty well trained, and I miss you. Not to mention we need to talk about all the things going on and I would much rather do that while having a nice dinner with you overlooking the creek. What d'ya say? I can probably be there by 4:30."

"That would be amazing! And about the video, are you sure it was okay? It was kind of a spontaneous decision to make a video instead of do a written post."

"It was perfect; absolute perfection. I will call you when I get on the road."

"Thanks, Mitch. I love you, and I can't wait to see you."

"Same, honey. I will get out of here as quick as I can."

Margaret climbed out of the hammock and took a short walk by the creek to stretch her sleepy muscles. After a few minutes, she made her way up to the cabin to get things ready for her extra special visitor.

∾

Mitch pulled hastily into the driveway at 3.33 p.m. He hopped out, leaving his bag behind as he went in search of his bride. Margaret heard the truck come to a grinding halt in the driveway, stopped what she was doing, and ran to meet him.

"Wow, you got here fast. Did you happen to notice the speed limit as you were driving?"

"Huh? What speed limit?" Mitch smiled and squeezed her tight.

Margaret and Mitch spent the rest of the day outside, exploring every inch of the property. They marveled at what Joseph had created and the great fortune of finding this little piece of heaven.

The property was perfectly crafted with touches of natural beauty everywhere. Beautiful trees, shrubs, and flowers looked as if they had always been there. It looked effortless, but they knew it had taken years and a lot of hard work for this paradise to exist.

Bird houses and wind chimes hung from several of the trees, offering a welcome retreat for the many birds and soft, gentle melodies to calm the most worrisome day.

A pebble pathway and a series of rock steps led to the bubbling creek, which slow-danced its way through the back of the property. Handcrafted chairs surrounded the large rock fire pit with string lights glistening from above. The now familiar hammock casually stretched out between two huge oak trees, which created the perfect canopy.

Margaret and Mitch ended their hike with a dip in the water.

"This cabin is quite possibly the best idea I have ever had," Mitch said while floating on his back in the shallow swimming hole.

Margaret leaned over him, with her face only inches away from his. "Umm, I'm pretty sure it was my idea for the last 20 years to find a place like this."

He smiled, squinting as the sun rays hit his body. "Well, it may have been your idea, but I made it happen."

She nodded her head and closed her eyes, feeling the warmth

of the afternoon break through the trees. "Yes, you did, and now, it's going to be—"

Margaret's words cut off when Mitch dropped his lower body into the water and jumped toward Margaret, who let out a loud shrill.

"Oh Mitch, you scared me!" she laughed, splashing him with water.

"Just making sure you are awake," he said, stepping in closer.

"What were you saying?" he asked with his eyes locking in on hers.

Margaret felt her heart beat faster when he pulled her body toward his.

"I have no idea," she replied, wrapping her arms around his waist.

~

~Margaret's Journal~

Mitch and I just shared two of the most glorious days of my life. I have traveled the world, and I cannot remember a place that has brought me more happiness or contentment. We enjoyed romantic dinners under the stars and deep conversations about a future that seems more like a fairy tale than real life. The Best Is Yet To Come.

Chapter Fifteen

SALLY WAS out in the pasture helping her dad with the newest addition to the farm: Bessie, a spunky golden-red calf.

"We got quite a fighter in this one," he said as Bessie gulped and pushed and shoved her way with the bottle Sally was holding.

The milk replacer oozed down Bessie's auburn face and onto Sally's shoes.

"Oh, Sally, you're getting your shoes all wet. I know you like to help, but I got this."

"I know you can do it, Dad, but after your heart issues, I hate to see you working so hard."

"I've never felt better. After they unclogged my darn arteries, I'm like a new man. You oughta go do something fun on your day off. Getting splattered by this here calf ain't no fun."

Sally closed her eyes as Bessie sneezed and all kinds of liquids spewed from her foamy mouth.

Sally and her dad began laughing.

"This is obviously a fun time," Sally said with a big, messy grin.

Sally's dad reached out, took the empty bottle, and put his hand on her shoulder. "I can handle this, really. Now, go do something for yourself. Me and your Momma are fine."

Sally wiped her face with the sleeve of her shirt. She stepped away from Bessie and reached for her dad, giving him a hug. "Thanks, Pop."

Sally walked back into the house and went to her room to change. Her phone lit up as she walked by. She had just missed a text from Margaret. She grabbed her phone and read the short message.

- Hey! I was wondering if you are available today?

Sally smiled a huge smile. She typed her response.

- YES!

- Would you like to come over this afternoon and stay for dinner?

- I would love that!

- Any time after 4 will be fine.

Sally did a little dance as she typed her reply.

- Thanks! See ya soon!

SALLY ARRIVED AT THE CABIN AT 4:01 P.M. MARGARET had prepared chicken salad, blueberry scones, and iced chai tea. They took their early meal to the deck and sat for a couple of hours enjoying the food and each other's company.

Margaret showed Sally the outline of the legacy book she was working on and told her what she knew about the interviews that were lined up so far. As the afternoon wound down, Margaret suggested they take their conversation to the creek.

When they arrived, they sat silently for several minutes watching the creek gently roll over the rocks.

"Is everything okay?" Sally asked, fearing the worst. "It seems like something is wrong."

Margaret took a deep breath and exhaled slowly. "Sally, I wanted to let you know that I am going home soon."

The color drained from Sally's face.

Margaret kept talking, but Sally didn't seem to hear her. She hung her head and fixed her gaze on a tiny caterpillar inching its way across a nearby rock.

"Sally, did you hear me?"

"Hello? Sally, are you okay?" Margaret reached and put her hand on Sally's shoulder.

Sally continued looking down, swallowing hard.

"Sally, did you hear me? I said we are buying Joseph's cabin."

Sally leaned forward, her eyes widening. "What? Are you kidding?"

Margaret smiled and shook her head.

"Please don't joke with me about something like this."

Margaret took both of Sally's hands and leaned in closer. "I am not joking. I am buying the cabin. Well, I should say that Mitch and I are buying the cabin."

Sally squeezed Margaret's hands. "Oh, my goodness, that is amazing! How did this happen?"

"Well, after Mitch and the boys came for their first visit, we all felt such a deep connection to the cabin that I couldn't stop thinking about how amazing it would be if this could be our permanent retreat. It is such a different pace of life here. Mitch and I began talking about how wonderful it would be if we could own it, so, we began praying about it, and when it felt like the right decision, Mitch contacted the owner. Because she held no sentimental attachment to the cabin, we let our offer do the talking and thankfully, she accepted."

"Wow, just wow. I felt so sad when you said you were going home." Sally shook her head in disbelief.

"I'm sorry that I left you hanging. I knew after I said I was going home you seemed to zone out."

"It's okay, it just felt too soon. I wasn't ready for you to leave permanently."

"Well, I won't be here full time, but I will be here as often as I can."

"I am so happy for you and Mitch. I have no doubt that Joseph would be thrilled!"

"Well, there is more."

Sally jumped up and gave Margaret a big hug. "I don't think I can take any more. I am so excited."

Sally let go of Margaret and began dancing around.

Margaret smiled and leaned back, taking a slow sip of her tea.

Just wait ... the time will come, Margaret's soul reassured her.

SALLY LEFT SHORTLY AFTER MARGARET SHARED THE BIG news with her. An early shift at the cafe made it difficult to stay out late. She pulled into her driveway, noticing the full moon lighting up the cornfield beside the house. The air was still and quiet. Sally tiptoed across the front porch and down the hall to her small bedroom.

She lay on her bed for several minutes, thinking about the cabin and Margaret. Her eyes grew heavy, and her heart full.

"I know Joseph probably can't hear me, Lord, but would you please tell him that the most amazing family is buying his little piece of Heaven on Earth. Thank You. Amen."

MARGARET GOT UP EARLY THE NEXT MORNING AND wrote a letter to Sally that explained what she wanted to tell her the previous night. She decided to walk to the cafe instead of driving.

A few feet down the dusty driveway, Margaret became aware of her heart beating against her chest, her lungs filling with air, and the way the breeze blew through the trees. She kept walking, pausing at the end of the driveway and remembering the first time she had pulled up to the mailbox.

"I'm so glad I didn't turn around that day." She ran her fingers along the hand-painted numbers and letters. She could almost envision Joseph, a man she had never met, pounding the post into the ground.

I wonder if he painted the address or was it his lovely bride?

Margaret kneeled, smelling the fragrant pink roses that were climbing up the back of the post. She gazed down the long, windy driveway, grateful to soon call this place her own.

She picked one of the roses and began her walk to the cafe.

Sally stopped what she was doing when Margaret walked in the door. "I still can't believe y'all bought Joseph's cabin. Gosh, I'm sorry, I guess I shouldn't call it Joseph's cabin anymore."

"You can certainly call it Joseph's cabin; he will always be a part of our story. The history of him and his bride was one of the selling points for us."

"Oh good, that's a relief. So, what's next for you guys?"

"Well, we are still working on the details. I will definitely keep you posted." Margaret reached into her purse and pulled out the letter she had written to Sally.

"For now, I want you to take this and read it when you have a chance to be alone. Take your time getting back to me."

Sally's eyes widened as she accepted the envelope. "Okay..."

"I was going to talk to you last night about this opportunity, but I thought this might be a better approach. I hope you have a good day."

Margaret walked out of the cafe and back toward the cabin.

Three hours later, Sally sat on the soft, green grass in the back pasture of her parents' farm. She leaned against the old pecan tree and began reading Margaret's letter.

Dear Sally,

I am so grateful to have met you. You are like a ray of sunshine in a rather dimly lit world. Perhaps I've never met anyone more genuine or fuller of potential.

When we first leased Joseph's cabin for the summer, I would have never guessed that in a few short weeks, Mitch and I would own this wonderful home and property.

We feel honored to carry on the legacy of love that Joseph began. As we look ahead, we are humbled by all that the cabin will offer us. We are so grateful to have a place of retreat as a couple and a family. As an author, I feel blessed to have a place to come to when I need to work on a project.

But, in reality, the cabin will be empty most of the time. Our lives are busy, and we aren't yet in the season of life that would allow us to move away from our main home. With all that in mind, we have a proposition for you.

Would you consider becoming the caretaker of the cabin and property and acting as my assistant? You could live in the cabin free of charge in addition to a generous salary.

Please know that we will respect your decision no matter what you decide. I encourage you to pray about this opportunity. Listen for His voice; there will be your answer.

With much love and appreciation,

Margaret

Sally reread the letter two more times before folding it and placing it back in the envelope. Her eyes filled with tears. She leaned against the tree and watched the clouds roll by, clutching the letter tight. Her mind was spinning with doubt.

Does Margaret understand that I've never been anything but a waitress? I never even went to college.

Act as her assistant? I am completely unqualified and inexperienced.

Caregiver of a beautiful home on a perfect piece of property? I live with my parents in a tiny bedroom that doesn't have its own closet or bathroom. How would I manage all that space?

"I need to talk to Margaret. I just don't see this working," she whispered while wiping the tears rolling down her cheeks.

Chapter Sixteen

Sally slept with the letter from Margaret under her pillow. She woke several times during the night, feeling for it as she doubted it was real. At 5 a.m., she sent Margaret a text.

- I really appreciate the offer, but I will need to pass. Perhaps you can find someone who is more qualified. I think that would be best. But thank you for thinking of me.

Sally hit send, shuffled her way to the tiny bathroom in the middle of the farmhouse, and stepped into the tub to take a shower. When she got out, she wiped the steamy mirror. She leaned in, looking deep into her own eyes.

"She doesn't know me, or maybe she just feels sorry for me. Either way, I could never be the person she needs me to be. I'm not like her," Sally muttered.

She stood still, glaring into her big, teary eyes. She shrugged her shoulders, put on her uniform, and headed to the cafe.

～

Sally's phone chimed as she poured coffee for the church ladies' group that met every week at the cafe.

"Is that your phone, honey?" one of the ladies, Mrs. Marie, smiled and asked as she sipped the perfectly prepared coffee.

"I guess so. Sorry, usually it's in the back."

"Well, go ahead and check it. It could be important."

Sally raised her brows. "I'm sure it's fine. I'll check it later," she said with a hint of irritation in her voice.

"Listen, sweet Sally. This morning, I woke up early with you heavy on my heart. I can't help but wonder how such a precious treasure like you is still waiting tables after all these years? If somebody is trying to contact you at 7 a.m., you better check and see if it's God trying to get through to you."

Mrs. Marie sipped her coffee and looked down at her pancakes, leaving the weight of the moment on Sally's shoulders.

"Okay ..."

Sally stepped to the side of the booth and read the text.

- Good morning. I will honor your decision if that's what you truly want, but I want to remind you of these truths. We chose you. You are capable. All you need is already within you.

Mrs. Marie looked up from the table and gazed at Sally. Sally looked back astonished at her insight.

Somewhere deep inside, Sally felt her soul whisper *it's okay to let go of your old story.*

Sally stepped into the kitchen, leaving the church ladies behind. Mrs. Betty looked up from the griddle. "Are you okay?"

Sally stood silent.

"Sally, what's wrong?

"Oh, nothing. I'm just tired, I guess."

Sally finished her shift not convinced that Margaret, Mrs. Marie, or her inner voice knew what was best.

~

A SUMMER STORM WAS BREWING IN THE CITY AND WAS headed toward Margaret. Mitch looked out across the cityscape and called her.

"Well, hello handsome," she answered with a grin.

"Hey babe. I just wanted to make sure you are in for the evening. A pretty big storm is heading your way."

"Yes, love. Thanks for always looking out for me."

Mitch closed his laptop and moved to the windows, spotting lightning in the distance. "How is it going with Sally? Have you heard from her other than that first rejection text?"

"I invited her to come over so we could discuss her concerns about our offer, but she politely declined. I can certainly relate to how she feels. You know what a battle it was for me to believe I deserved success."

Mitch looked at a photo on the wall of Margaret from early in her career. "Yes, I remember. You were shaking like a leaf when you stepped in front of the crowd at your first book signing."

Margaret laughed. "I can't believe you still have that photo in your office."

"It's one of my favorite photos of you. You worked so hard to get that first book published. It was amazing to see you in front of all of those people."

"I know. I didn't think I was smart or talented enough to make it as an author."

Margaret sat at the kitchen table and looked at the rough draft of her latest manuscript, which was book 25 of her career. She shook her head in disbelief and continued, "I worried that people who didn't know me would think I didn't measure up, and people who did know me would think I was a fraud."

Mitch smiled deeply. "But look at you now. I am so proud of you."

She ran her hand over the pages and sighed. "Thanks honey. It's been quite a journey, that's for sure...Thank you for warning me about the storm. Be careful driving home. I love you."

"Love you too. Good luck with Sally. I will be praying for her."

Margaret hung up and walked through the cabin making sure all the doors and windows were secure. She decided to sleep on the lower level in the hopes of sleeping through the storm. Thunder boomed in the distance and rain began to beat against the windows. She closed her eyes and pulled the quilt up.

"Lord, as storms rage around us tonight, I want to thank You for each and every time you brought me out of what seemed like an impossible situation. Thank You for Your divine guidance and love. Thank You for giving me the courage to continually seek the best version of who you have created me to be. I pray that You fill Sally with that same courage and that You create in her the desire and the confidence to boldly step into this next chapter of her life, and may I continue to do the same. Amen."

Chapter Seventeen

SALLY WORKED BACK-TO-BACK shifts at the cafe for three days after reading Margaret's letter. She maintained her usual hard work ethic and smile, but the letter replayed over and over in her mind. Her body was exhausted and her thoughts jumbled.

When her last shift of the three days ended, she opted to take the long way home. She rolled down the windows and savored the time alone. Her radio was off, but her thoughts were not.

Why did Margaret even ask me? Me of all people?

She pulled into the driveway, smiling as she spotted her dad in the garden. The sun was just beginning to drop behind the tall trees. He looked up and waved. She waved back feeling at home and loved.

Not to mention my parents, they need me. It's crazy to even consider moving out right now.

She saw her dad still looking her way. She continued smiling, feeling sick inside.

Snap out of it, Sally. For heaven's sake, enough already. It isn't even a real possibility. You already said no. Stop thinking about it.

She grabbed her purse and began walking toward the house, waving to her dad one more time.

Sally walked into the kitchen, kicking off her shoes as she went. "Hey, Mom."

"Hey sweetie, did you have a good day?"

"It was fine. I helped Mrs. Betty with some of the Fourth of July preparations. Oh, and a new girl who just moved into town came in looking for a job. She was oddly enthusiastic about wanting a job in the cafe. She brought in some pies that she'd made. She said she thinks she can make the cafe a spot on the map."

"Make Bluebird Cafe a spot on the map? You don't hear that every day. Did Mrs. Betty hire her?"

"No, but she told her that she would call her later this week, if she could find a few available hours in the schedule."

"Good. Maybe Mrs. Betty will hire her and you can work less, or better yet, you can finally do something bigger with your life."

Sally's mouth dropped. After a long pause, Sally cleared her throat. "Excuse me, Mom, what did you just say?

Her mom calmly replied, "You heard me. Maybe it's time you move on with your life. You have served and loved on every person in this town in that rinky-dink cafe, but you deserve better, Sally. I don't have any idea what that would be, but maybe it's time you figured it out."

Sally began to tear up, then dropped her head as the tears flowed onto her stained work shirt. Her mom rubbed her back. "It's okay. Change is hard, but staying stuck is even harder."

Her mom walked her to her bedroom, turning off the lights as she went.

SALLY TOSSED AND TURNED AND EVENTUALLY GOT OUT of bed as the roosters welcomed the new day stretching out over the horizon. Thirty minutes later she was driving to the cafe to help Mrs. Betty set up for the annual Independence Day parade and celebration. The parade, complete with steam engines, makes its way through the narrow streets each year as families gather in the Georgia summer heat.

The parade runs right past the cafe, and Mrs. Betty sells apple pie in a cup for $1.00, which probably doesn't even cover the cost of the cup, but she is deeply patriotic and wouldn't hear of over-charging for something as American as apple pie.

Sally carefully filled each Styrofoam cup to the top with warm, gooey pie. A tiny American Flag was then stuck in each cup as Mrs. Betty hummed "God Bless the USA."

"Honey, is everything okay? You sure aren't saying much" Mrs. Betty asked while licking the spoon after the last cup was filled.

"Yes. I'm okay."

"You know, I could have got one of the other girls to come in."

"I'm more than happy to help. I love our town's parade. It reminds me of when I was a little girl, and my parents would bring me. We would stand over by the bank and watch it from begin-ning to end."

"I know, I remember you running over and getting some of this apple pie for your daddy. Your parents don't come to the parade anymore, do they?"

"No, they don't seem to do anything fun, unless you consider farming fun," Sally smiled half-heartedly.

"Well, I sure hope you don't get stuck in that same old rut that everybody around here gets stuck in. You deserve better than that." Mrs. Betty placed the little flag in the last cup.

Stunned, Sally felt her heart beat a little faster as her serving spoon dripped the last bit of apple goo onto the counter. "What do you mean?"

"I've just always known you were different than everybody around here, but in a good way. Darlin', you must know this about yourself. You seem to see and feel things different than every other waitress that has ever worked here and most every person that walks through that door. Don't you see that about yourself?"

"Yes, ma'am, I guess I do." Sally felt her face flush.

"Why do you think I made you manager when you were only 18? Why do you think you are every customer's favorite? And why do you think that fancy writer that comes in here likes you so much? She sees something in you. I can tell when y'all are talking."

Tears spilled out of Sally's eyes and began to drop like wet summer rain on her worn apron.

"Honey, I didn't mean to make you cry," Mrs. Betty wrapped her arm around Sally.

"It's okay. I'm sorry I'm crying. Do you have a few minutes to talk?"

"Of course. We got plenty of time. You and I could win a pie serving contest—we got those cups filled lickety-split."

They laughed and found their way to the old corner booth that was Margaret's regular spot. Sally shared her heart and the opportunity that was before her. Mrs. Betty showered her with love and grace. In less than ten minutes, Sally's future had taken a drastic turn and she was fresh out of excuses.

SALLY DROVE HOME AFTER THE PARADE WITH THREE cups of apple pie and a bag full of candy that had been thrown her way. She found her parents sitting at the kitchen table when she walked in.

She felt her body heat with apprehension, but then she remembered the last words Mrs. Betty had said to her as the bell rang against the cafe door. "God's hand is upon your life, Sally. Don't you be afraid."

Her parents looked up from the table and smiled. Her mom noticed Sally's hesitancy. "Is everything okay, Sally?

"Yes, I just have something I need to talk to ya'll about. Is now a good time?"

"We always got time for you," Sally's dad said, smiling as he sunk his spoon into the cup of apple pie that Sally had placed before him.

Sally's voice shook as she read Margaret's letter out loud to her parents.

They sat quietly, their faces showing no emotion.

Sally finished the letter and then sat between her parents. "And I talked to Mrs. Betty today, and she gave me her blessing. She was very supportive, and said that the timing is perfect because of the new girl in town who wants a job."

Sally's mom patted her dad on the back as he remained quiet. Sally began to breathe faster as her doubts resurfaced.

Her dad looked up from his empty cup, licked his spoon, and nodded his head. "I was wondering when you were going to spread those pretty little wings of yours and fly."

"Oh, Daddy. Do you mean it? I was so worried that you would be upset with me and not understand why I would choose to move out."

"Sally, you've been here for me and your Momma long enough. It's time you live your own life."

"Oh Daddy, thank you!" Sally stood and wrapped her arms around her dad, feeling the roughness of his work coveralls and breathing in the smell of his aftershave and the fresh hay he had cut that morning.

Sally's dad held the hug and kissed her gently on her cheek. "Go make us proud, baby girl."

Her mom joined the hug, knowing that her daughter was embarking on a life that she herself had always been too scared to live.

Sally walked back to her bedroom and looked in the mirror that hung above her small desk. She smiled. "Today is Independence Day indeed."

Chapter Eighteen

MARGARET WOKE to the sound of birds chirping. Over the last few weeks, a Carolina wren couple had built a nest in the cabin eaves right by the master bedroom window. She didn't mind the noise, and she enjoyed watching the process, from the nest building to momma bird sitting patiently each day waiting for her little babies to hatch. New life was ready to erupt.

"Good job, Momma," Margaret whispered as she headed to the kitchen. With her favorite mug in hand, she reached for her phone and gasped when she read Sally's text that had arrived during the night.

-I hope I am not waking you. I was afraid if I waited until tomorrow morning I would chicken out. I say yes to the most amazing offer that has ever existed. If you have changed your mind, I understand, but if you still want me to work for y'all, I say yes.

～

SALLY WAS MAKING A FRESH POT OF COFFEE FOR THE church ladies when Margaret's return text chimed nearby. Sally felt her face redden while staring at the screen.

- Great! I am thrilled, and I know Mitch and the boys will be so happy! Why don't you come over after work today and we will discuss the details? I'll make us an early dinner.

Sally almost dropped the coffee pot as she reached for the counter to steady herself. A huge smile spread across her face. She reread the text multiple times.

"Looks like those prayers might be working," Mrs. Marie whispered to Sally, who poured the piping hot coffee into a well-worn, bright yellow mug.

Mrs. Marie winked at the waitress, who had faithfully served her for the last ten years.

"Yes, ma'am, I think you are right. Thank you. I sure appreciate your prayers and your encouragement."

Sally finished her shift with the same excellent service her customers were used to, then rushed home to tell her parents the great news.

THREE HOURS LATER, SALLY'S HEAD WAS STILL spinning with the reality of what lay ahead as she pulled up to the cabin, which would soon be her home. She walked onto the front porch, biting her lip along the way.

Margaret opened the door, noticing Sally's nervous demeanor. "How are you?"

"I guess I'm just feeling a little unsure that I will be able to be the assistant you need or want. You do realize I've never been anything but a waitress …"

Margaret motioned for her to come into the cabin.

"Sally, you are not your job. You excelled at that role for more than a decade, but it doesn't define who you are any more than me being an author defines who I am."

Margaret took both hands and placed them on Sally's shoulders, looking her in the eyes. "You have been such a wonderful friend for the last several weeks, and I have no doubt that you will do an excellent job. You can do this, I promise. And, as a reminder, I'm also doing something I've never done before by writing this legacy book, but we will figure it out together."

"Thank you seems so inadequate after everything you have done for me, but I don't know what else to say." She leaned in and hugged Margaret.

Margaret smiled and walked over to her bag. She pulled out a small Bible. "I've never told you, but you and I have more in common than you realize," Margaret's voice began to crack, her eyes glistening.

Sally looked confused. Margaret continued, "When I wanted to go to college to study creative writing, it was impossible for my parents to help me financially because we were very poor. My mom didn't understand why I would leave everything I knew and go out into the unknown, scary world.

"I feel so selfish. We've spent so much time talking about me since we met, we've never talked much about your childhood," Sally looked at Margaret with compassion in her eyes.

"It's okay. I learned a long time ago that our past doesn't define us any more than our titles or our roles do, unless we let it. I am not ashamed of my past—quite the opposite. I am proud of where I came from and the love I was shown, but I am also proud that I followed God's call on my life to step out of that so-called comfortable way of living and embark on a path that has been more amazing than I could have ever dreamed possible."

"I did wonder sometimes what your life was like before you were rich and famous, but I didn't want to seem nosy."

Margaret softly laughed. "Our stories are very similar as far as our humble beginnings. I just left the nest a little sooner. I haven't mentioned it because I wanted you to find your own way, and I didn't want you to compare what I have done with where God is leading you."

"Oh, Margaret. How can one person be so wise?"

Margaret smiled and opened the weathered Bible.

"Sally, my dad never even graduated high school. He couldn't read or write very well. I can still see him sitting in his old rocking chair on their front porch. He would sit for hours staring into this old Bible. I used to think he was reading it, but that was before I knew just how illiterate he actually was."

Margaret inhaled long and slow, remembering her dad's face. His smile, his gentle yet gruff voice ... for a moment, she was transported back to her childhood.

"Daddy, watch me. I can fly." Nine-year-old Margaret called out as she ran past her dad rocking on the front porch with his old King James Bible open in his lap. The soft breeze carried the kite higher and higher, as little Margaret opened her arms and pretended to be flying through the clouds as well.

He watched with a wide smile on his sun-leathered face. "You sure can, Margie girl. You sure can."

He laughed as Margaret flew around the parched South Georgia yard, gracefully following the shadow of the colorful kite that reached high into the sky.

After several minutes, Margaret came in for a landing at her dad's feet, knocking dust off his old work boots covered with red Georgia clay. She sat at the edge of his tattered rocker, catching her breath. "Daddy, read me a story from your Bible."

"Margie girl, I sure wish I could, but I can't read very good."

"Then why do you sit with the Bible in your lap all the time, looking through the pages, if you don't know what it says?"

"Well, Margie girl, I can read some, but mainly I hold this 'cause I know it's alive and it makes me feel right good to be holding the very words of God."

Young Margaret nodded her head. "Oh...," she said.

"You see, you don't have to have smarts to know God. He loves us no matter how He finds us. He don't care that I'm not smart or can't read good."

"Does He love me like that, too?"

"He sure does, Margie girl. He sure does."

Her dad looked down and rubbed the Bible's soft cover. He

closed his eyes, praying a simple prayer. "Thank you, God, for this little girl of mine."

"Daddy, would you like me to read to you? I'm a pretty good reader."

He opened his eyes, looking at his daughter, his proof that God still performed miracles.

"That'd sure be nice, Margie girl."

Young Margaret laid down her kite and opened the Bible. "What's your favorite story in here, Daddy?"

He rubbed his prickly chin. "Hmmm, how 'bout David beatin' that great big giant?" He reached his arms above his head as if he were a giant and laughed.

Margaret giggled, "Oh, Daddy, that's one of my favorites."

Sally honored the quietness of the moment, allowing Margaret to savor her memory. Margaret opened the Bible, which was full of notes scribbled in messy handwriting.

"What are those pieces of paper, if you don't mind me asking?"

"Those are reminders from my dad. The day I found out he couldn't read very well, I began reading to him. He was especially interested in the miracles of Jesus, because he always called me his little miracle."

"Why did he call you that? Did something miraculous happen?"

"No, that's the funny part. I guess it was just a bit out of the ordinary for an uneducated farmer from South Georgia to have such an inquisitive little girl who liked to dream such big, lofty dreams. Maybe that seemed like a miracle to him."

"Oh my goodness, that is so sweet." Sally thought of her own hard-working dad and grinned.

Margaret pulled out one of the notes, which was placed deep in the pages of scripture.

"When I read to Dad, he would copy his favorite part of the verse, word for word, and then add his own little note. It took him such a long time to write each letter and word, but he was determined. He gave me the Bible when I went away to college, and I bought him a brand new, large print Bible that same year for Christmas."

"Oh my," Sally responded, while shaking her head in amazement.

"This is the first note he wrote: 'I come against you in the name of the Lord, 1 Samuel 17:45. *God is for us. dont giv up.*'"

Sally held the note and read the powerful words that had been written over 40 years ago.

"Margaret, this is incredible."

"Sally, my dad never attempted to learn to read or to get out of that tiny little South Georgia town, but he still believed God for big things. Not necessarily for his own life, but he knew that God could still work miracles. The memories I have of him holding this Bible and rocking on the front porch of our teeny house have forever impacted me. I don't talk about it much, but Sally, you have to believe me; God can use anyone, from any background, at any time to absolutely change the world."

Sally swallowed hard and reached for the Bible. She flipped through the pages, feeling her confidence rise.

Margaret stood tall with her shoulders back. "Sally, I am a wealthy, best-selling author, yet my dad could barely read or write. It's not what we do or where we come from that defines our future."

Sally closed her teary eyes, breathing in possibility.

Margaret's thoughts slow danced back to her dad.

"*Daddy, watch me. I can fly.*" "*You sure can, Margie girl. You sure can.*"

SALLY STAYED UNTIL THE EVENING TURNED INTO A starry night. They shared more details of their pasts, but more significantly, they focused on the bright, new future that was in store for them.

As Sally drove away, Margaret walked around the property looking up into the twinkling night sky, absorbing the miraculous story God was weaving together.

"Who would have ever thought that we would end up buying this beautiful cabin? And then hire a precious, small-town waitress to be the caretaker and my personal assistant? Only You, God, could orchestrate such an oddly beautiful story."

Margaret strolled around for several minutes. Fireflies flew in and out of the shadows, and a distant owl could be heard hooting in unison with tree frogs.

Margaret breathed in the night, feeling a slight chill in the air.

"Thank You, Lord," she whispered as she made her way back to the front porch. She traced the outline of the heart that was etched into the wood beside the front door.

"And thank you, Joseph, for creating such a beautiful place."

Chapter Nineteen

MARGARET SLEPT PEACEFULLY for almost nine hours, waking with a spring in her step and a song in her heart. She found her phone and pulled up Mitch's number, hoping she wouldn't wake him. He answered on the first ring.

"Hey, babe, you're up early. How did it go with Sally last night?"

"It actually went great. She is so excited, Mitch, and so am I."

"That's great! It's certainly been an amazing few weeks."

"Sally said she can basically start working for us whenever we need her. She will be helping to train the young lady who will be taking her place at the cafe, but I assured her that it was okay if it took a few weeks for the transition to be in full effect."

"I'm glad Sally is excited. I know you are eager to get more organized with the legacy book, and from what you've said, she should be a great help."

"Yes, I think we will make a great team. I'm going to spend the next couple of days showing her what she needs to know about the cabin, and I've outlined some of my basic needs for the new book, so she can start helping with that, too." Margaret scanned the cabin, excited to get to work.

"That all sounds good. I am so proud of you, babe," Mitch said.

"Thank you. Every detail is working out. You don't think we moved too fast, do you?"

"Not at all. We prayed about it, we have the resources, and we have certainly learned to never take life for granted, so I think it's all perfectly timed."

"Good, I think so too." Margaret sat on the sofa and watched the morning sky lighten while the birds enjoyed an early morning feast. She smiled, enamored by it all.

"I am getting ready to go work out. I'll see you later. I love you."

Margaret closed her eyes and breathed in the moment, "And I love you."

She hung up and made herself a light breakfast. When she finished eating, she made her way through the cabin, taking notes of things she wanted to purchase to make the cabin their own.

The current owner sold the property fully furnished, and because Margaret was the first person to lease the cabin, it was like buying a brand-new home that was professionally decorated. Very few changes needed to be made, but Margaret wanted to add a few personal touches.

She and Mitch decided that the lower level would become Sally's primary dwelling place. It had a spacious bedroom, well-equipped bathroom, and nice living area with a walkout terrace to the creek. Margaret made a few notes, making plans to create a small kitchen area, which would help the space feel more like a fully independent apartment. Margaret smiled, nodding her head in approval, knowing that Sally would love every detail.

The upstairs loft was perhaps the most astonishing part of the cabin. Rustic stairs in the center of the cabin led to the second floor, which was rather small, but perfect for Margaret and her writing. An oversized, cozy chair was nestled into the roof eaves, with a small table nearby that held a copper coaster and a small fern in an antique vase atop a couple of old, worn books.

The other side of the loft had a built-in desk with beautiful stationery and pens, an old glass bottle with fresh flowers from the yard, and an antique Bible.

In the middle of the room was a queen-size bed covered in a beautiful array of linens, blankets, and pillows. A small decorative tray with chocolates and mints adorned the corner of the bed on top of a luxurious, soft throw that was flawlessly ivory, as if it had just been sheared from a sheep that had lived the plushest of lives.

Margaret scanned the loft, touching each beautiful element and decided it was exactly as it should be. No changes were needed. It felt as if the Lord had gone before her, preparing this place and her heart for this new season of life.

When Margaret felt confident that her list was complete, with a section for what to buy and an additional section for what to do, she packed up her SUV and began the drive back to their home in the city. As she traveled the winding mountain roads, she dialed Ernie's number.

"Hey, young lady. How's my favorite author doing?"

Margaret grinned when she heard Ernie's voice. Margaret and Ernie talked the entire drive back to her house. They laughed, reminisced, and planned for the days ahead.

MARGARET WALKED INTO THE EMPTY HOUSE AND spotted a bright yellow note on the fridge. *Welcome home! I love you and I can't wait to see you.*

Margaret brushed her fingers across the note, breathing in the scent of Mitch's cologne and knowing she must have just missed him.

She made a couple of trips to her vehicle to bring in her things, but soon found herself annoyed by the noise all around her. A neighbor's dog was barking each time she walked outside, a garbage truck grunted down the street, banging and compacting as it went, and a child could be heard screaming a couple of houses over. Her home in the city, while beautiful, seemed overly loud and cumbersome after her peaceful time at the cabin.

Be grateful for where you are, Margaret told herself as she pulled herself away from negative emotions. She poured herself a hot cup of coffee that Mitch had left for her, grabbed a snack, and headed to her office.

She sat in front of her computer and began browsing through her emails. She gasped when she saw an email from her previous agent, Tom.

Margaret

I wanted to wish you well on your new ventures and apologize for my actions during our time working together. I almost booked myself on that same flight, but changed my mind and decided to go one day earlier. I could have been on that plane. I tried to push you to be on that plane, too, and thankfully, you chose to honor your family instead of me.

I have wrestled daily with who I am and what kind of agent and person I have become. I read your press release and watched your video countless times. Your words, "When you take your last breath, what will your legacy be?" haunted me for days as I tried to pretend that my life mattered and that I wasn't that bad. I have now accepted that I was often more concerned with ratings and status than I was with being a man of God.

For now, I am taking time off to seek what God wants me to do next. I got caught up in what I thought success looked like, and I was wrong. Dead wrong.

I wanted you to know that I am sorry. I wish you and your family well. I look forward to following your future work. I am proud of the stand you took for yourself and for your family. Lastly, thank you for unknowingly leading me back to God.

Tom

Margaret leaned back in her chair and closed her laptop, breathing a heavy sigh. Her heart pounded in her chest, but her anxiety was replaced with shock and amazement. The email confirmed what she knew. Although Tom professed to be a Christian, he hadn't been walking with the Lord.

"I don't want to deal with this right now," she whispered under her breath.

The pit in her stomach tightened as memories of Tom resurfaced in her mind.

I was such a fool.

How could I have been such a fool?

She closed her computer and tried to forget that his email reached her inbox.

Chapter Twenty

MARGARET LAY beside Mitch as the moon still shone through the windows, her mind racing. She was thinking about the impending interviews, the last-minute details of buying the cabin, and, most of all, Tom. She quietly got up and headed to the family room, turned on the lamp, and grabbed her laptop, surrendering to the not-so-gentle nudge she was feeling in her soul.

"Please give me the words, Lord."

In the silence of the room, Margaret felt her heart beating harder than normal against her chest. Her hands felt clammy.

Why does this feel so hard?

Margaret sat with her thoughts. She retraced her relationship with Tom. Amid all the heartache and anger she had been feeling toward him, Margaret often felt the Lord urging her to pray for him, so, reluctantly, she began praying for him.

In the quiet, less bitter places of her heart, she felt sorry for Tom. When she put her hurt aside, she saw him as a broken man, lost in a world that was trying to consume him and everyone else around him.

Extend the same grace that you have been given ... whispered her soul.

Dear Tom,

I very much appreciate you reaching out to me. First, I forgive you completely. I will admit that I spent many months blaming you for my problems. However, I now fully recognize that I was a willing participant and the mess I made of my life during that season was not your fault. You never forced me to do anything. I chose to step away from who I knew myself to be as I sought a younger, 'more relevant' version of myself.

I am pleased that you are once again walking with the Lord. As we both know, the only true peace we will ever experience is when we are in step with Him or when He is carrying us when we can no longer move ourselves.

I am far from perfect, and I feel certain that God is not done refining me, and that's okay. I find myself longing for the most authentic version of me that only He can produce. I pray the same for you.

Seek Him, love Him, and get to know Him once again. He is the answer. I wish you much love, joy, and peace along your journey.

Margaret

She closed her laptop and returned to the bedroom. She pulled the comforter up, nestled herself beneath Mitch's arm, and drifted back to sleep, remembering a phrase she learned many years ago: *The only person you hurt when you withhold forgiveness is yourself.*

◈

A FEW HOURS LATER, MITCH AND MARGARET ENJOYED breakfast by the pool. The water was shimmering in aqua blue, and the ferns had never looked lusher and more vibrant. Petunias in lavender purple, deep fuchsia, and vibrant yellow brightened the sunny day even more as Margaret soaked up the sun.

Mitch reached over and took hold of her hand. "I can't believe the cabin will be ours in less than 24 hours."

She placed her other hand on top of his. "I know, this has

been a crazy year, but I wouldn't change any of it, except for hurting you and our boys."

Mitch caressed her hand while leaning in for a kiss. Margaret felt the physical strength of him, which was perfectly balanced with his soft, gentle spirit. He lovingly pulled her up into his embrace.

"The mistakes we both made are helping us see life more clearly," he said, while holding her. "And it sure feels good."

As the afternoon sun began its descent, Mitch and Margaret drove to the closing attorney's office and signed all the documents required to make the cabin theirs. Mitch dangled the keys when they reached the parking lot. "Well, it's official. The cabin is ours."

"What a miraculous turn of events," Margaret replied with her eyes wide. She smiled and her soul whispered, *The Best is Yet to Come.*

Mitch and Margaret drove to the cabin, both giddy with excitement. On their arrival, Mitch placed each item that had been purchased in the exact spot Margaret had envisioned. The outdoor space was a collaborative visionary effort of Mitch and the boys, complete with fishing gear, kayaks, outdoor games, and two more hammock loungers.

After each item was perfectly positioned, Margaret and Mitch lay in the hammock down by the creek and gazed up at the night sky as the sound of rushing water lulled them into a deep rest. Katydids serenaded them as a falling star streaked through the night sky.

Chapter Twenty-One

SALLY ARRIVED at the cabin the next morning at 9 a.m. Margaret and Mitch stood in the front door, arm in arm and smiling as Sally pulled into the driveway. She sat in her car, took a deep breath, and then slowly walked to the front door.

"Come in, friend. We have a lot to show you," Margaret reassured her.

Mitch and Margaret gave Sally a brief tour of the few changes they had made throughout the main cabin and then walked her downstairs. When they reached the bottom of the stairs, Margaret spread out her arms, beaming deep down to her soul. "I hope you like it. We tried to make it feel like your own apartment. What do you think?"

Sally stood, unable to speak. She looked around and her face and neck began to flush.

"We will be using the main floor and the loft; this space is just for you. Of course, nowhere is off limits, but we thought it was important to provide a private area for you," Mitch said.

"I can't believe how perfect this is. Oh my gosh, please pinch me, I must be dreaming …"

Margaret had been to Sally's parents' house and gathered a few items with the help of her mom. A large vase held several large magnolia blooms from her parents' yard, and tiny jars held cuttings from several of the plants from her mom's kitchen. A close-up picture of the baby calf, Bessie, was perfectly framed, with Bessie's playful face brightening up the room even more.

Margaret had truly outdone herself. A beautiful antique hutch now housed a tiny refrigerator and a small convection oven. All the impersonal touches had been removed and were replaced with things Sally would love.

Sally walked around the space, carefully noticing each item. She touched each special thing and began to laugh when she got to Bessie's picture.

She made her way to the bedroom and stopped in the middle of the doorway. "Oh, my goodness, is that my great-grandmother's quilt?"

Margaret stepped forward and put her arm around Sally. "Yes, it is. I went to your parents' house and your mom and I found some things we thought you might enjoy."

"Oh my gosh, that quilt has been on the top shelf of my parents' bedroom closet my entire life because Mom feared it would get damaged. I can't believe she gave it to me. It's so perfect."

Sally ran her hand over the delicate stitching and soft fabrics that had been lovingly sewn together by women who had gone before Sally to make this very opportunity possible. Women who had loved, sacrificed, and endured to be of service to those they held closest to their hearts.

"Your mom was so excited to give you the quilt. She told me that she had been saving it all these years because it felt too special to be thrown on their bed each day. She went on to say, 'What good is a beautiful thing if it isn't being shared with the world.'"

Margaret grinned and looked at Sally, whose eyes were full of tears and love.

"My parents live a simple life, but I wouldn't be who I am today or have the courage to be who I can be without them. "

Margaret reached out and ran her fingertips across the

different squares on the quilt, feeling the various fabrics and the legacy rising.

"Those who seem to live simple lives, are often the ones who support and encourage others to live bigger, bolder lives, which means that God still uses their lives in a mighty way."

"Wow, I've never thought about it like that."

"Good or bad, we are always learning how to live from those closest to us. I know your parents are very proud of the amazing young woman you have become."

"Thank you." Sally continued to look around her new living space.

A brand-new laptop lay atop a small desk in front of a window that filled the room with sunlight. Pens, journals, and notepads were stacked and ready for use. A new camera was lying beside the laptop.

"Is this all mine?" Sally whispered.

"Yes, ma'am, it's all yours. Hopefully, everything you need is here. If not, we will get it," Margaret replied.

"I can pay you back. Please just let me know how much I owe. It might take a while, but I will pay for all of it."

Mitch spoke up, "Sally, please know that we did all of this for you because we wanted to. You don't owe us anything. We appreciate your willingness to live here and look after the cabin, and I know your help will be invaluable to Margaret."

Margaret smiled, nodding her head in agreement.

"Thank you so much, seriously. I don't really know what to say. I promise I will try my hardest to do a good job for you."

"I know you will, Sally. I have no doubt in my mind that you and I will make a beautiful team." Margaret walked to Sally, and gave her a hug. Sally looked into Margaret's eyes as she said, "Thank you, really, thank you."

∼

- Sally's Journal ~

I moved into Joseph's cabin today, except now it belongs to Mitch and Margaret. It feels like I am living in a dream, like this can't really be happening.

Mitch and Margaret see something in me that I still don't see in myself, but I am trying to believe that I am capable of what they need from me and that I deserve this opportunity.

I feel lucky and blessed and favored and all the things. Today marks the beginning of a future I never dreamed possible.

Chapter Twenty-Two

MITCH AND MARGARET began the drive back to their home in the city. Even with all the wonderful things that were happening, doubt and nervousness filled Margaret's mind as they traversed the wet mountain roads.

Maybe this legacy book is a dumb idea. I am certainly not qualified to deal with other people's grief. I barely got through my own grief when my parents died; her thoughts swirled as they neared their home.

Keep going her soul urged.

She sat with her eyes closed, listening to that quiet, calm voice within. *Keep going.*

She looked over at Mitch, who was singing along with the radio. She smiled as her hand found his. He returned the smile and began singing even louder.

~

THE DOUBTS AND NERVOUSNESS CONTINUED AFTER Margaret got home. Mitch left for The Ranch, and Margaret headed to the pool with her laptop in hand, hoping to find some reassurance within, although apprehension was pressing hard.

Her breathing felt shallow and quick. Her eyes danced around the lush garden area surrounding the pool, and her mind felt scattered.

She breathed in and held her breath, closing her eyes, then she slowly exhaled while reaching for her phone.

Ernie answered on the first ring.

"Well, whad'ya know, it's my favorite author," Ernie said with a chuckle.

"Good morning, Ernie."

"Uh oh, I detect sadness in that pretty little voice of yours. What's going on?"

"I have been struggling with doubt this morning. I thought maybe I could update you on the plan for the new book and get your thoughts."

"Alright, let's hear it."

"I am considering the title *The Ripples We Create*. As of now, we have a total of seven face-to-face interviews to conduct, a few phone interviews, and dozens of short messages that individuals have sent us."

"Sounds good so far."

Margaret breathed in and exhaled hard.

"I will be adding in a bit of my story, some scripture, and promptings to encourage readers to evaluate their lives and legacy. Sally will also be helping with photography. I am hoping to capture some photos at each interview to help with the visual aspect of each story. What do you think? Is that a good idea? Too far-fetched?"

"I don't see any problems with your concept at all. It sounds great to me."

Margaret shifted, looking up at the billowy clouds floating by. "It's just so different from anything else I have ever written. I don't want to focus on the negative side of the crash, and I am worried what my audience will say after the last book was such a disaster."

"Hold on and take a deep breath. You've got yourself all worked up."

Margaret nodded her head in agreement.

"Listen to me, Margaret, and hear me loud and clear. Fear and doubt are liars, my dear. Of course, you have doubts; that's part of being human. You have a solid idea, and I believe in you and this project." His stern voice radiated through her anxiety.

Margaret leaned back in the chair and felt the warmth of the morning sun. She put her hand on her heart. "Oh, Ernie, your encouragement never ceases to amaze me."

"I am pretty wonderful," he said with a deep, belly laugh.

They ended the call, and Margaret closed her laptop. She made her way to the edge of their property, which overlooked the city. She missed the creek, the tall trees, and the simplicity of life at the cabin.

Live in this moment, she told herself as the neighbor's dog insisted on creating a distraction.

She sat in the cool, green grass and smiled a deep smile all the way to her soul. Her doubts were swept away in the peace of Ernie's encouraging, yet direct words.

Then, like a soft breeze, she thought of the loving words Mitch said when this all began, '*God will open other doors; you'll see.*' The feelings of doubt subsided as the desire to serve overpowered the enemy.

Margaret sat quietly for several minutes, eyes closed and heart open. When she opened her eyes, a brilliant cardinal was perched in a nearby tree.

"Well, aren't you handsome?" she said, amazed at the timing of the shy visitor. The sun shone on her new friend's brilliant red feathers. They both watched each other. The bird turned, gave Margaret one last look, and then swooshed down into the bushes below.

"Thank You..." Margaret felt grateful to be aware of God's presence, even in the little things.

THE NEXT MORNING, MARGARET AND MITCH ENJOYED breakfast on the patio, which proved to be the perfect send-off for Margaret. He prepared her favorite breakfast bowl along with a side of juicy ripe oranges and perfectly prepared coffee.

"So, are you ready to begin the interviews?" he asked.

"In some ways, I am. Thanks to you, I feel very organized with the files for each person, and I have all the things I need packed, but I am still nervous about how I will hold up under the weight of so many sad stories. I mean, you know how hard I took it when my parents died. I hardly feel qualified to be delving into this level of grief."

Mitch leaned over the table and looked into Margaret's eyes. "You are more than qualified. I have never known anyone who is better at relating to what other people are going through than you."

Margaret held Mitch's gaze. He took his hand and rubbed it down her cheek. The morning breeze blew her hair away from her face, and he leaned forward, brushing his lips against hers. He kissed her right cheek and then her left cheek. "You are more than qualified."

TWO HOURS LATER, MARGRET TRAVERSED THE WET road as rain spilled out of the sky. She slowly drove down Main Street, feeling a warmth in her soul that she had never felt back in the city.

The glow of the quaint stores lit up the little town. The cafe sign blinked OPEN while waitresses poured piping hot coffee into oversized mugs. The barber shop was bustling with activity as several local men waited their turn on senior discount day. The flower shop was filled with a soon-to-be-bride, her mom, and three bridesmaids, each oohing and awing in excitement over the proposed blush pink bouquet.

Margaret made her final turn onto Willow Springs Drive, and her mind went back to the first time she arrived at Joseph's cabin. The fact that she and Mitch now owned the cabin continued to amaze her.

She paused at the end of the driveway, remembering how close she had come to leaving that first day. She wondered how different things would have turned out if she had not stayed.

Her body, mind, and soul felt immediate relief as she continued down the wet driveway into her own paradise. She parked near the front porch and looked up in wonder when the cloudy sky gave way to a brilliant rainbow. She smiled when the sky brightened, displaying a visible reminder of God's faithfulness and a wonderful memory she shared with Mitch.

Sally was in the kitchen when she heard Margaret rolling to a stop in front of the cabin. She put the last dish she was drying into the cabinet and rushed to open the door.

"Welcome back," Sally said with slight hesitation in her voice, reaching to help Margaret with her bags.

"It's good to be back. Are you ready for our big adventure?"

"I guess so. I know you have told me over and over that I can do this, but I'm still so nervous."

"I know how you feel. Mitch and Ernie have also been reassuring me the last couple of weeks. I was talking to Matthew recently, and he reminded me of a phrase I used to tell him when he would get nervous before a big game or event, 'Do it scared.'"

Sally smiled, her eyes creasing as happiness spread across her face. "I like that. Do it scared. That's a simple, but direct way of speaking action over our fears."

Margaret and Sally spent the rest of the evening in quiet reflection and preparation for the upcoming trip. Before they each retired to their bedrooms for the night, Margaret prayed for their future endeavors.

"Father God, as Sally and I get ready to embark on the first step of this journey, I pray for Your tender mercy and love to see us through each moment. I pray that the families will be open and receptive to our presence and that You will speak through us. Fill us with words that will comfort and actions that will lighten the load they are carrying. Overflow us with grace, compassion, and love as we seek to make a difference. Thank You for this opportunity and for my second chance at living a life that matters. May my life be poured out to You as an offering. Amen."

Sally opened her eyes, her face relaxing. "Amen."

Chapter Twenty-Three

FLIGHT 7889 WAS A CONNECTING flight out of Chattanooga, Tennessee, which meant many of the passengers lived within a two-hour drive of the cabin. The first three interviews were close to the downtown area of Chattanooga, which was bustling with activity.

Margaret reserved a beautiful suite overlooking the city, thinking it was probably Sally's first time staying in a nice hotel. She also arranged for an early check-in, so they could get settled when they arrived. Margaret's assumption about Sally was proven to be correct as they entered the suite.

"Oh my gosh, you've got to be kidding. This place is beautiful!" exclaimed Sally as she walked through the door.

"I wanted to treat you to a really nice place, at least for this first outing. We won't always splurge like this, but the extra room will be nice while we get ourselves organized."

"Well, if you say so. After all, you are the boss," Sally grinned while walking to the large floor-to-ceiling windows overlooking the city. "Wow. Just wow!"

Margaret smiled while watching young Sally's innocence and wonder unfold. "We have all day, so feel free to take advantage of everything. There is a nice tub in the main bathroom, and the hotel also has a lot to offer."

"It will take me more than a day to get used to this kind of living. I can't get over this." Sally walked in and out of both bathrooms and bedrooms, shaking her head in amazement.

"You deserve to be spoiled, Sally. You took a big chance leaving what was comfortable to start this new venture with me. I really appreciate you, and having you on this journey brings me a lot of comfort."

"Thanks ... I'm glad to hear you say that. I'm going to try really hard to do a good job, I promise."

Sally lowered her head, looking at the floor.

Margaret walked over to her. "You have already done an excellent job. Please don't doubt yourself for another moment. If I'm not happy or I want something done differently, I will tell you. Don't always assume the worst about yourself."

"I'm sorry."

"You don't have to apologize. From now on, can we agree that you are right where you are supposed to be?"

Sally's eyes lit up and her smile widened. "Okay. Although I doubt myself, I want you to know I did pray about this opportunity. I think what you are saying is true. I am right where I am supposed to be," Sally scanned the room, "which right now is in some kind of palace!" She giggled and walked back to the large windows to take in the view.

Margaret stood back and watched what looked like a butterfly emerging from its cocoon.

Both ladies were grateful for the evening to prepare and gather the items they would need for the first interview, which included their courage. Margaret was planning on conducting the interviews, and Sally brought a voice recorder, the camera, and a notepad to help properly document each person's story, with their consent.

Mitch had been handling the inquiries for the interviews because he wanted to be the first point of contact, in case any bogus requests came in. He had then created a small file for each of the families with the preliminary details.

The plan was for Sally to add her notes and any photos that she took to each file as information was gathered during the interview. That same file would be used throughout the process as each individual's story was gathered, documented, edited, and finally crafted into a short biography. Margaret considered herself old-school and much preferred physical material, which would eventually be transposed digitally.

Sally was much like Margaret—very detail-oriented and neat. She enjoyed the opportunity to create an organizational plan that would work for the project. Margaret gladly allowed Sally to manage these details, feeling thankful for her assistance. For most of Margaret's career, she felt as if she had to oversee everything. Her need to be in control and micro-manage every aspect of her professional life only created more stress and took her away from her true gift, which was to write.

As the cityscape shone brightly into the night's darkness, Margaret said goodnight to Sally and went into her bedroom. She leaned against the luxurious bed's headboard and opened her Bible. After spending several minutes silently reading through scripture, she became transfixed on a passage in Philippians 4. Margaret scooted up in the bed and began feeling peace radiating from deep within her soul.

"Do not be anxious about anything, but in everything by prayer and supplication with thanksgiving let your requests be made known to God. And the peace of God, which surpasses all understanding, will guard your hearts and your minds in Christ Jesus," she said aloud.

Margaret closed her Bible and laid it upon her chest. Her eyes were heavy, and her heart was full.

Chapter Twenty-Four

THE NEXT MORNING, Margaret mapped the first address and confirmed it was less than ten minutes from the hotel. When it was time to leave, Margaret and Sally sat on the edge of Margaret's bed and said a prayer of protection, provision, and purpose as they readied themselves to meet Bill Baker's widow.

Pam Baker had been the first person to respond on the website. Two hours after the social media post went live about the legacy book, Pam left a long message and requested a face-to-face interview as soon as possible.

Pam, now a widow, called herself a strong believer as she wrote at length about her husband, Bill, in the first message. She was passionate about this opportunity to spread the word about her dear husband, whom she had loved for over 40 years. Bill and Pam had one daughter and two grandsons, who would also be at the interview.

At 9:40 a.m., Margaret and Sally pulled into the driveway, neither saying a word. As the vehicle came to a stop, Margaret simply stated what her heart felt. "God go before us."

Pam met Margaret and Sally in the driveway, tears already streaming down her face. "Thank you so much for giving my Bill one last voice in this world." She hugged Margaret and then Sally, and then Margaret again. Sally was speechless as her own tears started to form.

Margaret only managed to say a faint, "It is truly our honor," before Pam hugged her again. Margaret suddenly realized this assignment would be much harder than she thought.

Margaret and Sally spent three hours with Pam, her lovely daughter, and her precious grandsons. They listened to many stories about Bill that made them laugh and cry.

They wished they had known Bill while feeling like, in some ways, they did know him. They learned he was a loving husband, a devoted father, and a grandfather determined to have the two most spoiled grandsons that could ever live.

Pam put together a delightful brunch and showered Margaret and Sally with true Southern hospitality and genuine love. Sally decided that hand-written notes were more personal and less technical than typed ones, so she wrote endless details about the life of Bill Baker.

As the room grew quiet and everyone seemed to marvel at the legacy Bill had left behind, Margaret laid down her things and looked at Pam. "This has been so wonderful. I cannot tell you how much I appreciate your openness and the time you have spent with us."

"It has been my honor, truly. I know Bill would be tickled to live on in this way."

"That's great, I am so grateful we can tell his story. As we wrap up our time together, is there anything you would like us to photograph while we are here that we could include in the story?" Margaret asked.

Pam's eyes widened, and then she hopped up with great intention. "Yes! You ladies need to see the treehouse!" Pam's daughter and grandsons perked up and smiled when the treehouse was mentioned. "That's a great idea, Mom."

Pam walked Margaret and Sally to the backyard, where they were met with a marvelous three-story treehouse.

Sally was the first to speak. "Oh, my gosh, I have never seen anything like this. This is amazing!"

Pam looked up at the treehouse with a wide grin.. "It really is amazing. My Bill was always a dreamer, and he had the biggest imagination of anyone I knew. When we bought this property 40 years ago, we were newlyweds and hadn't even thought about having children yet, much less grandchildren. But my Bill insisted that he plant three trees that he knew would grow fast and strong so his future grandchildren would have a treehouse like no other."

Margaret grinned, gazing at the structure and imagining that Mitch would have done the same thing. "Now, that is planning ahead."

"That was my Bill, always dreaming up these wild plans for the future. I remember saying, 'Sweetie, shouldn't we think about what we will do for our kids first?'" Pam laughed as she watched her grandsons climb all over the impressive structure that Bill had imagined all those years ago.

"What did he say?" Margaret was amused by the sweetness of every story about Bill.

"Oh, he said something like, 'The kids will get to enjoy those trees too, but they won't be big enough for a long time to build what I am thinking of.' And you know what? He was right."

"Our daughter did enjoy the shade of the trees and climbing all over them, but around the time our first grandson was born, the trees were the perfect size. Bill began building, and he never stopped. As the boys grew, Bill would adapt the treehouse to meet their needs. What started as a simple treehouse is now more of a play-fort, complete with a telescope for viewing the night sky. Bill would sit up there with the boys for hours, telling them outlandish stories and gazing toward Heaven." Pam's voice became strained as the emotion surfaced on her face.

Bill and Pam's daughter, who had been very quiet the entire interview, spoke up, "Dad was always gazing toward Heaven, right, Mom?" She put her arm around her mom and held her tight.

Margaret walked all around the structure. "Is it okay if Sally takes some pictures now?"

"That would be wonderful. If you would like, feel free to climb the ladder and see for yourself what a masterpiece the treehouse really is," Pam beamed with pride at what Bill had left for all to enjoy.

Sally laid down her things except for the camera and made her way up the ladder. The boys were quick to give her a tour once she arrived on the first level.

After several minutes and dozens of pictures, Sally leaned over the railing and urged Margaret to join her, "Margaret, you have to see this. It is so perfect in every way."

Margaret was more than happy to join Sally and the boys. Bit by bit, she climbed, and as she reached the top, she saw four simple words etched above the opening to the wooden door: *God, go before us.* Margaret stood stunned as she recalled saying those exact words only hours before when she and Sally arrived at Bill and Pam's home.

Margaret leaned over the edge and called down to Pam and her daughter. "Can you tell me more about this phrase that is etched above the doorway?"

"That was the phrase he said all the time. Daddy was a dreamer, as Mom said, and he believed that God created each of us with passions and purposes that we could only carry out if we were walking with God. So, Dad would have these wild ideas, but the words that kept his feet on the ground were, God, go before us. Daddy was willing to go anywhere and try anything, but he never wanted to feel like he was in front of God. He would always tell me to make sure I was chasing my dreams, but never forget who should be leading the way."

"What a wonderful, wise man," Margaret stood at the railing overlooking the home that Bill and Pam had built and created a family in, amazed at the majesty of it all. Margaret considered telling Pam and her daughter that she had just said those very words when she arrived, but instead, she looked to Heaven, which is what Bill would have done. She quietly thanked God for this family, this opportunity, and her blessed life.

~

THE DRIVE BACK TO THE HOTEL WAS PEACEFUL, WITH Margaret and Sally both processing what had just happened. The words that were spoken, the love that was shown, the dreams that were realized, and the legacy that, without a doubt, was created.

Margaret thought of Mitch and what a wonderful husband and father he was. Her heart was overflowing with love as they pulled in front of the valet. They got out of the SUV and slowly made their way through the hotel lobby.

"Want to order room service or eat at the restaurant?" Margaret asked.

Sally stopped walking and raised her eyebrows. "Whatever you want to do. It doesn't matter to me."

"Okay, in that case, let's go get comfy. We can work on the book, enjoy the suite, and order some yummy food to our room."

"That sounds absolutely perfect."

~

~Margaret's Journal~
  A love so pure. A man so great.
  Oh, Bill, how I wish I'd known you on this side of Heaven.

Chapter Twenty-Five

MARGARET WOKE as the start of another day glistened off the tall windows of the downtown buildings. She longed to hear Mitch's voice, but figured he would still be asleep. She didn't want to wake Sally, so she grabbed her phone and sent him a text instead.

- Hi, are you up yet?

Mitch was making his first cup of coffee for the day when the text came in. He smiled as he put his mug down.

- Hi, beautiful bride of mine, yes, I just got up. I have a full day, so I set my alarm so I could get my workout in and hopefully hear your sweet voice.

Margaret took a deep breath, feeling happiness and peace radiate throughout her body.

- Aw, well, isn't that sweet! I just wanted to start my day by saying I love you!

Mitch stirred his coffee and dialed Margaret's number. Margaret felt her pulse quicken as her phone lit up. She tiptoed into the bathroom.

"Well, hello," she whispered.

"I love you, too!" he exclaimed.

"Thanks, honey! It's so good to hear your voice."

"Same here, babe. I won't keep you, but I wanted to let you know that I will be praying for you and Sally today."

"Thank you. I'm actually feeling a little anxious. Yesterday was so perfect, I don't know what to expect today."

"Just remember what you told me last night. God will go before you. I truly believe that."

They said their goodbyes and Margaret laid down her phone, went back to her bedroom, and quietly grabbed her journal, her Bible, and that day's file as she prepared her heart for another day of love and service.

THE SECOND INTERVIEW WAS SCHEDULED FOR 1 P.M. AT the church where Tristan Cartwright attended and worked. The later interview time allowed Margaret and Sally an opportunity to look over the remaining files and begin to organize the notes from the day before.

A late brunch satisfied their hunger and continued to spoil Sally beyond her comprehension. Margaret sat back and watched as Sally was served by the excellent wait staff in the restaurant. Perhaps there had never been a more grateful patron than Sally. Ten years of being on the other side of the table gave Sally great perspective and appreciation.

It felt like Tristan would be a harder case than Pam. Perhaps it was his young age, or perhaps because Margaret's boys would have been in a similar situation had Margaret gotten on that plane. Whatever the case, she already felt deep sympathy for this young man who, at 24 years of age, had just buried his mother.

Tristan was the youth worship leader at an up-and-coming church in Chattanooga. His mother, Penny, was on board flight 7889 on her way to Tampa to attend a worship conference. She was also involved in ministry, but at a much smaller church.

When Margaret and Sally arrived, they found the doors of the church locked. It was a huge building with multiple entrances, but Tristan had specifically said to meet him at the main entrance. It was a beautiful day, so standing outside waiting for him to arrive was not a problem.

Margaret's heart skipped a beat when he appeared from behind the glass. Tristan fumbled with the door to get it open.

"Ummm, sorry you had to wait so long. I was in the middle of changing out one of the stage lights. I'm Tristan." He extended his shaky hand and exhaled a long, deep breath.

Margaret immediately felt her mother meter go into overdrive as her heart became deeply burdened for this grieving young man. "We've got all day, we aren't in a rush. Is there anything we can help you with?"

"Ummm, actually, I do need to put away the ladder and the supplies, but I don't want to bother you with that." His voice was getting quieter with each word.

Margaret reached out her hand and touched his shoulder. "This is all very hard, isn't it?"

Tristan looked away and nodded.

"Why don't you let Sally and me help you, and we will just take our time getting to the interview?"

Tristan took another deep breath, smiling at Margaret. "Okay," he replied.

Tristan turned and walked down the hallway. Margaret and Sally followed behind and spent the next hour switching out stage lights and sharing dried-out pastries and cold coffee in the lounge. Little by little, Tristan warmed up, and Margaret and Sally were slowly ushered into the life of his wonderful mother, Penny Cartwright.

Tristan sat in a chair just beyond the stage. He spent several minutes telling Margaret and Sally what a wonderful mom Penny had been and what an inspiration she was in his life. As they continued talking, it was apparent that Tristan was feeling more comfortable with Margaret and Sally.

"Mom was truly one of the Godliest people I have ever known. I've spent my whole life around people in ministry, but

Mom was different. She was the same whether she was in front of five people, 500 people, or just me. I don't think I realized how much her faith shaped mine until she was gone."

Margaret and Sally listened intently, honoring his quiet ways and his hesitancy to share too much too soon.

"Would you guys be open to going to my Mom's church for the rest of our time together? I really think that will give you a better idea of who Mom was."

"Of course, Tristan. That would be wonderful." Margaret stood and patted him on the back. He returned a warm smile and led them back to the parking lot.

Penny's church was about ten minutes away on a sleepy little road just outside the city. It was quaint, yet elegant. Margaret parked while noticing the old baptismal pool and the long cinder block structure that, most likely, housed various outdoor church gatherings. She sat for a moment before getting out, recalling fond memories of her childhood church.

Tristan parked closer to the church, got out, and slowly started walking toward the open courtyard between the church and the fellowship hall. The courtyard was circular with a red-brick path that wound through hundreds of beautiful flowers and lush plants. In the middle of the courtyard sat a simple angel statue with a small etched stone in front that read, "In memory of Mrs. Penny."

Tristan approached the angel with tears forming in his eyes. "I still can't believe she is gone."

Margaret and Sally allowed him time to be with his feelings as they stood off to the side.

"My dad died five years ago from cancer," Tristan said, staring vacantly at the angel.

"Mom started this garden when he was on hospice. They only lived a couple of minutes down the road, so in the evening, when he was resting, she would come here. It was like therapy for her. I was away at college, but I would call and check on her and Dad every day after my classes."

"I'm so sorry, Tristan, that must have been so hard." Margaret thought of her boys and felt the weight of Tristan's despair.

After several moments, Tristan broke his fixed gaze and leaned over to pull some weeds that were growing nearby. "Mom was very active in church, especially with the preschoolers. She taught Sunday School here for the last 30 years. I got my love of music from her. She led worship for the kids and all the women's events."

"She sounds like a wonderful person, Tristan." Margaret followed Tristan's lead and plucked the last remaining weeds near her feet.

Tristan smiled. "She really was. Everybody loved Mom, and she loved them back, especially me."

Tristan sat on a wrought iron bench just beyond the statue.

"Mom was so strong when Dad died, and although she was devastated, she sacrificed everything for my life to be as normal as possible. Every time Mom and I talked, she would say, 'Remember who you are, and whose you are. Go be the light that God has created you to be.' She probably said that phrase to me at least 1,000 times over the years. I used to ignore her and think she was being too preachy, but I have to admit those words got me through some pretty serious setbacks and saved my life a time or two."

Tristan leaned back, took a deep breath, and closed his eyes, sitting still with his thoughts.

"Mom is the reason the church I am working at is so solid. When some of their choices and philosophies began to waver and go down a road that wasn't scriptural, I talked to Mom, and we began to pray about it. Ironically, the person behind the unbiblical movement at church suddenly put in their notice and left the church. I talked to the remaining leadership team, and things have been so much better. They have gotten back to the real truth of scripture. It's like they remembered who they were and who He is."

Tristan paused and began to smile. "Gosh, I never thought about it quite like that. Mom probably prayed that over my church, too." He stared at his mom's name on the plaque.

"Isn't it amazing how God works in all the little details of our lives?" Margaret noticed a butterfly gracefully flying above the angel statue. "He never ceases to amaze me."

The butterfly landed on the plaque and seemed to be tiptoeing over the letters etched in love. They all stood still, watching and waiting for the delicate insect to make its next move. A gentle breeze began to blow, and within seconds, the wind escorted the tiny marvel to a nearby cluster of flowers.

Sally made a note about the encounter with the brilliantly-colored butterfly and looked to Tristan, whose eyes were fixed on the plaque. "Tristan, I think it's great that you talked to your church. I don't know if I would have the courage to do that."

"I would have never been able to go to them without Mom's suggestions and prayers. Mom was the greatest encourager of my life. If it wasn't for her, I would have long since forgotten who God created me to be, and so many lives would have been different without her."

"There isn't a doubt in my mind that your Mom's impact will be felt for generations to come. What a beautiful legacy she has left. Thank you so much for sharing her with us."

Margaret took Tristan and Sally's hand and the three of them circled around the angel statue in the courtyard, lifting their voices to Heaven and thanking God for Penny Nicole Cartwright, mother to Tristan, and daughter of the King.

~

~Margaret's Journal~
Today was day two of interviews. I can't possibly convey in words

how I feel after spending the day with Tristan. He is such a wonderful young man, and his faith is awe-inspiring.

So many emotions fill my soul as I try to rest for the evening. I think of my boys and how they would have felt if I had boarded that plane. I think of who I am as a mother and a believer. I consider my own legacy and the words that will be said when I am no longer here.

As we were leaving, I gave Tristan my private number and encouraged him to call me anytime. He didn't say a word, but instead, gave me a hug that I felt for hours after we left.

I called Matthew and Luke once we got back to the hotel. I caught up with their lives and reminded them of how much I loved them both.

I have never felt so divinely directed. Thank You, God, for this opportunity and for going before us.

Chapter Twenty-Six

DAY three of the interviews began with an early breakfast in the hotel and a stroll downtown by the river. The fresh air breathed new life into the day and Margaret and Sally's purpose.

They were working well together, as if they had worked together for years. There was a quiet, relaxed ease to their partnership. There was no need for endless chatter; they were simply there for each other, working, serving, and aiming to make a difference as they walked through this new season in their lives.

The last interview in Chattanooga was set to take place at a local coffee shop. Margaret felt relief wash over her as she read through the file and became reacquainted with Miguel Martinez's details. Margaret naively believed this interview would be less intense and heart-wrenching because they were meeting with Miguel's brother and sister-in-law, which felt less intimate than a spouse or child. She would soon find out that her assumptions were incorrect. Legacy and grief know no bounds.

~

SALLY AND MARGARET WALKED INTO FRESH ROASTERS Coffee Shop at 11:55 a.m. and spotted a couple in the back who appeared to be waiting for someone. The middle-aged man got up and walked to where Margaret and Sally were standing.

"Hi, are you Margaret?"

"Yes, you must be Antonio." Margaret extended her hand and felt it engulfed in both of Antonio's hands as he smiled warmly at her and Sally.

"And this is Sally. I believe Mitch told you that I would be bringing Sally with me."

"Yes, it's very nice to meet you both." Antonio reached out and took Sally's hand, gave it the same warm embrace, and ushered her and Margaret to the back of the coffee shop. "Come on back, my wife is excited to meet you, Margaret. She is a huge fan. She has read all of your books; I hope that doesn't make you feel uncomfortable."

"Not at all. I truly appreciate the support," she replied as she and Sally joined Antonio and his wife, Elena.

"They spent the next half hour becoming acquainted, and Margaret joyfully signed Elena's favorite book, which Margaret had written before the contract fiasco.

Elena held the newly signed novel close to her chest. "I just want you to know how much it meant to me when you did that video down at the creek. You know—when you owned up to what you had done and apologized."

"Yes, I am so glad it resonated with you. I meant every word."

"That video is what made us call you about Miguel, and it totally restored my love for you as an author," Elena replied with a huge grin.

"Well, I can't wait to hear about Miguel, and thank you for the encouragement; it means a lot."

Miguel Martinez was almost 50 the day he stepped onto Flight 7889. He and his younger brother, Antonio, along with their parents, were refugees from Cuba. When the boys were only three and five, their father courageously snuck the family out of Cuba and defected to the United States.

Miguel and Antonio learned the meaning of hard work and

perseverance as they watched their father work hard every day of his life until he literally took his last breath while tilling his garden. Their mom soon followed and died of what appeared to be grief. When their parents passed away, the bond Miguel and Antonio had always shared grew even stronger.

Miguel never married, and he worked for the same company his entire life. He was engaged to be married, but at age 29, his fiancée contracted a rare form of cancer and passed away. Miguel begged her to go ahead and marry him before she died, but she refused, knowing he was the type of man who would only marry one person, and, according to Antonio, she didn't want him to be alone after she died.

Miguel's fiancé knew him well because, although they could never make the marriage official, he was, indeed, the type of man who would only love one woman. He loved his deceased fiancée with no end, and ironically, he was headed to Tampa to honor their love story when he lost his life.

Each year, on the anniversary of their engagement, Miguel would fly to Tampa and drive to the beach, where he got down on one knee and pledged his devotion to his forever love. The yearly trip became a time of reflection for Miguel.

As Margaret and Sally learned the intimate details of Miguel's life, Margaret found herself thinking of Mitch and wondering if he might have responded the same way Miguel did. She smiled and encouraged Antonio to tell them more.

"Miguel was a man of deep faith, although he wasn't much of a church man. It was the impact he had at his job that was his biggest testimony."

"Oh, how so?"

"Miguel didn't lead a traditional Bible study or anything like that. He was the kind of guy who was always taking a depressed friend to lunch or inviting a lonely person to our Thanksgiving dinners. He was even the godfather to the son of one of his child-hood friends."

"That's really special," Sally said as she listened and thumbed through the pictures that Antonio and his wife had brought. There were images of Miguel at the park with his godson playing baseball, and an old picture of Miguel and his fiancée standing on a beach with the sunset perfectly illuminating the diamond ring that he had just placed on her finger. The last picture was of Miguel at a cookout he had hosted only days before the plane crash, which would be the last picture Antonio would have of his brother.

As Antonio poured out his heart, Margaret couldn't help but notice a young man sitting two tables over who appeared to be listening and hanging on every word. She looked at the young man and smiled as if giving him permission to be a part of their conversation. He slowly stood and walked toward their table.

"I apologize for intruding. I didn't mean to be eavesdropping, but I heard Miguel's name, and I just couldn't let it go. Are y'all talking about Miguel Martinez?"

Antonio sat up straighter, "Yes, we are. Did you know him?"

"Yes, I was an intern at Miguel's company last year and he literally saved my life."

Margaret couldn't believe her ears as she felt her body tingle with chill bumps from head to toe.

Antonio shook his head and raised his voice. "I'm sorry, did you just say he saved your life?"

"Yes, I can tell you what happened, if you want me to."

Antonio stood and shook the young man's hand. "Yes, please. I am Antonio. Miguel was my older brother. This is my wife, Elena. And this is Margaret, who is writing a book about Flight 7889, and her assistant, Sally."

Everyone welcomed the young man to the table.

"I was so sad to hear that Miguel died. I think about him every day. My name is Logan, by the way."

Logan sat and exposed his soul in ways only God could orchestrate. Two years before, Logan's dad had been sent to prison for embezzlement, and his mom couldn't handle the embarrassment, so she took her life. Logan was only 18 and found himself homeless and essentially an orphan who had just aged out of the system. A friend's dad managed to get Logan a paid internship at the company he worked for, which is where he met Miguel.

Logan said he found a cheap apartment in the worst part of town and tried to make a new life for himself, but it was almost impossible. Miguel was quick to see that Logan was struggling, so he began to mentor Logan professionally and, eventually, spiritually. Things were mostly looking up for Logan until he tried to reach out to his dad in prison.

"I sent my dad a letter trying to reconnect in some way, and the only reply I got was a short letter that told me to leave him alone. He blamed me for my mom's death."

Logan sat with his eyes looking vacantly across the table. "I decided that my dad was right—it was my fault, all of it. Maybe if they hadn't had me, my dad wouldn't have needed more money, and maybe he would have never stolen from his company. My mom would still be alive if my dad hadn't gone to prison," Logan took a deep breath and paused.

"I sank really deep into blaming myself, so I took the lockbox that held my dad's old handgun from underneath my bed. I sat on the edge of the mattress, and I loaded the gun."

Sally closed her eyes and clutched the notepad she was using for notes in total disbelief of the unfolding story.

Logan leaned back in his chair, taking a deep breath, holding it, and then exhaling as the memories came rushing back.

"Right after I loaded the gun, my cell phone began to ring. I was annoyed that I hadn't thought to turn it off, but as I reached to throw the phone across the room, I saw it was Miguel calling me. I can't explain it, but I knew in that moment that I couldn't pull the trigger. Before my phone rang, I had decided the world would be better off without me, but when I saw Miguel's name on the phone, I knew he would be devastated if I took my life. He had done so much for me."

Logan began to choke up.

"Logan, I'm grateful you are sharing this story, but if this is too hard for you, you don't have to continue." Antonio grabbed Logan's shoulder and held it tight. Logan cleared his throat and closed his eyes. The table remained silent as the last barista began closing the shop.

"It's okay, I want to tell you the rest." He took another deep breath and continued. "At first, I didn't answer the phone, I just fell to the floor and cried. I eventually unloaded the gun and put it back under the bed. Miguel called again, and I answered. I didn't plan on telling him what had happened, but he could hear something was wrong. He told me I'd been heavy on his heart that day, so I ended up telling him everything. He stayed on the phone with me as he drove to my apartment. He came into my apartment, put his hands on my shoulders, and kept saying, 'You are loved; God has a plan for your life. You are loved; God has a plan for your life.' He stayed with me all night and slept on my sofa. He even paid for me to see a Christian counselor, helped me sell the gun, and prayed with me every day for weeks."

All eyes at the table were wet with tears as Logan's demeanor shifted into one of gratitude. "Miguel was there for me when no one else was. Three weeks after I almost took my own life, Miguel led me to the Lord, and I put my trust in Jesus. The next day, he was leaving to go out of town, and he never came back. If Miguel had given up on me like everyone else in my life, I wouldn't be here."

Antonio began to whisper, "Thank You, Lord" over and over as Elena rubbed his back with tears soaking through her silk shirt.

Logan pulled a carefully crafted cross from underneath his shirt. Three small nails had been bent to create a cross. The cross was wrapped in thin wire and hung from a thin leather strap. "As a matter of fact, Miguel made this cross that I wear every day."

Antonio nodded his head, reached in, and pulled the same type of cross from under his collared shirt. "Our Papa started making these crosses when we were teenagers. When he passed away, Mama gave Miguel all his supplies because Miguel was always crafty like Papa. I've often wondered if he was still making them. I've worn the one Papa gave us for years, with little thought, if I'm being honest."

Logan rubbed his fingers back and forth on the smooth, cool metal of the nails that lay across his chest, directly over his heart. "I figured there was a backstory, but I never got the chance to ask Miguel. The day he led me to Jesus, we were having lunch at his place, and somehow our conversation landed on my faith, or lack thereof. He was so patient with all my doubts. He answered all my questions, and he read several passages of scripture to me. After I prayed to receive Christ, he went into his bedroom and came back with the necklace. He put it around my neck and said, 'It is finished. You are His. No longer an orphan, you are now part of the kingdom.' I'm not going to lie, I cried like a baby. It felt like, for the first time in my life, I belonged to a family. Like my life finally had meaning and purpose."

Antonio sat back in his chair and exhaled a long, slow breath. "Papa would be so proud. He began making those necklaces for that same purpose. Papa taught us to lead with Jesus. I haven't always done such a good job of that, but Miguel sure did."

The table fell into silence as each person considered the majesty of the moment.

Logan continued to run his fingers over his cross, feeling the warmth of love and acceptance surround him.

Antonio lowered his head, thinking about the great legacy left behind by his father and brother, and how he had not lived with the same intention.

Elena gazed out of the windows toward the puffy clouds floating above the city, awed by the fact that her husband was finally emerging from years of lukewarm faith.

Sally looked around the coffee shop, considering what a miracle the chance encounter with Logan had been, and smiled at the barista, who seemed overwhelmed with her own internal struggle.

And Margaret sat taking it all in. She felt as if the whole world had stopped, and she was merely a shooting star passing through a holy moment that would leave a trail of stardust for eternity.

After several moments, Margaret said, "Would you all mind if I pray for us. It feels as if we should lift our voices to the Lord."

There was a gentle nod from each person at the table. The barista turned her back to the group and bowed her head.

Margaret got up from her chair and knelt between Logan and Antonio. She laid her hands on them and began to pray, lifting her voice to the Author of faith, love, grace, mercy, kindness, and so much more.

The prayer could be heard throughout the empty coffee shop. The barista found herself moved by the encounter she was witnessing. For several moments, the Holy Spirit worked through Margaret as the words flowed and the prayer erupted into previously hardened hearts.

They all said "Amen" in unison, and Logan stood and hugged Margaret as if he was desperate for human touch. She held him as if he were her son, and then Antonio stood and took her place. Logan wept in his strong arms.

Antonio began to speak with a calm yet bold confidence, "I will always be here for you, Logan. I can never replace Miguel, but I promise that I will pick up where he left off. I will work hard at being the man of God that I now realize I should be."

Antonio placed both his hands on Logan's shoulders and continued, "What Miguel said to you is absolutely true. You are not an orphan; you are a beloved child of God. Don't you ever forget that."

"Thank you ..." Logan murmured through his tears.

The interview concluded with rounds of hugs, exchanging of telephone numbers, and genuine love and concern for one another.

Miguel had lived a life few dare to live. He had loved deeper than what felt comfortable and served in the most challenging of circumstances.

Miguel lived out his faith in action and words. Margaret felt certain that God had brought forth a special encounter at Fresh Roasters that would extend well beyond that little table.

As the door shut and the coffee shop was finally empty, the barista began to tremble as she replayed the conversation and powerful prayer she had overheard. She picked up the phone to call her mom, whom she had not spoken to in six months. When her mom answered, the barista began to sob, "Mom, I am so sorry for everything I said to you and for everything I've done to hurt you. I love you; will you please forgive me?"

Chapter Twenty-Seven

MARGARET AND SALLY walked slowly back to the hotel, neither saying a word. Margaret felt as if every sense in her body had been heightened. She noticed the perfectly blue sky, smelled the aroma of fresh pastries from the open door of a little bakery, and heard children laughing in a nearby park.

Sally was walking a step slower than Margaret, with her head held high, looking up, and breathing in life. As they approached the hotel, they looked at each other, shrugged their shoulders, smiled, and kept walking. When they rounded the corner three blocks from their hotel, Margaret spotted a cute café with outdoor seating. "Want to grab a late lunch?"

"That would be great."

After they ordered lunch, Margaret and Sally began to unpack the many emotions they were both feeling. Tears came and went as they laughed and marveled at the amazing turn of events.

Sally pushed her salad plate to the side and leaned back in her chair with a confused look. "What are the chances that Logan would be the only other customer in that coffee shop this morning?"

"Honestly, Sally, in my 30-year career as a writer, I have never felt so blessed. From finding you, being spared from the crash, meeting Pam, then Tristan, then Antonio, and now Logan, I honestly don't feel worthy of this calling." Margaret sipped her water and looked away, still unsure of what to make of the situation.

"Margaret, I don't know why God chose you, but I'm glad that He did. And I'm glad that He realized how much I needed you. I mean, for goodness' sake, I was a waitress a few weeks ago. Now, I feel like I'm living some kind of dream life that I don't deserve to be living." Sally hung her head.

Margaret, feeling just as unworthy, suddenly thought of a Bible verse. She grabbed her phone and opened her Bible app, remembering the words but wanting to get in the Word so she could accurately share it with Sally.

"Sally, we are obviously both struggling with feeling unworthy, right?"

Sally nodded her head.

"What if we could just step into the truth, step into what God says about us? A couple of minutes ago, I was feeling all this doubt and insecurity rise in me, and then it was as if the Holy Spirit reminded me that those emotions are not of God. Sally, fear is not of God. Doubt is not of God."

Margaret reached out and took Sally's hand. "A Bible verse comes to mind. Would you like to hear it?"

"Of course," Sally's voice returned to one of joy instead of defeat.

"Okay, listen to this: For we are God's handiwork. That's us, Sally. God made us. Do you think He makes mistakes?"

Sally shook her head, hanging on Margaret's every word.

"Me neither. I think, actually, I believe, that we are here for a purpose; we are not mistakes."

Sally's face changed, her eyes brightened, and she sat up in her chair, longing for the truth that Margaret was pouring forth.

"Okay, so listen. For we are God's handiwork, created in Christ Jesus to do good works, which God prepared in advance for us to do. God knew, Sally. He knew you would need me, and I would need you. He knew that I would make a royal mess of my life, but He also knew that He would redeem my mess and would take that mess and create something beautiful, which is what I am doing; it's what we are doing. Don't you see, Sally? We are right where we are supposed to be, doing exactly what He wants us to do."

Sally began to nod, "You are right... It may take me my whole life to understand why He chose me to be involved in something so wonderful, but I promise you, I will do everything I can to stay on the path that He has set before us."

"Me too, Sally. Me too."

Chapter Twenty-Eight

As the sun rose over the city, Margaret and Sally checked out of the hotel and began the drive back to the cabin. Margaret's mind was racing with all she had experienced over the last three days, her heart filled to the brim and overflowing.

Sally leaned against the window, her face filled with wonder as she peacefully slept. The early morning wake-up call had roused her, but she was far from rested. She had stayed up late the previous night organizing her notes from the interviews instead of sleeping.

Margaret grinned as she watched Sally sleep so soundly. "Just like my boys," Margaret whispered, and continued driving. As they stopped in front of the cabin, Margaret put her hand on Sally's knee. "Hey, friend. We've made it back to the cabin."

Sally woke up in a daze, confused for a moment.

"I can't believe this is where I live," Sally said as she stretched and yawned, eyes opening wide as she looked around.

"Well, it's no 5-star hotel, but it will have to do," Margaret replied jokingly.

"Don't get me wrong, the hotel was amazing, but this place—this place is perfect. There is nowhere I would rather be." Sally continued to look around with a big smile on her face.

"I agree, it's pretty perfect." Margaret noticed her humming-bird friend feeding in a nearby cluster of flowers. "I need to head home after lunch, so I am going to go for a walk. Feel free to go on in."

"Sounds good, enjoy your walk."

Sally unpacked the SUV and then went straight downstairs to get back to work.

Margaret walked toward the creek and felt her phone vibrate in her back pocket. It was Ernie. She answered, anxious to tell him about the interviews, which she did in rapid fire without taking a break for almost five minutes.

"Young lady, that is unreal. I can't believe how these people opened up to you. And the Logan story, you know that's all God, right?"

"I know, Ernie. I went into the weekend with little to no expectations. Obviously, I am used to my world of fictional stories, which I create with my imagination. I have never experienced anything even remotely as personal as what I just witnessed with each interview."

"Well, I hope you realize you are smack-dab in the middle of an amazing opportunity to glorify God."

"Ernie, perhaps I have never been more sure of anything in my life."

MARGARET DROVE BACK TO THE CITY AFTER A QUICK lunch with Sally. She was happy to see Mitch and her boys, who were home for a few days. She much preferred the cabin over life in the city at this time, but the life she and Mitch had built was solid, so she would ignore the traffic and the noise and focus on the love she felt when she was with her family.

Love really does conquer all she thought as she unpacked her things. Mitch was outside with his smoker preparing dinner, and the boys were hanging out by the pool.

She changed into her swimsuit, then walked outside to reconnect with her family and enjoy the warm summer sun.

Luke walked over and gave her a hug. "Hey, Mom, how are the interviews going?"

"They are going great. The people Sally and I have met are all so amazing."

Matthew stood and gave Margaret his own bear hug, slightly picking her up off the ground. "Are you allowed to tell us about them?"

"Yes, my strong young man!" Margaret laughed. "We have full consent to share the details of each interview, although I will maintain a certain level of privacy for each family. Do you guys want to hear about the three people we are honoring so far?"

Matthew squinted as the sun bounced off the water. "I know this may sound bad, Mom, and please don't take it the wrong way, but are the stories really sad?"

"I get it, buddy. Of course there is sadness, considering the topic. You know me, I try to be all sunshine and roses, but I have found myself blown away with how gratifying and blissful I have felt as I've learned about each of these people. And the families we have met are incredible. So, while it's very sad that these people died, I can't ever remember feeling more hopeful about my own life or more encouraged to live a life that matters."

Mitch walked up, brushing Margaret's windblown hair from her face and wrapping his arms around her. "Okay, babe, we would be fools to pass on these first-hand accounts, so fill us in. I think we can handle it, right, boys?"

Matthew and Luke agreed, and they soon found themselves immersed in a new world of grief, acceptance, and joy. Margaret felt both energized and exhausted as the stories poured from the deepest part of her soul. As she talked, she realized that she already felt a deep connection with each person who had passed away and with the ones who had shared their stories.

Margaret spent the remainder of the weekend fully immersed in her family. She did not check her phone or her emails. She forgot social media even existed by temporarily removing the apps from her phone. She completely unplugged.

She and her family went hiking, enjoyed the pool, visited their favorite coffee shop, and played board games into the wee hours of the night. Her physical body was beginning to transform, and her mind and soul felt renewed in every way.

～

~MARGARET'S JOURNAL~

Writing an entire book filled with stories of grief would be about the last thing I would choose to do. I feel certain I cannot do these beautiful stories adequate justice, but I will give my all to honor each of them and the Lord with the words that overflow from the blessing of each interview.

In the deepest part of my soul, I believe this project will, indeed, save lives and will lift, encourage, and inspire countless individuals. It has already shaped me in immeasurable ways.

Chapter Twenty-Nine

FRANK CONTACTED Mitch as a broken man, desperate to try anything to help him make sense of the fact that Trudy, his wife of 20 years, was gone. Frank and Trudy had lived and worked in a small town in the suburbs of Atlanta. They were both cashiers at a local grocery store and appeared to be living a very unassuming life. However, the news of the plane crash and Trudy's sudden death had sent a wave of grief through their little town.

Frank heard about the legacy book the day after Margaret's post went live through one of his long-time customers. He rushed home that same day and called the number the customer had given him. He talked to Mitch for several minutes during that first call and knew, without a doubt, that Trudy's story needed to be told. Frank was relieved when Mitch set up an interview a few days later, and that Mitch was willing to tag along for the extra support.

~

MITCH, MARGARET, AND SALLY MET FRANK AT HIS AND Trudy's humble home, which was less than an hour from the cabin. Mitch stood at the door, knocking with no sign that anyone was home. After the fourth attempt, Frank answered the door. He was unshaven, un-showered, and reeked of cigarette smoke. Thankfully, he smoked on the back stoop, so the house smelled strongly of cheap vanilla candles instead of smoke.

Four jar candles with dollar store stickers still on them sat on the old wood-burning fireplace. Frank must have seen Margaret and Sally look at the candles, because the first words out of his mouth were, "Vanilla was Trudy's favorite."

The flames danced in the breeze from the ceiling fan that wobbled dangerously. The house was oppressively hot, and Frank either did not have air-conditioning or it wasn't working. Several peace lilies and other potted plants, with funeral bows still attached, drooped in desperation. Frank seemed unconcerned with the heat as sweat gathered in the deep creases of his frown lines.

"Does anybody want anything to drink? I got water and sweet tea. We don't keep alcohol in the house. I got sober a few years ago because Trudy didn't like me drinking. I would do anything for that lady—well, almost anything," Frank's voice became muffled as he looked away and sat in one of the matching recliners. It was obvious that he and Trudy must have loved these chairs because they were both worn down to the springs.

No one took Frank up on his offer of a beverage. Instead, introductions were made, and Trudy's story began to unfold. As Frank poured out his heart, they learned that Trudy was a Christian and Frank was not. The only thing that Frank would not do for Trudy was go to church. He said that when he and Trudy met, she was already a believer, but she was still a lot of fun. In the beginning of their relationship, Trudy would go to church on Sunday and live the other six days as she wished.

"Over time, Trudy changed and became more spiritual, but she was still my best friend, and she loved me just the same. She never tried to force me to go to church, but she would ask me every single week if I wanted to go with her. I never went, not once. I don't know why I was so pig-headed. I was just a stubborn old fool," Frank's plump face got redder as he held back the tears.

Margaret smiled warmly. "I know this is hard, Frank. Do you need a minute? Maybe Sally and I could step outside."

"No, it's okay. I want to tell you about Trudy. She deserves to be in that book of yours."

"Okay, just take your time. We aren't in a hurry," Margaret reassured Frank as Mitch watched his wife in her element.

Frank wiped the sweat from his brow and continued, "I knew my Trudy was special, but it wasn't until her funeral that I really understood how special. The owner of the grocery store we work at helped pay for a really nice funeral for Trudy. He said it was because she was the best employee he had ever had. The night of her viewing, there must have been 200 people there. All her church people and so many customers, all sharing stories about how Trudy had shown them love or helped them in some way. Then I got all these plants and flowers and cards telling me what a fine woman she was. I don't know how she had time to be so nice to everybody; taking care of me was a full-time job." He hung his head and closed his eyes.

Margaret silently began praying for strength for Frank.

"She was so patient with me. I wasn't always nice to her. I never hit her or anything, I just didn't always treat her good. She was always so calm and sweet. I didn't deserve her. She would tell me, 'It's okay, God knows your heart.' I got so sick of hearing her tell me that God cared about me, but maybe she was right. I should have went to church with her, that was all she ever asked from me." Frank buried his head in his hands and began to sob. "Why didn't I listen to her? Why didn't I listen to her?"

Mitch stood and put his hand on Frank's shoulder. "Frank, do you mind if I pray for you?"

Frank kept his head buried in his hands but managed a muffled "Okay." Mitch got down on his knees and firmly placed his hand on Frank's back. His boldness radiated throughout the tiny mobile home. The Holy Spirit coursed through Mitch as he began to pray,

"Father God, I boldly come to You today, and I lift up Frank and his grief. Only You know how he feels and the pain he is experiencing, please God reassure him that he is not alone.

We humbly ask that You speak into his heart now, Lord. Cover him with Your mercy and grace. Please take away his regret and his shame and anything else that would keep him from Your presence. May this day be a turning point in Frank's life. May he look to You and put his faith in You alone. May You use this tragedy for Your glory. Thank You, Lord, for Trudy. Thank You for the reassurance that she knew You and that You welcomed her home. May her legacy and light live on forever. In the name of Jesus I pray, Amen."

Frank had never encountered a man of God like Mitch, and as the words seeped into his soul, his sobs subsided. Frank slowly opened his eyes, looking at Mitch with a childlike wonder. "I'm not sure what's happening, but I think maybe Trudy sent you."

Mitch looked into Frank's tear-filled eyes. "Frank, I think it's God who sent us here, although I am sure Trudy would rejoice knowing that we are here with you. I believe that God wants you to lay down the broken parts of yourself and turn to Him. Do you think you can do that?"

"I think so. I know that's what Trudy would want." Frank looked at Margaret with deep concern on his face. "I mean, you are a wife. Don't you think that's what she would want?"

Margaret reached for Frank's hand. "Yes, that is exactly what she would want. That is where you will find your peace, Frank. You are still going to grieve and miss your precious wife, but having a relationship with Jesus will change your life. That is why your Trudy was so wonderful, Frank. She knew Jesus."

Mitch, Margaret, and Sally spent the next 30 minutes praying with Frank and talking through salvation, and then, as the cuckoo clock struck 3 p.m., Frank stood up with tears flowing down his face and said, "I believe what ya'll are telling me. I believe Jesus died for me and that I can have a new life in Him."

Frank stood still for a few moments, with his eyes closed, a wide smile emerging from his once weary face. He walked over to a photo hanging on the wall, which displayed Trudy on their wedding day. "Well, I did it, sweetie. I finally met Jesus." He ran his finger over the dusty frame. "Oh, sweetie, I'm sorry I didn't listen to you."

Mitch, Margaret, and Sally sat quietly, amazed by what had just happened as they witnessed Frank's transformation from a broken man sobbing on the floor to a believer.

Margaret and Sally quietly walked outside to give Frank and Mitch another few minutes together. When the men emerged and walked onto the front porch, Frank had a radiance about him. He was holding his head high and breathing deep and rhythmic breaths as if he was breathing for the first time.

Mitch and Frank exchanged phone numbers, and the good-byes faded as the afternoon sun lit the angel wind chime hanging on the front porch. *Trudy JoAnne Bailey* was etched in the wood, and the soft, gentle breeze created a beautiful melody. Everyone stopped and listened, looking up to Heaven in awe and appreciation.

As they were driving away, looking back at Frank waving from the porch, Margaret closed her eyes and spoke from the depths of her soul. "Just when I think my heart cannot grow an ounce more...."

~

~ SALLY'S JOURNAL ~

We got back to the cabin late this evening, then Mitch and Margaret headed back to the city. I am sitting on the back deck, wondering how could I be a part of something so amazing?

Each interview shows me even more of who God is and how deep His love runs for each of us. He really does leave the 99 for the one.

Chapter Thirty

SALLY ENJOYED her time at the cabin more than she ever dreamed possible. She primarily worked on her assistant duties for Margaret on the lower level or outside. More than half her waking hours were spent beyond the walls of the cabin, either on the back deck or down at the creek.

She organized and typed up the notes from each interview and did a soft edit on the photos she had taken. She then placed each item back in the file. On the outside of the file, she wrote a summary of each story, color-coding the pertinent information. One by one, Sally completed her part and gave the files back to Margaret. Sally was grateful that Margaret preferred written documentation over digital in those early stages. The creativity and flow felt more natural.

~

MARGARET'S HOME OFFICE IN THE CITY WAS BRIGHT, sunny, and littered with inspiration and ideas. The legacy book was only one of many ideas that danced in Margaret's mind.

One large wall of her office was covered with cork-board pinned with bright yellow notes, and three large dry-erase boards hung on another wall with multi-colored scribbling covering most of the surfaces. The wall behind Margaret's desk was floor-to-ceiling windows that overlooked the shimmering pool and luscious garden area. The remaining wall was covered with awards, photos, and memories of a career that pointed to a loving, gracious God.

As Margaret looked over each file that Sally had carefully prepared, she felt a sense of overwhelming gratitude. Her fingers ran over each name, pausing to remember their life and their legacy.

Bill Andrew Baker

Penny Michelle Cartwright

Miguel Jose Martinez

Trudy JoAnne Bailey

Each person had taught Margaret so much already.

How to dream, how to love, how to serve, and how to never give up on those you love.

As Margaret's fingers typed away on the keyboard, she began considering her life, what she had been through, and what she had put her family through over the last several months. She stopped typing and walked into Mitch's home office. His face lit up when Margaret walked into the room.

"Hey, listen, my beautiful wife just walked into the room. Can I call you back in a few minutes?" He winked at Margaret, motioning for her to come closer.

"Okay, thanks. I'll get back to you." He ended the call and stood, pulling her in close.

"To what do I owe this pleasure? I figured you would be working non-stop today."

"I am working, but I was thinking about us and what I did with the whole contract mess. Mitch, I am so sorry for lying to you and the boys."

"Honey, we have covered this several times. That is in the past. You realized your mistake and you did what needed to be done to rectify that mistake. Not to mention, you have asked for my

forgiveness multiple times. I forgave you the first time you asked."
Mitch kissed her wet cheek.

"I will never understand why you are so good to me."

"Well, I will never understand why you put up with me and
all the stupid things I say and do. But here we are, all these years
later, making it work."

"I guess part of my insecurity right now is that it feels like God
has assigned me a task that is too important for who I really am."

"Oh, Margaret, honey. That is the enemy lying to you. You
know he wants you to feel stuck and incapable. He is a liar, plain
and simple. God is using you, you Margaret—imperfect, beautiful
you. He chose you, and He loves you. He knows the real you, and
He still chose you. Please, darling, you have to believe me."

Margaret felt her knees go weak and her body relax into his
arms.

She buried her head in his chest. "Thank you...I believe you."

Margaret felt herself be swallowed up in the all-consuming
grace of her husband and the mercy of her Creator.

THE NEXT MORNING, MARGARET DROVE BACK TO THE
cabin. Sally had breakfast ready when she arrived. They walked
down to the creek, sat by the fire pit, and enjoyed a simple but
healthy start to their day.

"I don't know why I am so anxious about our next interview."
Sally bit her bottom lip as she watched the creek flow through the
ferns.

"I feel the same way. I can't imagine how this young man
must be feeling, having lost his mom, dad, and younger sister.
Since Mitch told me about Austin, I am ashamed to say I have
been dreading this interview."

"Well, it makes me feel better that you are uncertain too."
Sally took a deep breath and finished the last of her hot tea.

"When I gathered the list of passengers, I noticed there were several families on board, which is typical of most flights. But, for me, it feels so much heavier to think of a family losing their lives, especially for those left behind."

Sally set down her mug and looked up. "I don't want to live in fear, but all of this has certainly reminded me how fragile life really is."

"I couldn't agree more. I think of all the meaningless things I have distracted myself with over the years, and I wish I could go back and shake myself and say, 'Wake up!'"

Sally shook her head and smiled. "It's surprising to hear you say that because of everything you have accomplished."

Margaret nodded. "I see how you could perceive it that way, but I am left wondering what else I could have done. Who else could I have helped? What opportunities did I miss when I was chasing the world or distracting myself?"

"Oh gosh, I guess that's true. We could probably always be doing more."

"I don't think it's just about doing; I think it is also about becoming. Becoming more like Jesus. More of who He created us to be. Sometimes that requires doing more things, and sometimes that requires us to stop doing things."

Sally nodded her head. "Wow."

"I'm sorry if I sound like I am preaching. It's just that the clearer and healthier my mind and body are becoming, the more I am seeing things about my life that I have never seen."

"Preach on, I love it," Sally said with a huge grin.

"I guess ultimately, I can no longer ignore how precious each day is and what a gift it is to be alive."

"Amen and Amen," Sally said, reaching forward and giving Margaret a hug.

Margaret held the hug for a moment and then pulled away. She placed one of her hands on Sally's knee. "Thank you for taking a chance with me. I know it must have seemed crazy to leave your job and home for someone you haven't known that long. I don't tell you often enough how much I appreciate you."

"I'll admit it was super scary, but mainly because I didn't know if I was capable of what you would need from me. I never once doubted that working for you would be anything other than wonderful. You came into the cafe in the pit of your valley, and even then, you were the most inspiring person I've ever met."

Margaret leaned back in her chair. "Thank you, that's a very sweet thing to say." Once again, she heard her soul whisper, *The Best is Yet to Come.*

Chapter Thirty-One

THE NEXT DAY, Margaret and Sally drove to the residence of Jeff and Joy McCain, which was nestled in one of the most beautiful spots in all North Georgia.

"Please don't let this be three times as hard," Margaret whispered as she parked in front of the black horse fence that peacefully led to a beautiful modern farmhouse.

The young man saw them coming and opened the door before they got to it.

"Hello, I'm Austin. Do you ladies need any help with your things?" His smile was big as he held the door open.

Margaret was surprised at the amount of joy that seemed to be exuding from this young man who had just lost his parents and younger sister.

"I think we have it, but we appreciate the offer," Margaret replied, looking at Sally.

"Yes, thank you," Sally blushed as she walked in behind Margaret.

Margaret extended her hand. "It's so nice to meet you, Austin. I am Margaret, and this is Sally."

Austin shook both ladies' hands. "First, thank you for coming. My sister, unfortunately, won't be able to join us; her little girl is sick. She said we can call her if we need to, but she trusts me to take the reins, so I guess we will see how it goes."

Austin led Margaret and Sally into the open, beautifully decorated great room that overlooked a sweeping pasture with horses and a perfectly positioned red barn.

Margaret noticed a young colt running playfully through the tall grass. "This is a beautiful home, and the land is breathtaking."

"It is something to behold, for sure. It was my parents' dream to live on a spread like this. They built this place about fifteen years ago; just a couple of years after my younger sister surprised the family with her appearance." Austin laughed gently and sat on the soft leather sofa.

"Well, it is certainly impressive. Sally's parents also live on a farm, don't they, Sally?"

"Yes, but it doesn't look like this," Sally's face reddened as she avoided eye contact with Austin.

"Dad and Mom worked really hard to establish the farm. That's one of the things you should know about them both; they were extremely hard workers, and they taught us to be the same way. My older sister has her own decorating business that she began when she was 21, and I have done pretty well for myself. I own a remodeling company that specializes in renovating barns and farmhouses."

Margaret smiled deeply. "That's wonderful. I know your parents must have been so proud of you both."

As Austin began telling his parents' story, Margaret realized she was not the only one spared the day of the crash. Austin's entire family had initially planned to fly to Tampa for a mini vacation. However, when the time to purchase tickets arrived, Austin and his sister realized their work commitments conflicted with the dates.

The party of seven was chiseled down to a party of three, and while he and his sister could have opted out of their commitments, their mom encouraged them to "show up strong" for the commitments they had, which was a common phrase around the McCains' home.

Their mom lovingly assured them that another trip would be around the corner. Of course, she didn't know that she, her husband, and their 17-year-old daughter would perish on Flight 7889.

Austin could have been bitter, but instead, he seemed relaxed and fully present. Margaret couldn't help but notice how calm he seemed about the whole situation. It didn't seem as if he didn't care, because it was obvious that he loved his family, but something about this interview was different.

Margaret continued to listen to Austin as he recounted and retold family vacation memories, unforgettable birthday celebrations, and, perhaps, the sweetest of all, the day-to-day stories he recalled so fondly.

"Mom was that mom, you know, the one who seems to live to serve. She and I would go hang out for the day, and it was always about me. We would go where I wanted to eat and do what I wanted to do. She was easily the most selfless person I knew." Austin nodded, recalling the sound of her voice the last time she called.

"Mom actually called me the morning of the crash to check in with me and wish me luck on a proposal that I was presenting that day to my biggest client ever."

He took a deep breath, and after a few moments of silence, he continued,

"Mom somehow always made each of us kids feel like we were her favorite." He walked to the rock fireplace, where frame after frame held photos that displayed lives well lived and love abounding.

"Here is Mom and me last year on a hike we took for Mother's Day. Isn't she beautiful?"

Margaret nodded as the lump in her throat intensified. She was trying to focus her attention on Austin and his family's story, but her mind kept skipping back to her own family. *What if I had gotten on that plane?*

Sally took over the conversation, realizing that Margaret was struggling. "She really is beautiful. I see her eyes in you." Sally looked at the photo he was holding. Margaret smiled as she witnessed Sally coming out of her shell.

"That's what everybody has always said. I got her eyes and Dad's smile."

He picked up a picture of him and his dad standing beside their dirt bikes, grinning ear to ear and covered in dusty, Georgia red clay.

"And then there was Dad ... he was the best man I ever knew." Austin took another deep breath that he held for several seconds, and then breathed out slowly as he released the grief that had previously lived in the deepest, most secret parts of him.

Margaret pushed away her own sadness and stood looking at the picture, curious as to the sort of father that could raise such an incredible young man.

"Tell us more about your dad."

"Dad taught me everything about being a man. He was strong in every possible way, and he loved us all with every ounce of who he was."

Austin continued by telling Margaret and Sally about some of his fondest memories of his dad. Camping trips complete with long chats under the stars, riding dirt bikes at a nearby track, and their never-ending talks about music, cars, and guns.

"Dad was a man's man, but he was wise enough to know that he couldn't lord over his own life; only Jesus can do that. So, the primary lesson in our home has always been God first, family second, and country third. Dad bled red, white, and blue. He was never in the military because when he was the age that he would have enlisted, his dad was terminally ill. So, he stuck around and helped care for him while putting himself through college. He planned to go to Officer Candidate School after college, but he met Mom when he was a senior, and they got married right after graduation and he took over his dad's construction business instead."

Sally held the frame containing the picture of Austin and his dad on their dirt bikes. "Gosh, your parents sound amazing."

"That's why we called you. Words really can't do justice to who they were. My older sister saw your announcement about a legacy book, and she called me right away and told me that we had to tell you about our family. She really did plan on being here, but even if she had been, she's pretty quiet. I have always been the talkative one." He sat as a wave of grief washed over him. His face changed as his mind began to wander.

"I am sure all of this is extremely difficult," Margaret said with compassion.

"Look, I don't want to deceive you ladies. I have prayed and prayed about this meeting. I could hear Mom saying, 'Show up strong,' and Dad encouraging me to be in the moment and to give it my all. So, that's what I have been trying to do, but I've got to be honest, trying to keep living normally is the hardest thing I have ever done."

"I can't imagine how you must feel. I think we have plenty of information to create a really lovely section about your parents, so we can conclude the interview." Margret stood, "Really, it's okay."

"I don't want you guys to leave yet. Maybe we could just go for a walk or something, and I'll tell you about my sister."

"That sounds like a great idea." Margaret patted Austin on the back, and he stood and gave her a light hug. "I really appreciate you doing this and for being so kind. Not many famous people seem to care about the average family."

"It is honestly an honor to be here with you today. And, just so you know, I do think people care; it's just real easy to get caught up in your own world and forget what others are enduring. I am sad to say, I have spent much of my life as that person," Margaret said with a deep look of compassion in her eyes.

"Well, either way, thank you." Austin extended his arm, with his hand outstretched toward the door. "After you, ladies."

And just like that, Austin had snapped back into the strong young man that his parents had shaped him to be.

~

FOR THE NEXT TWO HOURS, AUSTIN, MARGARET, AND Sally walked the 20-acre farm and took in all the sights while learning more about Austin's parents and younger sister, Cheyenne, who was a senior in high-school. He reminisced about the joy that exuded from his sister and the impact she made in their local community, especially her high-school.

"Cheyenne wasn't your typical teenager. She was so full of life and joy. She was known for saying, 'Smile, God loves you,' everywhere she went. I must have heard her say that phrase a thousand times..." Austin looked out over the sprawling pasture and sighed a heavy sigh.

He continued, "When we were at the funeral, a young man timidly approached me. He told me that Cheyenne was the reason he went to school each day. She was in his first period class and he knew that she would say or do something that would help him get through the day. He later posted a photo on Instagram of her lone desk with a sun ray illuminating where she once sat...Even in high-school, when many kids are selfish, and mean, Cheyenne sought to be a light."

Margaret and Sally both stood still, hanging on Austin's every word. He laughed and teared up a few times, but overall, he was confident, present, and a shining light of hope amid great heartache.

"I can't imagine how much harder this would be if my family had been like some of my friends' families. They seem hardly to know each other. I had dinner at a friend's home a few days ago, and every member of the family spent more time looking at their devices than they did looking at each other. I know that's the way of the world, and I sound totally old-fashioned for saying that, but Mom and Dad gave me their full attention when we were together, and in a weird way, that has made their death easier. I know they squeezed every bit of life out of their time here on Earth. They taught me and my sister to do the same."

Margaret and Sally marveled in awe of the stories that were being shared and the life lessons they were learning.

"I mean, don't get me wrong, we weren't perfect, and we sometimes had little squabbles, but Mom and Dad wholeheartedly believed in the power of forgiveness, so apologies were commonplace in our house. I never once saw Mom and Dad go to bed mad at each other, although they were up really late working through a huge spat a couple of times." Austin laughed as he opened the fence gate and walked toward the young colt.

"I think that's the great thing about living on a farm. The cycle of life is always present. This little gal was born right before my parents and sister passed away. Cheyenne named her Jasmine. The man who has been the farm's caretaker since Mom and Dad moved here said Jasmine is the strongest filly he has ever seen."

Margaret and Sally spent several minutes visiting with Jasmine, her mother, and fellow horses. The evening sun began to set beyond the tree line as Austin looked into Sally's eyes. "I can tell Jasmine really likes you. Do your parents have horses, too?"

Sally felt herself blush unexpectedly, "Actually, my dad has always just raised cows and a few chickens and, most recently, a couple of goats. Of course, my mom had to beg him for the goats."

Austin chuckled. "I know what you mean. That's why we have JoJo, our little miniature donkey. One of Mom's friends sent her a video of a guy with a little donkey as a pet, and Mom begged Dad for a donkey of her own. He resisted for a few weeks, but JoJo was delivered with a big red bow around his neck for her birthday two years ago. You should have seen him when they let him loose in the pasture. He took off and went wild with that bow on his neck. He was more like a wild stallion than a donkey. When he became exhausted and we could catch him and remove the bow, he calmed down, and he's been Mom's favorite ever since."

"Oh, I love that story. That must have been so funny," Sally replied as Margaret had casually disengaged from the conversation while watching the gentle summer breeze blow through the family's large garden. Ripe red tomatoes glistened in the sun, and corn stalks seemed to be bowing down to the splendor of such a perfect day.

The tour of the farm and the interview concluded with rounds of hugs and well-wishes. Austin stood at the front door of the house and watched them drive away. He made no sound as he waved goodbye, but tears fell loose from a part of him that he tried to keep hidden. When they were out of sight, he wiped away the tears and walked back into the house. *Show up strong*, echoed in his heart.

Chapter Thirty-Two

SALLY WAS MORE chatty than normal on the ride back to the cabin as she brimmed with admiration for Austin. Of course, she didn't realize she was doing this, but Margaret noticed early in the interview that there was a bit of a spark between them. It would most likely come to nothing as they lived in different cities and came from different worlds.

Sally talked for the entire journey as they ate their very late picnic lunch in the car while winding down mountain roads. As they passed through town, Sally finally took a breath, "So, who are we interviewing next? Do you know any details yet?"

"I glanced at the file before I left home, but Mitch was still gathering the details. Apparently, the mother of the deceased woman called the first week the inquiries began, and when she and Mitch talked, she changed her mind about being interviewed. However, she called back last week and said she would like us to come. I think Mitch set up the interview for this Friday."

"Okay, sounds good. I am kinda sad that this will be the last interview. As hard as this has been, it has been an amazing experience."

"I completely agree. . I do have one phone interview to conduct, but we are definitely winding this project down."

THE NEXT MORNING, AFTER AN EARLY BREAKFAST WITH Sally, Margaret headed back to the city to be with Mitch for a few days. Once she arrived home, she told Mitch all about Austin and how amazing their time had been on the farm. "You should have seen Sally; she was quite smitten with this young man. Of course, he was pretty remarkable, considering everything he has been through."

"Well, I can't think of a better catch than Sally. If she didn't seem almost like a daughter to you, I would have been trying to matchmake her with one of our boys."

Margaret laughed. "Don't think I haven't considered that, but you are right, she does feel like the daughter we never had."

Mitch took Margaret's hand and kissed it softly. "I am sure her perfect match is out there. I am certainly glad I found mine."

Later that day, Mitch briefed Margaret about his conversations with Rose Cunningham, who would be the final in-person interviewee. The more Mitch talked about Mrs. Cunningham, the more anxious and unsettled Margaret became. She placed the file containing all the gathered information about Mrs. Cunningham and her daughter in her office, deciding to focus on today's phone interview instead.

A lady named Ingrid had sent a very detailed email last week and requested a phone interview. As Margaret read through the file, she couldn't help but smile at the wonder of it all. A perfect stranger sending such detailed information about the person she loved most in the entire world.

Who am I to be the recipient of so much trust?

Mitch's words came rushing back into her heart and lovingly pulled her out of her doubt. *God is using you, you Margaret. Imperfect, beautiful you. He chose you. He loves you. He knows the real you, and He still chose you.*

Margaret laid down the file, closed her eyes, and sat with gratitude for several moments. As she opened her eyes again, rain began to fall against her office windows, while the sun was still shining brightly through the clouds.

Margaret continued gazing out of the windows as a brilliant rainbow gradually appeared in the distance. It started very faint, and then, little by little, the colors deepened, and the arc extended. She hit the intercom and paged Mitch. He responded with a simple sentence that warmed her even more. "I am headed your way, and yes, I see it."

Mitch met Margaret in her office, and they walked onto their back patio as the warm rain continued to fall. They made a point to notice and marvel at rainbows because it was a symbol of God's faithfulness and a reminder of their love for one another. "Remember how this all started?" Mitch gently nudged his bride.

"Of course I remember. Let's see ..."

Margaret turned to face Mitch. "We were young and carefree, and a month after we met, you asked me to marry you."

Margaret continued, "Seventy-five days later, we were standing on the sandy shore of Coronado pledging our lives to each other. It rained so hard that the locals were freaking out, but you and I were so in love, we barely noticed."

They both laughed and paused, remembering the moment.

"Then, right as our little beach wedding was supposed to begin, the rain stopped and a glorious rainbow appeared. It was perfect."

Mitch kissed her. "Perfect then and perfect now."

Several moments passed as the rainbow diminished and the clouds gave way to sunny skies. Mitch returned to his office, and Margaret sipped on her morning tea. She turned down the worship music and opened the file for Stanley.

"Okay, let's meet Ingrid and Stanley."

It took several rings for Ingrid to answer the phone, and her voice was shaky as she managed a faint, "Hello?"

"Hi, Ingrid. This is Margaret. I am so thankful to connect with you today."

"Thank you. I find myself a bit run-down. We just had a

women's conference at our church, and I worked several hours each day. I must have talked and sang just a bit too much. It seems that my voice is trying to leave me."

Margaret smiled, recalling having felt that same way on several occasions. "No problem, I understand. Would you like me to call you another time?"

"I actually typed what I want to say about my dear Stanley. I am happy to email you that if you would like, and then we can talk another day."

"That sounds wonderful."

$$\sim$$

MOMENTS LATER, MARGARET FOUND HERSELF immersed in Stanley's life as she read Ingrid's email.

Thank you for allowing me to write about Stanley. I guess because I was an English teacher for so long, I tend to relay my feelings through written words much better than by speaking.

My name is Ingrid, and I was married for 38 years to Stanley, the love of my life. Stanley was on Flight 7889 so he could go help a friend who was moving after the death of his wife. Although I loved Stanley with my whole heart, he was a simple man who led a simple life.

Stanley worked at the same accounting firm for 30 years. He never tried to make partner, and he declined a bigger office with windows. He was content in his cubicle. Stanley began working there right out of college and was probably the most loyal employee the company ever employeed.

We never had children. I suppose it just wasn't in our cards. We shared the same two-bedroom house that we purchased 35 years ago. I guess you could say Stanley lived a boring life. He didn't have any hobbies, unless you include accounting as a hobby.

Margaret's puppy, Roscoe, walked into the room and bumped his head against Margaret's hand, requesting a little love.

She extended her hand and rubbed under his chin, causing his tail to spin in circles.

"Love is really something special, isn't it, buddy?"

Roscoe stepped in a little closer and leaned his full weight on Margaret. She embraced the affection of her sweet visitor and took a sip from her warm mug. She leaned back in her chair and scrolled to a new page.

We didn't attend a church and weren't involved in the community, so I'm not sure how far my Stanley's legacy will reach, if anywhere, but I will be forever lost without my dear husband. He was my rock when times were hard, my smile when times were good, and everything in between. Stanley was dependable and trustworthy. The few friends he had were for life. It was ironic and fitting that Stanley died on his way to help a friend.

Right after the crash, I was extremely burdened by the thought of how it all happened when the plane was in distress. But then, I thought of my cool, calm Stanley, and I began to imagine that he was probably a great voice of peace in those final moments.

Margaret took a deep breath and reached for a tissue on her desk. She wiped her eyes and shifted in her chair. "Wow, these stories never get easier."

She rubbed the top of Roscoe's head and kept reading.

I never once saw Stanley look afraid, even when he was diagnosed with cancer 10 years ago. He dealt with two years of treatments and three surgeries, but he remained faithful and strong, even when I wasn't.

Stanley didn't go to church very often, but he did know the Lord. I suppose he would have been a faithful church servant if I hadn't been so resistant all those years.

A few days after his death, when I was really struggling with my grief, I went into his office and sat at his desk. His Bible was open, along with his notebook, which he used to journal and create his own Bible study.

I sat there recounting our last morning together. I remember how he hugged me deep, kissed me on my forehead like he always did, and then began telling me how special his time was in the Word that morning. He began telling me about the verses he'd read, and I responded by telling him he should hurry to get ahead of traffic.

"Oh my, how many times have I done that to Mitch? Rushed him out of the door or been rushing myself. This could so easily have been us," Margaret whispered to herself.

She felt her throat tighten, finding it hard to see the computer screen through her glassy eyes. Roscoe was snoring beneath her feet now, and a soft rain began to hit the windows. The nearby candle flickered in the dimly lit room, as clouds covered the sun. Margaret drank her last bit of tea and switched on her desk lamp.

I have been in a season of doubt in my own life as I have watched everyone else on social media sending their kids off to college, having grand-babies, and sharing big family gatherings. Occasionally, I still deal with bitterness over never being able to have children, but my husband, ever faithful but never pushy, continued to love me just the same.

The last words Stanley said to me were, 'Ingrid, always remember God is good; He loves you, and so do I.' I smiled as he held the hug longer than normal. I replied, 'I love you, too.' I was still unsure about the God is good part.

When I got the call about the plane crash, it reaffirmed to me that God is not always good, but then, I began to wrestle with how I was feeling. I felt like I owed it to Stanley to at least try to look to God to relieve my pain, but I didn't want to. I was doing it for Stanley, not God.

"Oh, Ingrid, you poor dear lady," Margaret said through her tears. Roscoe, who would have made a good therapy dog, stood when Margaret began to audibly cry. He began nudging her with his head over and over, and whining while he consoled her.

"I am okay, sweet boy." She grinned and gave him a firm rub behind his ears.

"Let me try to get through this."

Roscoe retreated under the desk, and Margaret continued reading.

I sat at Stanley's desk and looked at his Bible, which was turned to 2 Corinthians 12, knowing it was open at the words he'd read the morning before he'd left this Earth. These verses were highlighted with the date written to the side and a tiny note that said, 'For Ingrid, my forever love.'

The verses read, 'But he said to me, My grace is sufficient for you for my power is made perfect in weakness. Therefore, I will boast all the more gladly about my weaknesses, so that Christ's power may rest on me. That is why, for Christ's sake, I delight in weaknesses, in insults, in hardships, in persecutions, in difficulties. For when I am weak, then I am strong.'

I sat at his desk, crying and praying for probably an hour. I couldn't believe that Stanley witnessed to me, even after his death. I really never deserved such love and dedication.

I got down on my knees with Stanley's Bible clutched to my chest, and I surrendered my life to Jesus for the first time. I would have told you that I was a Christian before that day, but I wasn't. I believed in God and Jesus, but I had never asked Him to be my Savior.

So, with that in mind, Stanley's biggest legacy is leading me to eternal life with him one day in Heaven. He planted the seeds years ago, and he kept watering them and watering them as I resisted and fought him every step of the way. It took his death for me to see how wrong I was and how right he was.

Stanley didn't do great things according to the world's standards, but he was a great man, and he was a great husband, a great friend, a great employee, and a great man of God. I pray these words will encourage someone who thinks they know who God is, yet lacks peace.

I needed to understand and accept that God had a son and he sent that son to die for me, a worthless, bitter sinner. And He not only died for me, He also rose again in victory, and I can do the same. I started going to church the day after I was saved, and I was baptized on Stanley's birthday last week, praise be to God.

I will always miss Stanley, but thankfully, now we will be together again one day. Thank you for this opportunity and for caring enough to share some of the lives and light of Flight 7889.

In His love,

Ingrid

MARGARET SAT MOTIONLESS IN HER OFFICE CHAIR, feeling torn to her core. Roscoe snored beneath her feet. The rain clouds parted, and brilliant sun rays broke through the horizon. Several minutes passed as if the world had stopped. She stared at the words Ingrid had so beautifully shared and decided to forward the email to Mitch, Ernie, and Sally with the simple caption: "God is good."

Chapter Thirty-Three

MARGARET WAS FILLED with dread as she thought about the day ahead of her. She didn't want to climb out of the cozy bed where she was snuggled with Mitch, and she especially didn't want to conduct the final interview.

With each interview, Margaret felt somewhat anxious and nervous, but the meeting with Mrs. Cunningham felt oddly uncertain and dark. Mitch had given his word that Margaret and Sally would meet with her, but if it were up to Margaret, the interview would have been canceled. Margaret's intuition was telling her not to go, but she ignored her feelings and pushed on.

The drive back to the cabin seemed longer than normal as Margaret's mind began unraveling. Her relationship with Mitch had never been better, her boys were doing great, yet she felt deeply unsettled.

As she worked through each legacy story and immersed herself in the lives of so many hurting people, she found herself carrying burdens that weren't hers to carry. She knew that her role was to be a listening ear, to pray for those grieving and then present their stories, but she was struggling to let go of the details and the pain.

With only 20 miles left before she arrived at the cabin, her mind became fixated on the last interview and Mrs. Cunningham. She felt a shiver go up her spine and decided a call to Ernie was in order.

"Well, isn't this a nice surprise?" Ernie answered with his usual cheerful tone.

"Hey, friend, you got a minute?"

"Of course, what's up? You sound like someone just punched you in the gut."

Margaret let out a soft laugh as the knot tightened in her stomach.

"I'm doing okay. I mean, everything around me is okay, better than okay, really, but I am struggling."

"What's wrong? Did something happen?"

"No, nothing happened. I'm just battling with how much I hurt my family, and all these interviews are really heavy. For some reason, I am more nervous about the last interview. I guess I'm just overwhelmed and sad if I am being completely honest."

"Well, your family issues are in the past, and I know that man of yours has forgiven you. You gotta remember that it wasn't that many years ago that Mitch was the one begging for forgiveness. He knows how to forgive and move on because he experienced it himself, so you need to let that shame go once and for all."

"I know you are right, but Mitch never lied straight to my face."

"Good gracious, he's not some kind of saint. You just happen to be overly enamored with him right now," Ernie chuckled.

Margaret nodded her head and grinned. "That's true. We are pretty smitten with each other right now."

"Don't you remember all those times you would complain because he spent more time with the guys at The Ranch than he did at home? Mitch hit some rough patches along the way, too. That's what marriage is, give and take. Not to mention that contract fiasco put me back on your team, so that seems like a good thing to me."

"Of course, us working together is great ... I just still feel so worthless at times."

"Sounds to me like you are stuck in some old thinking. As long as you see yourself as the Margaret who makes bad decisions and label yourself as guilty, you'll keep expecting the worst from yourself. You make up stories for a living. Maybe, you need to write a new story for your life and then live it."

Margaret smiled and nodded her head again. "Wow, Ernie, that was pretty profound."

"I'm not done. As for those interviews, you better believe you should be feeling something. You would have to be emotionally dead inside not to feel something. You just need to remember to lay down those burdens at the end of every day. It's all too heavy for you to carry, darling."

"Oh, Ernie, have you any idea how wise and wonderful you are?"

"Well, I don't like to brag, but I am pretty wonderful."

They ended the call, and Margaret rolled down her windows. She began noticing the trees and the sun spilling onto the road; the fresh smell of the mountain air and birds flying above. She felt her tensions diminish and her purpose rise back up.

"Maybe Ernie is right. Maybe I can keep writing a new story for my life, one in which guilt and shame are not part of who I am," she said, as if declaring truth that sat in the deepest parts of her soul.

When Margaret arrived back at the cabin, she said hello to Sally and then went for a long walk to get her body moving and clear her thoughts. The higher she ascended, the deeper her thoughts traveled.

She marveled at the beauty of Creation, stopping several times to be fully present in the moment. The tall trees that seemed to stretch to Heaven, the thriving, green vines that brought magnificent vibrancy to the forest, and the lowly insects that marched to the beat of a brilliant Creator.

When she arrived back at the creek, she drank her entire bottle of water and stretched her warm muscles. She grabbed her journal, which she had placed in the chairs by the fire-pit before her hike, then slipped off her shoes and dangled her feet in the creek's cool water as day became evening.

~

MARGARET'S JOURNAL

I continue to be amazed at how this new season of my life is unfolding. Everything I was searching for, I already had—love, acceptance, grace, and belonging.

I am reminded of the saying, 'Home is where your heart is,' and I am fully aware that my heart is in many places. It is with my boys at their school and with Mitch back in the city, but I also believe that home is where a path forges through the forest and a winding creek flows ...

Chapter Thirty-Four

MARGARET AND SALLY packed up the SUV and began the drive to Mrs. Cunningham's house as the first sign of daybreak stretched out over the horizon. Margaret was quieter than normal on the drive as she was still dealing with lingering feelings of apprehension. She recalled Ernie's words, *You need to write a new story for your life and then live it.* She took a deep breath and considered how she wanted to show up for the interview, and then felt her body relax. *Be confident, yet humble, with a servant's heart,* she thought to herself.

~

MRS. ROSE CUNNINGHAM WAS AN ELDERLY WOMAN who lived alone in the foothills of the Smoky Mountains of Tennessee. Mrs. Cunningham had called and spoken with Mitch immediately following the public announcement regarding the legacy book. However, as she and Mitch were finishing up the initial phone call, she changed her mind about going public with her daughter's story. One week later, Mitch received another phone call from Mrs. Cunningham. She apologized for her previous indecision, said that she was ready to talk, and asked if Margaret could come as soon as possible. Mitch obliged and got to work putting her on Margaret and Sally's busy calendar.

When Margaret and Sally entered the long gravel driveway, there was an ominous feeling about the property. 'No Trespassing' signs were posted in several places, along with two 'Beware of Dog' signs nailed to the front porch. There wasn't any evidence of a dog on the property, but both ladies felt nervous about getting out of the car.

The house was old and in need of repairs. The curtains were pulled tight, and there was no sound coming from inside. Margret knocked as she tried to swallow the lump in her throat. Sally, picking up on the oddity of it all and on Margaret's hesitancy, looked at her phone to check the time, only to notice they had no cell service. Normally, that would not have been an issue, but in this case, Sally felt panic press in.

After a couple of minutes of standing on the front porch with flies buzzing all around them, Margaret and Sally heard someone inside. A rough, raspy voice that was almost shouting called out from the other side of the door, "Who's there?"

"It's Margaret and my assistant Sally. My husband Mitch spoke to you about an interview."

The door opened just a crack, and Margaret caught a glimpse of a frail, thin elderly woman. The chain lock was slowly removed as Mrs. Cunningham stood scowling and motioned for them to come in. She pointed to the couch.

Mrs. Cunningham left the room as soon as they entered. Ten minutes later, she was still nowhere to be seen. Margaret's heart raced as they sat waiting in the small living room. Neither Margaret nor Sally said a word. Margaret looked at her watch: 11:42 a.m. *If she doesn't come back in here by 11:45, we are out of here*, Margaret decided within.

At 11:44 a.m., as Margaret was just about to stand up, Mrs. Cunningham walked into the room carrying a teapot, teacups, and an assortment of cookies.

"I am sorry to have kept you ladies waiting. I am having a rather challenging day. Would you like some tea or cookies?"

Margaret responded in a shaky voice full of adrenaline, "I am sure this is difficult. Why don't you and I touch base another day when you are feeling better?"

"No, I would like to get this over with. It seems like the right thing to do."

Mrs. Cunningham proceeded to tell Margaret and Sally all about her 30-year marriage, the town she lived in, her church, and even her quilting group.

Margaret was gracious and patient as Mrs. Cunningham rambled on at length. It became increasingly awkward as they sat listening to her life story, which did not include her daughter. Margaret realized early on that Mrs. Cunningham was avoiding any mention of Samantha.

Mrs. Cunningham excused herself to the restroom twice, and then answered her phone and talked to a friend as if she did not have visitors. At 12:30 p.m., she looked at Margaret and Sally with a blank expression, stood up, pulled off her apron, and neatly folded it into the tiniest of squares.

"I am done now. You ladies need to be leaving."

Mrs. Cunningham began tidying up. Margaret and Sally glanced at each other, unsure what to say or do.

Margaret smiled warmly. "Sure, that's not a problem. It took me months to deal with my parents' death. I know this must be very difficult."

Mrs. Cunningham stood over Margaret. "What do you know about my grief? You have no idea the torment I experience every waking hour of my life. I am sorry to have bothered you, ladies, but you need to get out of my house before I call the police!"

Margaret calmly stood and gathered her things, and Sally followed behind, not saying a word. Margaret got to the door and looked back at Mrs. Cunningham, who appeared to be filled with rage. "Thank you for your time."

Margaret and Sally walked quickly to their vehicle, not

looking back. When both doors were closed and locked, Sally was the first to speak.

"What in the world just happened?" she asked in a shaky voice.

"I suppose my intuition was right on this one. That was possibly the most tense, awkward interaction I have ever had with another person."

"I have never seen anyone get so mad, so fast," Sally exclaimed.

Margaret stopped at the end of the driveway when she knew they could no longer be seen from the house. She turned to face Sally. "I am sorry I put you in that situation. Are you okay?"

"Yeah, I'm fine. Mrs. Cunningham actually reminds me of this lady who sometimes attends our church. She will turn on you in an instant, and she can be so hateful."

"That must be challenging," Margaret said, looking concerned.

"We eventually discovered that her entire family had died in a car wreck right before she moved to our town."

"Oh, my goodness, that's terrible!"

"It really is. My mom has always said that grief can really get a hold of a person. Some people eventually release the stranglehold it has, and some people don't."

"Hmm. That is some sound wisdom," Margaret said.

Sally shook her head and leaned back. "It's obvious that Mrs. Cunningham is being held tight by her grief."

"I guess so ..."

Margaret and Sally drove to the hotel, neither saying another word. When they arrived, they grabbed their things and went up to their room.

"Let's order room service and a movie and call it a night. We can get back to work tomorrow."

"Sounds like a plan." Sally kicked off her shoes and loosened her ponytail, grateful for a break.

≈

~SALLY'S JOURNAL~

Working with Margaret is like a dream come true, but not a dream I ever imagined. It's funny because I have learned so much from her on the good days, but just as much on the bad days.

The way she handled the situation with Mrs Cunningham today was so courageous. I wanted to run out of that place, but Margaret was patient and kind. I guess it's true that you learn as much from watching what someone doesn't do as you do from watching what someone actually does. Consider me inspired.

Chapter Thirty-Five

SALLY AND MARGARET were nibbling on a light breakfast the next morning when Margaret's phone rang. It was Mitch.

"Hey, honey, I wasn't expecting to hear from you this early. I figured you would be sleeping after I kept you on the phone so long after that weird interview yesterday."

"About that. Mrs. Cunningham called me this morning. She wants you guys to go back. She said it's really important."

"Um, no can do, Mitch. She looked at me like she wanted to kill me."

"It can't be that bad. She's like 80 years old."

"Trust me, it was that bad."

"Okay, I trust you to know what is best. I will let her know that your schedule won't allow you to return, and I will suggest a phone interview in a few days."

"Thanks, honey." Margaret ended the call feeling simultaneously relieved and conflicted.

"Did she want us to come back?" Sally asked in a low, fearful voice.

"Yes. I'm sure you heard me. I told Mitch no, but now I am wondering if that was the right thing to do. I mean, after all, anger is one of the stages of grief, and I can't even imagine how

I would feel if either of my boys had been on that plane. What do you think, Sally? Are you willing to give her another chance?"

"Well, I'm pretty sure that's what we are supposed to do. You know the whole turn the other cheek thing. God never promised us easy. But I completely trust your judgment and decision, so I am good either way."

"That's what I figured you would say. Let me see if I can catch Mitch before he calls her back."

Mitch answered on the first ring. "Hey, babe."

"Have you talked to Mrs. Cunningham yet?"

"No."

"Okay, I think I changed my mind."

"I thought you might. That's why I was waiting to call her. I know this must be so hard. Want me to have the cops on stand-by?" Mitch chuckled.

"Maybe."

"Honey, if you really feel that way, don't go. We can go together later."

"It's okay, Mitch, I put myself in her shoes for just a moment, and you know what? I would probably be angry too. I think we will be okay. I promise to let you know how it goes as soon as possible. We don't really have cell reception in her home, but it seemed okay in the driveway."

"Alright, please call me if you need me. I love you. And Margaret?"

"Yes, babe?"

"I'm really proud of you."

"Thank you, Mitch."

∼

RAIN BEGAN TO FALL, AND THUNDER RUMBLED AS Margaret and Sally pulled back into Mrs. Cunningham's long driveway. The angry host who Margaret and Sally had encountered during the first visit was no longer the person who met them at the door.

Mrs. Cunningham stood with her eyes bloodshot and shoulders slumped, looking as if she had aged ten years overnight. Margaret and Sally smiled politely as she closed the door behind them, neither brave enough to speak.

Mrs. Cunningham sat and motioned for them to do the same. She stared vacantly as if looking through her guests. Margaret began to feel nauseous as she considered whether they should stay or leave. Her main concern was Sally's safety, who looked fearful and unsure.

Two minutes passed.

Three minutes passed.

Complete silence filled every inch of the dark room.

Four minutes passed.

Margaret held her breath and exhaled long and slow. "Mrs. Cunningham, perhaps we could do a phone interview at a later date?"

Silence.

Another minute passed.

The tension within Margaret felt too much. She looked to Sally and then to the door.

"I never really knew her, you know, the real Samantha." Mrs. Cunningham's eyes remained vacant as a single tear rolled down her right cheek.

Margaret and Sally sat motionless.

"I told her to never take a drink. I knew what would happen. When Daddy drank, all those horrible men would come around. It was just awful. I was only trying to protect her."

Margaret swallowed hard.

"We named her Samantha Grace Cunningham. She turned 40 the day she got on that airplane. A friend was meeting her in Florida. They were going to drive to Key West for her birthday. We got in a big fight about her going. I never told her that I was sorry."

Unsure whether she should speak or remain silent, Margaret's heart was breaking for the pain she witnessed in Mrs. Cunningham's eyes. "I'm so sorry."

Mrs. Cunningham continued as if she were speaking into thin air. "I wanted more kids, but me and Samantha almost died when I was having her; that's why her middle name is Grace.

She was the perfect daughter until she went away to college. I begged her not to go away. I knew there would be trouble, but she wouldn't listen to me. She met some friends who were into the party scene, and she began drinking, and just like Daddy, she became hooked."

Margaret felt a bead of sweat prickle on her forehead. The room seemed to be getting hotter by the minute.

"Samantha was a full-blown alcoholic by the time it was legal for her to drink. My daddy, who she called Poppy, battled and lost his war against alcohol when Samantha was only 13. Samantha resembled Daddy in every way—their quirky sense of humor, their round, freckled faces, their wavy, auburn hair, and their love of hard liquor."

Margaret was listening intently, yet she began thinking that Mrs. Cunningham had missed the point of creating a "positive" legacy book. *Perhaps, if nothing else, the time will be therapeutic for Mrs. Cunningham,* she thought.

"Samantha never got married and never had any children. She went from job to job and lived either in small apartments in the worst part of town or on a friend's sofa. I was embarrassed and ashamed of how she turned out, or how it seemed she turned out. I didn't really give her a chance."

The left eye joined in as tears gently rolled down both of Mrs. Cunningham's cheeks. Sally reached into her bag and found a tissue to pass along. The gesture seemed to break the trance that she was in, as she sat back in her chair and unfolded her hands. Deep, rhythmic breaths came easier as she slowed the pace of her words.

"When you both were here earlier, I was so terrible to you. I felt sure you would never come back, but I believe Samantha's story is worth sharing, so I began writing you a letter about her. The more I wrote, the better I felt. It was like mercy was pouring from the sky."

Mrs. Cunningham's face changed as she began to tell them about Samantha, the Samantha that she discovered after the plane crash.

"When I got the call from the coroner's office confirming Samantha had died in the crash, I was furious with her for going on that trip. I told her the day before she left that she had no business going out of town when she barely had any money. Of course, she didn't listen to me. I should have been devastated when I found out she died, not mad, but I'm just telling you how I felt."

Mrs. Cunningham leaned over and began to weep. "She was a good girl. How did I never see what a good girl she was?"

Margaret stood, walked over to Mrs. Cunningham, and knelt beside her. "I am so very sorry, Mrs. Cunningham."

Unlike the day before, Mrs. Cunningham allowed Margaret to console her. Several minutes passed as Sally watched grace in action while praying silently for peace and mercy for Mrs. Cunningham.

"Mrs. Cunningham, I am sorry that we are stirring up all these very difficult feelings for you. Would you be more comfortable if we talked another time?" Margaret gently rubbed the top of her back. Mrs. Cunningham took a deep breath and leaned back in her chair, looking at Sally and then Margaret with kindness in her eyes.

"I don't want you to leave. If it wasn't for you, I may have never learned the truth about Samantha."

Margaret sat back down and leaned forward, looking into her eyes, "I'm not sure what you mean?"

"Please call me Rose, and please accept my apology for being so rude yesterday. I know this must be hard for you both to be here with me acting such a fool." Rose lowered her head, looking exhausted.

"Apology accepted. You have been through so much, we just don't want to make things more difficult for you," Margaret reassured her.

"I have been the one making things hard for myself." Rose took a deep breath and wiped the tears from her face.

"You see, as soon as Samantha started drinking, I began seeing her as a lost sinner, and I wasn't tolerant of her and her actions. I only saw the bad things she did. But, you know what, even when I shunned her, she was always good to me. I really didn't deserve her kindness, because the love I had for her must have seemed very conditional."

Rose began to shake her head. "But, it wasn't, I just didn't know what to do. I didn't know how to show my love. I hated that she drank like Daddy, and I thought if I made it harder for her, she would stop."

"That is understandable. Being a parent is certainly difficult."

"It really is. I am ashamed to say I didn't do a very good job."

"I'm afraid we all feel that way at times. I have two boys, and I've lost track of how many times I have let them down. I am sure Samantha understood how much you loved her."

Rose shrugged her shoulders, looking doubtful. "Do you ladies have time for me to show you something? It's rather important."

"Of course. We've got all day." Sally offered Rose another tissue.

Rose went into her kitchen and brought out a large wooden box. She set it down in front of Margaret and Sally. She slowly opened the box while smiling for the first time since they had arrived. Inside the box were letters and cards that Rose had received after Samantha's death. There were dozens of them.

"When Samantha died, I began receiving cards and letters from various people who knew her. She went to AA meetings on and off for years, and apparently, she was really encouraging to everyone there.

When I read the first letter, I didn't believe what I was reading. It made me mad that this person I had never even heard of thought so highly of Samantha. They were paying their respects to me because I guess she never told them what a terrible mother I was. When the second letter arrived and it was the same, I couldn't stand the thought of what I had missed all those years, so I threw it in the trash and vowed I would never look at another piece of mail about her."

"Then I heard about your idea for the legacy book on the Christian radio station I listen to, and I thought maybe I owed it to Samantha to tell her story. The letters and cards kept coming, but I didn't have the nerve to open them until after your visit yesterday. There are 32 of them still here. I threw the first two away."

Margaret ran her hand across the weathered wooden box. "Oh my goodness, Rose, that is unbelievable. Do you mind if we look through them?"

Rose's smile widened. "Please do. It turns out that God was using my Samantha, even in the trenches of her life."

For the next hour, Margaret and Sally read through every letter and card about Samantha. She had helped countless numbers of other broken people as she battled her addiction. Rose looked on and felt something she had long since forgotten: pride for her daughter.

-*Samantha was the nicest person in our meetings and genuinely cared about me when no one else did.*

-*Samantha is the reason I am sober today.*

-*Heaven gained an angel when Samantha left this Earth, because she was certainly an angel while she was here.*

Every card and letter pointed to one thing: Samantha was a follower of Jesus. Flawed, yes, but it was evident that she was a kind, wonderful woman who made a difference.

For every sad story, job loss, and broken relationship Samantha experienced, she impacted those around her positively. Because Samantha had accepted Jesus as her Savior, the light within her kept on shining, even when she was wrecking her own world. Her faith and light certainly grew dim at times, but God's grace was with her every step of the way.

When Samantha was drinking, she would distance herself from her mother and God because deep in her soul, she knew being an alcoholic was not God's plan for her. She would straighten up, and then she would think of her Poppy, who passed away because of his alcoholism, and she began to believe that she also wasn't strong enough to fight the daily desire. So, although she was continually trying to do the right thing, her belief about who she "thought" she was, was stronger than the truth of who she really was.

Rose admitted that, for a very long time, she was embarrassed and ashamed of her daughter and the life she lived. But when she began to think about Samantha's legacy of love, the lives she touched, and the perseverance that it took for her to make it through one more day, she realized what a gift Samantha was to the world.

Sally laid down the last letter. "Rose, is there anything you would like me to photograph to add to Samantha's legacy story?"

"Yes." Rose escorted Margaret and Sally into Samantha's old bedroom, which was basically untouched since she was a teenager. The light reflected perfectly through the soft, white drapes that fell behind Samantha's little desk. On top of her desk was a journal from the last summer camp she ever attended. The words, "Always Remember Isaiah 43," were written in bubble letters on the front of her journal song, with her own interpretation of that verse,

YES, GOD can make me new.

Several verses were written in cursive in various colors on the front and back of the journal.

When you walk through the fire, you will not be burned.
Do not be afraid, for I am with you.
See, I am doing a new thing!

A bracelet that read, *What would Jesus do? He would love first,* lay next to her journal while her Bible was perfectly positioned in the middle of the desk.

Rose noticed Sally looking at the Bible. "I tried to give Samantha her Bible several times, but she insisted that she had the words written on her heart and didn't want to chance losing or damaging it. Every time she straightened herself up and visited, she would sit at her desk and read her Bible while I made dinner."

"I am sure she loved that you kept her room so nice for her," Sally continued, looking around the small, yet very tidy room.

Clothes and shoes still lined the closet as if time had stood still. Rose insisted on sobriety to live there, so Samantha had not lived in the home with her mother since she was 18. For 22 years, Rose would clean Samantha's room and otherwise leave it untouched, waiting for the day that her daughter would claim victory over alcoholism once and for all. Sadly, that day never came, at least not according to Rose's previous standards.

As Margaret watched Rose and Sally interact, she stood in awe of this story of unrelenting grace and mercy. Her thoughts went to how she could possibly portray this story to her readers.

As they concluded in Samantha's room, Rose walked Margaret and Sally back into the family room and thanked them for the opportunity to share Samantha's story. Rose was holding her head higher, and her eyes looked brighter. "You know, maybe I will go help at the recovery group at my church. That might be a good way to honor my baby girl."

"That is a beautiful idea, Rose. I am sure that would have made Samantha very happy," Margaret smiled.

"I can never thank you enough for helping me to see my daughter for the wonderful angel she was. I know she is with the Lord and, for the first time in a long time, I feel at peace."

Once again, Margaret and Sally left an interview astonished at what they had just encountered. Only God could weave such an amazing turn of events. Margaret drove back to the cabin as the storm swept out of town. The clouds gave way to a glorious sunset that glowed yellow and orange over the mountains.

Words were not needed. Margaret and Sally wound their way through the mountains, realizing they had just witnessed 20 years of bitterness, shame, and disappointment come tumbling down.

∾

Margaret's Journal

How often do we as humans want to give up on our fellow man?

We somehow think we are better, but in God's eyes, we are all hopeless sinners in need of a Savior. Thank goodness Samantha knew Jesus and thank goodness that even in the trenches of life, she sought to please Him.

What the enemy meant for evil, the Lord used for good. Lord, thank You for giving me a new perspective on those who are struggling. I am sorry for all the times I made a quick judgment about someone, without knowing their story. Thank You for opening my eyes and my soul. I am so grateful ...

Chapter Thirty-Six

THERE WAS an unusual chill in the air when Margaret and Sally arrived at the cabin. They quietly began unpacking their belongings while noticing the cooler air.

"If you don't mind, I think I will go visit my parents for a little while this evening. It's been a while since I've seen them," Sally said.

"Of course, anytime you want to go, just go. Never feel like you have to ask me."

After Sally left, Margaret took a long shower, allowing her body the time it needed to relax. Steam bellowed out of the glass enclosure, filling the room. She stepped out and used her hand to clear the fog from the mirror. Her eyes twinkled in the reflection, looking bright and vibrant. Her skin was once again glowing, and the puffiness had subsided. She picked her wedding band up from the small ceramic bowl on the counter and placed the ring on her finger. It easily slid into place, unlike a few weeks ago when it would barely fit.

Margaret stared at her reflection and smiled.

"Welcome back," she said, reaching for her robe.

Margaret made her way through the cabin, noticing the door was already locked and her favorite candle was flickering in the middle of the kitchen table with soft worship music playing in the background.

Sweet Sally, you really are so good to me, she thought as she nestled into the sofa with a cozy blanket and her Bible.

Margaret spent the next hour reading through Romans and journaling. A little before seven, she got a call from Mitch.

"Hello ..." Margaret answered with a hint of flirtation in her voice.

"Well, hello, gorgeous. How are you?"

"If you want to know the truth, I am exhausted, but in a good way."

"Well, then you might not like my news."

"Uh oh, what does that mean?" Margaret sat up and laid her things to the side.

"I got an inquiry from a lady who would like to meet with you. She wants to share the story of one of her friends."

"Oh, honey, I'm basically done formatting the book. I don't have space for another story, not to mention the deadline for inquiries was two weeks ago."

"I know. I tried to tell her that."

Margaret sighed. "I'm sorry. She needs to understand there was a deadline for a reason."

"Well, the reason she didn't call originally was because her friend was dying from cancer when he got on the plane. He only had weeks left to live."

Margaret scooted to the edge of the sofa. "Oh."

"She said that as the news outlets continued to report on some of the more notable passengers, she felt as if she had to share his story."

"Oh ... well, that's a twist I didn't expect. I can certainly see how she would feel that way. Sally picked up the most recent edition of People magazine, which featured a huge spread on a handful of passengers. I do feel like I will be representing the passengers who would have otherwise been forgotten in the news."

"You just hit the nail on the head. Your story is so different from what pop culture presents to the world."

"Okay, I don't mind meeting her, but I can't promise anything more than a mention of him. There just isn't room for another full story."

"You, Margaret Taylor, are simply amazing."

"I think the word you are looking for is sucker, but I will take amazing," Margaret laughed.

Mitch chuckled. "Okay, I'll set it up."

$$\sim$$

LESS THAN 48 HOURS LATER, MARGARET AND SALLY opened the door of the cafe and secured Margaret's regular booth in the corner.

A few minutes later, a young woman walked into the cafe, scanning the room. Margaret waved, and the woman walked toward them.

Margaret stepped out of the booth and extended her hand. "Hi, you must be Tabatha."

"Yes, and you must be Margaret and Sally," she replied, shaking each of their hands.

"You look so familiar to me. Have we met before?" Margaret asked.

"I don't think so."

As Margaret listened to Tabatha's voice, the memory came flooding back, and Margaret was transported back to video footage from the day of the plane crash.

A reporter was standing in the terminal. People were screaming and crying.

The reporter pushed his way through the crowd, "Ma'am, did you know someone aboard Flight 7889?"

He was breathing hard, adrenaline rising to the surface.

Tabatha stood steady and silent, looking out to the runway as if in a trance.

"Ma'm, did you hear me?" he huffed.

"Yes," she whispered into the microphone.

"Yes, you heard me, or yes, you knew someone?" The reporter barked back.

Tabatha stared into the camera, her green eyes glassy and full of pain.

"Yes, I heard you, and yes, I knew someone."

Her words were clear and concise. It sounded as if each word could topple a mountain with the heaviness of her raw emotion.

The reporter stared at her with his brows pinched and a scowl on his face.

Tabatha didn't move and didn't say another word.

The reporter took the microphone, turned around, and began interviewing a red-haired teenage boy who was practically begging for a moment in the spotlight.

Margaret remembered the interview vividly and felt chill bumps cover her body. She brought herself back to the present, feeling her heart beat faster against her chest.

Tabatha sat and pulled her phone and a notebook out of her purse.

Margaret got the attention of the waitress and ordered coffee for the three of them. "I know this may be unsettling for you, and if you prefer not to talk about this, I completely understand, but I am pretty sure I figured out why I recognize you."

"Okay," Tabatha said with a curious tone.

Margaret felt her stomach tighten. "I was watching TV the day of the plane crash. I saw the reporter interviewing you. At least, I am pretty sure that was you."

The color drained out of Tabatha's face, and she closed her eyes. "Yes, that was me."

Margaret shook her head. "I am really sorry; I shouldn't have brought that up. I thought the reporter was horribly insensitive. When I realized it was you, I felt as if I needed to say something."

Tabatha opened her eyes and looked at Margaret. She picked up her mug, drank the creamy contents, and unfolded her arms.

"You are the first person who has mentioned the interview, and I know other people saw it. I know I must have looked like a fool just standing there."

"Oh, my goodness, not at all. The person who looked like a fool was that reporter. I thought you handled it with such grace."

The table sat silent for a full minute.

Margaret broke the silence. "Tabatha, I am really sorry that I mentioned the reporter. Please know that we met with you today because we care, and our hearts truly mourn your loss."

Tabatha inhaled and let her breath out slowly. "Thank you, that means a lot. But, truthfully, I am not here for me. I am here for Chris... He was like the big brother I never had."

Tabatha gazed out of the window and then back to Margaret and Sally.

"Chris and I met at the cancer treatment center. I had just moved to Georgia when I got diagnosed with breast cancer. Thankfully, my prognosis was good. Chris, on the other hand, had stage 4 colon cancer. The odds were stacked against him."

"Oh, that's terrible," Sally said, engaging with every word.

"At first, it was really hard for me to accept my cancer diagnosis. I was in a new city, I had lost touch with my family, and it all seemed a bit hopeless. But then.. I met Chris."

Tabatha began slowly stirring her coffee. "His wife used to bring him to all of his appointments. You could tell they were really devoted to each other. Most people there had someone, except me. Chris was the first to notice that I was always alone."

The cafe cleared out from the morning rush, and the waitresses began clearing the tables while soft music played in the background. Margaret and Sally sat quietly, allowing Tabatha time.

"I found out a few days into our friendship that Chris was not only battling for his life, but he was also a chaplain. He had taken an online course so he could better help others going through hard times." Tabatha smiled and chuckled under her breath. "His smile could light up the entire cancer treatment center, and his laugh—his laugh was contagious."

"He sounds wonderful," Margaret replied.

Tabatha picked up her phone and began scrolling through her photos.

"This is Chris and me the day I rang the bell and was declared cancer-free. He was so happy for me. I started my podcast that same day. I had no idea what I was doing, but Chris's encouragement made me realize I needed to do something. I was given a second chance at life, and I wanted to make the most of it."

Margaret smiled a deep smile. *I know how that feels.*

Tabatha reached into her purse and pulled out a small electronic tablet. She found the app she was looking for and pulled up the home page of her podcast, "Purpose in the Pain."

"This is my podcast. It was actually inspired by Chris," Tabatha declared.

Margaret studied the page and read through the awe-inspiring words.

Welcome to the "Purpose in the Pain" podcast, where we dive deep into real life and explore how God uses our pain to strengthen our purpose. Purpose in the Pain Podcast is hosted by me, Tabatha Allen, and inspired by my dear friend Chris, who taught me a life-changing lesson. "You never know what people are going through, and sometimes, the people with the biggest smiles are struggling the most, so be kind." -Chris

Margaret passed the tablet to Sally and leaned back. "Wow, I am almost without words. Essentially, you are telling me that this incredible man who was dying from cancer inspired you to start a podcast that now inspires others to live with more purpose?"

"Yes, that's exactly what happened."

"What about his cancer diagnosis? Could Chris heal his cancer? How did he end up on that plane?" Margaret asked.

"The cancer had pretty much spread everywhere, and his doctors had exhausted every effort. Chris was working through his bucket list of things he wanted to do while he could. Most days were pretty hard on him. He was on his way to visit his brother, Tim, who lives in Tampa. They were going to catch a baseball game together, and Chris wanted to see the beach one last time."

"Oh, my gosh," Sally said, just above a whisper.

"The reality is that Chris would have probably passed soon, but it still breaks my heart that he's gone."

"Of course," Margaret reached her hand back across the table, found Tabatha's warm hand, and gave it a squeeze.

Margaret shook her head and stared at the words on the tablet. *Purpose in the Pain.* She laid her hands on the table and looked around the cafe, attempting to gather her thoughts.

The manuscript is basically complete and ready to turn in.

There isn't a natural place for another full story.

The whole book would have to be reworked.

Margaret swallowed hard. "Tabatha, how would you feel if I added Chris and his story to our book?"

Tabatha's eyes opened wide, and a smile spread across her face. "I was hoping you would say that."

Margaret, Sally, and Tabatha spent the next two hours talking about Chris and about the lasting effects of grief. A call to Chris's wife, Wendi provided a few more details and confirmed that his story would, indeed, be added.

Margaret was surprised to hear that Chris often struggled with depression and anxiety, but at the same time was deeply committed to being a ray of sunshine in other people's lives. He was a Master Gardener, a woodworker, and loved all things aviation. His wife sent a few photos of Chris to Sally. There was one photo of him with the most beautiful peonies anyone at the table had ever seen. It was evident that Chris showered everything in his life with love.

MARGARET AND SALLY MADE THE SHORT DRIVE BACK TO

the cabin in silence. When parked, Sally finally spoke up. "Do you ever feel like this is a dream, like this isn't actually happening?"

Margaret shifted in her seat and faced Sally. "I was literally just thinking that exact thing. Like, how in the world did we get here? How can there be so many beautiful souls in the world, and we are the ones telling their stories?"

"I know, right? This has me wondering about every person I have ever served at the cafe, as well as all the people at church and school. I never really thought about how special each person is."

"Exactly. Of course, the reality is that we all bring something different to the table of life, and not everyone will leave such a beautiful, lasting legacy. But, at the same time, so many people who pass each day leave imprints on the world that will be felt for generations to come."

"That's so true," Sally said just above a whisper. She got out of the car and began walking toward the cabin.

"I'll be in later," Margaret called from the open window.

Sally looked back and smiled, "Sounds good."

Margaret couldn't break loose from the wonder of it all.

Why me? Why spare my life and then use me in such a mighty way?

Margaret closed her eyes, allowing the breeze to cool her.

I knit you together in your mother's womb. You are fearfully and wonderfully made. That's why.

"Thank You," she said, acknowledging the Holy Spirit working within her. She took her phone from her purse, pulled up Mitch's number, and typed a text.

- I am so glad I said yes to meeting Tabatha, yes to not getting on that plane, yes to writing this book, and yes to the Lord when He called me to be His. I love you and I can't wait to see you.

One minute later, her phone lit up with a reply from Mitch.

- I'm glad the meeting went well with Tabatha, and Amen to everything else!

Chapter Thirty-Seven

A SOFT BREEZE blew through the cabin's open lower-level doors. Sally shuffled through stacks of notes and dozens of pictures, double-checking that she had not forgotten any important details from the interviews.

Suddenly, she heard footsteps above and a soft whimper.

Sally stopped what she was doing, stood still trying to decipher the sound, then walked to the edge of the stairwell and listened.

She continued to listen until she was positive that Margaret was crying.

Sally started walking up the stairs. "Margaret are you okay?" she called out.

No response.

When Sally got to the top of the stairs, she saw Margaret in the corner of the sofa with her head buried in her hands and her knees pulled into her chest.

Alarmed, Sally stopped and whispered, "Margaret, I don't mean to bother you, but I thought I heard you crying ... are you okay?"

With bloodshot eyes and mascara running down her face,

Margaret looked at Sally and nodded her head as a soft smile emerged from the tears.

"Okay, I will let you have some privacy. I'm sorry, I shouldn't have come up."

"It's okay, please, don't leave."

"Okay ..." Sally sat on the other end of the sofa, passing Margaret a tissue.

The family room was mostly dark, illuminated only by the faintest glow of a small table lamp. The large windows displayed the night sky filled with countless twinkling stars. The visiting owl sang out across the silence, *hoot, hoot ... hoot, hoot.*

After several minutes, Margaret stood and walked to the kitchen.

"Want some tea?"

"Sure."

After preparing hot mugs of chamomile tea, Margaret sat back on the sofa with Sally.

She blew steam from her mug and gently smiled. "I'm sorry if I frightened you."

"It's okay, I was just worried about you."

"I have been struggling with all these layers of grief and legacy we have been uncovering."

Sally reached to the side table and handed her another tissue, then took one for herself.

"It's been rewarding and gut-wrenching at the same time," Sally replied.

"When Mitch called about meeting Tabatha, I was annoyed that we would have to go do another interview, partly because I had the book formatted, but I also didn't want to walk through another trench of grief with someone." Margaret hung her head. "I am embarrassed and ashamed to even say that, considering the grace the Lord has given us during this whole process." Margaret sniffled and looked out of the windows into the dark forest.

"Don't feel bad, I understand, really." Sally patted Margaret's leg and continued.

"Every story has been incredible, but something about Chris's story resonated differently for me."

Both women fell silent again, sipping their tea and listening to the hum of the air conditioner. Margaret shifted on the sofa, laying her mug on the table. "I think it was because he knew he was dying, yet still chose to live."

Sally's eyes widened, "I hadn't thought of it that way."

Margaret sat up and wiped her eyes. "I hadn't either until this very moment, but that's it. Everyone else who boarded that plane thought they had time. Time to make things right, chase their dreams, forgive, or move on, but Chris knew his time was coming to an end, and he still chose to live."

Margaret stood. "He found purpose in his pain, literally, and he lived out that purpose. He encouraged others, loved God, and used what time he had to make a difference in the world around him."

A smile spread across Sally's face as she watched Margaret's entire demeanor change. Margaret continued, "Chris's story is the perfect addition to the book because it is the final reminder that we must live as if every day could be our last. How long we are given is irrelevant in the eternal perspective."

Sally stood, walked to the kitchen, and got her Bible. "This conversation reminds me of something I was reading just a few days ago."

Margaret joined Sally in the kitchen, eager to hear truth.

Sally thumbed through the worn pages. "Here it is. This is from the book of James. 'Now listen, you who say, today or tomorrow we will go to this or that city, and spend a year there, carry on business, and make money. Why, you do not even know what will happen tomorrow. What is your life? You are a mist that appears for a little while and then vanishes. Instead, you ought to say, if it is the Lord's will, we will live and do this or that.'"

"Yes, that is exactly right."

Margaret closed her eyes and exhaled a breath that felt caught in her soul for months.

Chapter Thirty-Eight

OVER THE NEXT SEVERAL DAYS, Margaret began trying to finalize the manuscript. She laid out each section of the story on the kitchen table, recalling each interview and interviewee. She shifted the papers, rummaging through each stack countless times, while trying to put them in logical order. She tapped her fingers on the table with her brows squeezed together.

Sally walked through the front door. "Hey, you look puzzled. Everything okay?"

Margaret leaned forward, rubbing her forehead. "I had the book formatted before meeting with Tabatha, but for some reason, it all seems out of order now."

"I have no idea the kind of order it should be in," Sally said, laying down her watering jug and wiping her hands.

Margaret continued, rubbing her forehead, then moving her hand to her neck to rub out the tension.

"I wonder if you should just go with the order of the interviews to make it simple?"

"Hmm, I hadn't really thought about doing that, but maybe you're right. It's like we talked about yesterday, Chris's story at the end makes sense. That will leave the reader with a sense that there was indeed a purpose in the middle of all of the pain."

Sally smiled and began rearranging each section in the order in which the interview had taken place. "So, we will start with Bill, and then Penny."

Margaret spoke up. "Oh, I forgot to tell you. Tristan texted me a couple of days ago. He is still leading worship, but he is also heading up the missionary team for the youth group at his church. He said he is organizing a trip to the Dominican Republic next year."

"Oh wow, that's so cool. Can you imagine how proud his mom would be?"

Margaret thought of the angel statue at Penny's little church and the impact she had made. "His mom certainly led by example."

"Yes, she did." Sally pulled the next file and placed it beside Penny's file. So, we have Bill, then Penny, then Miguel."

"Sweet Miguel," Margaret sighed. "That story amazes me."

"I know, it's so crazy that Logan was at the coffee shop that day. What are the chances?" Sally asked while shrugging her shoulders.

"Well, apparently the chances are pretty good."

Sally grinned. "Good point. All right, so we have Miguel, and then Trudy."

"Sorry to interrupt again. Speaking of Trudy and Frank, Mitch told me that he and Frank talk a couple of times a week now. Frank has started attending the church that Trudy went to. He told Mitch that all the women swoon over him in an attempt to take care of the new widower."

Sally sighed, "Oh, that's so sweet. Frank was such a gentle giant."

"All right, back to it. Sorry, I keep interrupting," Margaret said.

"It's totally okay, I love that all of these people still want to be in touch with you and Mitch."

"Me too."

"Alright, so after Frank was the McCain family." Sally blushed and averted her eyes.

Margaret noticed the change in Sally. "Oh, yes, Austin. He seemed like such a wonderful young man."

Sally's face reddened further. "Yep, so anyway, then you had the letter about Stanley."

Margaret nodded, "Yes, what a beautiful letter. You could tell Ingrid was once a teacher. She had such a way with words."

"Then we have Samantha and Rose," Sally said, raising her eyebrows. "That was one of the craziest things I have ever been through. I didn't wanna say much because I would've never wanted to ignore or stop the interview, but I was scared out of my mind."

"Trust me, I have never experienced a more challenging interchange. I look back now and know that it was God's grace that kept us there. Rose honestly terrified me until her walls came down. I know that sounds awful, but she and her house were ominous to say the least."

"I completely agree, but Samantha's story is probably my favorite. And the impact reading those letters had on Rose was worth it all," Sally said.

Margaret took the notes that Sally had just typed up about Chris. "And then, the very last, unexpected story, dear Chris. When I first asked Tabatha about adding him to the book, my brain was saying no, it would be too complicated. Now, I can't imagine the book without him."

"Me either."

"Well, I think that is everyone." Margaret reached across the table and took hold of Sally's hand. "I really couldn't have done this without you."

Sally squeezed Margaret's hand. "I played such a small part but thank you for saying that."

Margaret lifted her mug. "I propose a toast."

Sally smiled and lifted her mug.

"To us. Two women who felt unworthy of such a calling but were courageous enough to answer the call anyway."

~

THE NEXT THREE DAYS WERE SPENT ORGANIZING THE stories and extracting the most intimate, honorable details of each person's life. Margaret spent hours down by the creek reading the notes that Sally had so carefully written. She thumbed through dozens of photos that served as tiny snapshots of the beauty and wonder they had encountered at each interview. Each photo represented a life well-lived and a physical reminder of a legacy that would continue beyond this generation.

-The treehouse that Bill had so lovingly built.

-The beautiful garden that Penny had created with her own two hands.

-The cross pendant that Miguel had crafted that hung around Logan's neck.

-The wind chime etched with Trudy's name that sang a sweet melody of love.

-The heartfelt letter that described Stanley with such detail and devotion.

-Jasmine, the young colt that represented dreams accomplished and the promise of new life at Jeff, Joy, and Cheyenne's home.

-The wooden box full of letters that showcased Samantha and her never-ending quest to live a life of significance.

-The picture of Chris and Tabatha at the cancer center, his smile radiating tremendous purpose in his pain, despite his diagnosis.

The book was a collection of mini biographies of each individual, along with details from the interviews. Margaret included her own faith journey, her story of surrender, and her experience of a second chance at life.

Between the stories, Margaret had created devotional entries, which contained accompanying scripture. Inspirational messages were spread throughout with a call to action, designed to spur the reader to live and love more fully. The book, which began as a simple idea, had transformed into an inspirational work of art that was sure to reach into the heart of every reader.

Tears were a regular part of the process as Margaret recounted the stories with a deep sense of love and grief. *My life will never be the same*, she thought repeatedly as she compiled what she believed to be the best work of her career.

When she felt satisfied with the layout of the book, she packed up her things and headed back to the city to celebrate the completion of the book and her anniversary with Mitch.

~Margaret's Journal~

From the baby in utero who never takes a breath out of their mother's womb, to the elderly person who lives to be 100, every life serves a purpose.

If this experience has taught me anything, it's that our lives are interconnected in ways that only a good God could orchestrate and that every single life matters more than we will ever know on this side of Heaven.

Chapter Thirty-Nine

MARGARET WALKED in the front door of her home and saw rose petals sprinkled on the floor leading to the veranda. She grinned as she set her things down in the foyer. She carefully walked around each delicate yellow petal as the smell of home-made pizza drifted through the sliding glass doors on the back of the house that led to the pool.

She spotted Mitch standing next to the brick pizza oven. He looked up from his lunch preparations and watched his bride step over the last of the petals and into his arms. He held her tight. "Gosh, I've missed you."

"I've missed you, too. Thanks for taking the day off. Oh, and the rose petals are certainly a nice touch." Margaret rested her head against his chest, taking a deep, restorative breath.

"Well, in case you have forgotten, that's what we found upon entering our honeymoon suite. It seemed only fitting, considering what day it is."

"I could never forget. Happy anniversary, babe, and thank you for standing by me the last 28 years."

"There is nowhere I would rather be."

Margaret and Mitch spent the rest of the day sharing good food, lots of laughs, and dreams of the future. As the sun began to drop below the trees, Margaret's phone began to ring with a familiar tone. A smile lit up her summer-tanned face as she saw Matthew's name appear on her screen.

"Hey, buddy."

"Hey, Mom. Happy anniversary! How's it going?"

"Thanks, we have had a great day. How are you?"

"I'm doing good. I'm finally getting a bit of a break, which brings me to my next question. Luke and I were talking about coming home for the weekend. Are you and Dad going to be around?"

"That would be great! We don't have any plans. Do you guys want to hang out here or go to the cabin?"

"I vote for the cabin, but we can do whatever you and Dad want to do."

Margaret looked to Mitch and whispered, "How about the cabin?" Mitch nodded and winked at his bride.

Later that evening, Margaret decided to call Sally to let her know about their upcoming family visit.

"Hi, Sally. I wanted to let you know that we are all going to head that way Friday for a few days."

"Oh, great! I'm so happy you guys will have some time together."

"You are welcome to stay. I just didn't want to surprise you. I did check at that lovely inn you have mentioned, and they have a room available if you would prefer to go there for a little retreat of your own. It's completely up to you."

"I will do whatever is best for y'all. I hate to intrude on your family time, but I also don't want you spending money on a room for me. I could just go to Mom and Dad's."

"Why don't we do this? I will get you a room for two nights as a treat for all the hard work you've been doing. At the end of the two days, you can decide if you want to stay there, come back to the cabin, or go to your parents. Does that sound okay?"

"That would be amazing, if you are sure. I don't want to be a bother."

"You are never a bother. You certainly deserve a break."

"I think you forgot about my former job; now, every day feels like a break," Sally giggled.

"That's a great perspective, and even more reason for me to treat you. I will make the arrangements and give you the details when we get to the cabin."

"That sounds great. Thank you so much, Margaret!"

SALLY HUNG UP THE PHONE AND WORKED HER WAY through the cabin, cleaning and organizing each room with precision. She then went into the yard and began gathering fragrant magnolia blooms, colorful zinnias, and droopy, bright yellow sunflowers. She placed the flowers in mason jars throughout the cabin, adding the perfect touch of summer vibrancy.

Her next mission was to pick perfectly ripe apples from the property. She gathered six green apples and six red apples, then made her way back to the kitchen. With her favorite worship playlist playing in the background, she peeled and prepared an old-fashioned lattice-topped pie for Margaret and her family. With the leftover apples, she prepared a small cobbler for her parents

"Dad will love this. I can take it on my way to Mary's Inn. Mary's! I can't believe I am going to Mary's," she exclaimed in excitement. She ate the last two slices of apple, then continued creating the perfect welcome for Margaret and her family.

When all the work was done, she sat on the back deck waiting for the pie and cobbler to cook. She looked over the deck railing at the creek dancing through the lush green ferns and the slippery dark rocks. "This cannot be my real life. Thank You, Lord."

MITCH, MARGARET, MATTHEW, AND LUKE ARRIVED AT the cabin around 10 a.m. Friday morning, laughing and enjoying

each other's company. Sally heard the laughter as she stepped onto the front porch, marveling at the family that had been disconnected and in despair only weeks before. They were a picture of forgiveness and grace.

"Are you excited about going to Mary's?" Matthew asked as they walked through the door.

"Yes, I'm so excited. I never thought in a million years I would get a chance to go somewhere so beautiful. One of my friends went there on her honeymoon. She couldn't stop talking about it."

"Well, you'll have to let us know if it's nice as it looks. Maybe this guy and I can go sometime," Margaret ran her hand across Mitch's back.

"That would certainly be nice," Mitch said, and then leaned down to kiss Margaret on the cheek.

"Could you guys be any more ooey-gooey in love?" Luke asked with a chuckle.

Margaret and Mitch looked at each other, then they both replied, "Probably not."

Everyone laughed.

"Okay, okay, Sally, you should be on your way. I asked for early check-in for you, so your suite should be ready when you arrive."

"My suite, that sounds so fancy," Sally said, blushing.

Sally reached and hugged Mitch. "Thank you so much."

She then hugged Margaret. "As long as I live, I'll never be able to repay you for how you have changed my life."

"Now who's being ooey-gooey?" Margaret nudged Sally with a gentle push on her back. "Now go, your suite is waiting for you."

"Eek! I still can't believe it!" Sally exclaimed as she rushed downstairs to get her bag.

Chapter Forty

SALLY PLACED her duffle bag in her car and headed 25 miles north to Mary's Mountain Inn & Spa, making a quick stop to drop off her parents' cobbler.

Sally's mom greeted her at the door. "Well, what a sweet surprise." They exchanged a warm hug. "Is Pop home?" Sally asked.

"No, honey, he just left for the Feed & Seed."

Her mom looked down at the towel in Sally's hand. "Wha'cha got there?"

Sally smiled and unwrapped the cobbler. "Fresh apple cobbler; it's Grandma Faye's recipe."

"Oh boy, your daddy will be so excited. Let me get that," Sally's mom took the cobbler. "I hope you are staying awhile," she said, while walking toward the kitchen.

"Actually, I am heading to Mary's Inn and Spa," Sally murmured, hesitating slightly.

"Mary's? Is that the fancy place Nicole honeymooned at?"

"Yes, that's it."

"What in the world are you doing going there?" her mom asked, her eyes squinting and her hands on her hips.

"Margaret's family came into town for the weekend, and she

and Mitch are treating me to some time at Mary's because of how hard I worked on the book."

Sally stood still, feeling her pulse quicken. She felt her face getting hot.

"Huh, that seems awfully expensive. You could have stayed with us."

"Margaret insisted. I know I can always stay here, but I think it's good for me to try new things, don't you, Mom?"

Her mom laid the cobbler on the counter and looked out of the small kitchen window with her back turned to Sally. She watched the clouds roll by and a small butterfly casually fluttering along. Almost a full minute passed before her mom slowly turned around with a soft smile on her face.

"Yes, I think it's great, Sally. Please go have a good time. You'll have to tell me all about it."

Sally exhaled a sigh of relief and hugged her mom again.

"Thank you, Mom, that means a lot."

Her mom gave her another hug and then urged her out the door in the pursuit of expanding her horizons.

AN HOUR LATER, SALLY PULLED INTO THE PRISTINE entrance with a faint smile emerging from her timidity.

I can't believe I'm here.

Slowly, her car wound its way up the long, narrow driveway. About a third of the way up the long ascent, she came to a sign that read, 'Mary's Mountain Inn & Spa, Registered guests only beyond this point.'

She felt her hesitation escalate.

I don't belong here.

This is a place for people like Margaret, not me.

A luxury car rolled up behind her, pressing in on her thoughts. Sally glanced in the rearview, feeling embarrassed for blocking the driveway, and continued up the mountain. When she reached the top, the SUV pulled off into a side parking lot, and Sally had no choice but to continue forward.

Mary's was more grand and luxurious than Sally had imagined. The inn was impressive in every sense of the word. A beautiful, well-appointed structure sprawled majestically on the crest of a North Georgia mountain peak, with spectacular views as far as the eye could see. The retreat had every luxury that a getaway should include, complete with a beautiful spa in an adjacent building that was sure to relax even the most stressed-out guest.

Sally parked her car underneath the massive porte-cochere and took a deep breath as she shook her head in disbelief. She thought back to the many times that wealthy customers would stop in the cafe for a bite to eat on their way to this exclusive destination. She recalled the other waitresses being smug and judgmental, but Sally had always felt differently. Sure, some people were not very nice, but most were.

There had always been a little voice in her soul that wondered if maybe, just maybe, one day she would be able to live beyond the walls of the cafe and her parents' farmhouse. But, never in her wildest dreams had she envisioned the life Margaret and Mitch were so graciously sharing with her.

Living in the cabin had provided Sally with a way out of her normal, mundane routine, but she still wasn't sure that she deserved this new life. She grabbed her phone and called Margaret.

"Hello," Margaret answered.

Sally scanned the lower parking lot that was full of expensive vehicles. "Hey, I'm really sorry to bother you, but I think I am a little out of my league up here. I don't think I brought the right kind of clothes for a place like this. Heck, I don't think I even own the right kind of clothes for a place like this."

Margaret grinned. "Please don't think for another moment that you don't belong there. The most precious asset you possess is yourself. Enjoy your time away; you deserve it."

"Okay, if you say so." Sally paused, giving herself a little time to process her emotions.

She recalled what Margaret had just said, *"Don't think for another moment that you don't belong there. The most precious asset you possess is yourself."*

She closed her eyes and felt a rush of confidence spring from the encouraging words.

I can do this, she thought to herself.

"Okay, Margaret. I trust you and I believe you. Thanks again, and please tell Mitch thank you also. You have both changed my life."

Sally freshened up her lip gloss and headed into the impressive mountain inn, clueless that her entire life was about to change.

She slowly walked through the expansive entryway and looked around, her eyes widening at the panoramic view of the Blue Ridge Mountains through the tall, spotless windows of the great room. The middle-aged woman at the front desk smiled.. "Well, hello, you must be Sally. We have been expecting you."

"Ummm, yes ma'am. I'm Sally."

"Welcome to Mary's. We are so happy that you will be joining us for a couple of days, or perhaps longer. Your friend Margaret was so kind when she booked your stay. She has some special things in store for you."

The nice lady laid Sally's welcome bag on top of the desk.

"Yes, ma'am. Margaret is one of the kindest people I know. Ummm, I wasn't sure where to park my car."

"I will alert the valet, and Kelsey will help with your bags. She will also give you a tour of the inn and the grounds, show you to your suite, and help you get your spa visit booked. Consider her your new best friend."

The lady smiled while handing Sally a luxurious bag filled with local treats, including handmade chocolates filled with creamy caramel, organic hand lotion made from a local farm, and a small satin eye pillow scented with freshly grown lavender.

Sally accepted the bag hesitantly. "Oh, okay. Ummm, I think I will have to pass on the spa, but thank you for the offer. My budget is a little tight. I'm just getting started with my job with Margaret, and I'm trying to be very careful with my spending until I get a new budget figured out." She looked down and began to blush.

She probably didn't need all that info, you dummy, Sally thought, with her head still lowered.

"I think it's wonderful that you are such a wise steward of your money, but I have great news for you. Your friend Margaret has already prepaid for everything, and she insisted that we spoil you rotten and that you don't spend a dime."

"Oh, okay, thank you very much, and I apologize for rambling. This way of life is new for me."

"No problem, dear, you are doing great. I am going to page Kelsey for you, and she will get you settled. Please let me know if I can be of further assistance. My name is Susie."

"Thank you very much, Susie. I really appreciate it."

"It is my pleasure, dear and Sally, one more thing ..."

"Yes?"

"We are all just ordinary people around here. No one is better than you or deserves to be here any more than you. Sure, some of our guests are quite wealthy, but we are just as grateful to have you join us."

Sally exhaled, realizing she had been mostly holding her breath. Her hand trembled, rattling the bag she was holding. "Thank you, Susie. That means more to me than you know."

Kelsey hurried around the corner to find Sally standing by the windows, looking out in awe and wonder.

"Hi Sally, it's so nice to meet you. My name is Kelsey, and I will be your inn hostess while you are here. I will help you with any needs that may arise during your stay with us."

"Hi, it's nice to meet you. Thank you so much." Sally glanced back outside and spotted three hot air balloons in the distance, floating into the billowy, white clouds. "I can't get over this view."

"I know, I have worked here for five years, and the view never gets old. I love driving up here every day from the valley."

Sally and Kelsey watched the balloons rise higher and higher into the clouds.

"You are going to love the view from your suite. We have you in the Garden Suite, which is my favorite one in the entire inn. Let's get your bags, and I'll have the valet move your car, and then I will show you around. You are absolutely going to love it here."

The valet moved Sally's car and handed her worn duffel bag to Kelsey, who brought it into the inn after much resistance from Sally. After Kelsey convinced Sally to relax and enjoy the special treatment, they walked through the inn, making their way to the terrace level, where the Garden Suite was prominently located.

When Kelsey opened the door to the suite, Sally gasped in surprise. They walked forward, looking at the expansive view. Two large windows and a glass balcony door overlooked the garden below. Sally's smile widened when she spotted the Koi pond, filled with eight brightly-colored fish that swam elegantly back and forth.

A large gazebo surrounded by native azaleas displayed bright fuchsia and gleaming white blooms. In the distance, the mountain range glistened in the afternoon sun with the hot air balloons drifting beyond the horizon.

"Oh my, this is absolutely amazing," Sally whispered, noticing the bouquet of flowers Margaret had arranged to be there upon her arrival.

Sally walked to the flowers and pulled the small, pale-yellow card from the bouquet. She opened the card and read the simple sentiment from Margaret.

Enjoy your time away. This is just the beginning.

Sally laid the card down and smiled a smile that reached deep into her soul.

Kelsey walked past the plush bed and over to the closet. "I'll lay your things down, and when you are ready, we will head to the spa so you can book your service."

Sally felt her face flush, unaccustomed to so much attention.

"Your friend has wonderful taste. She chose my favorite suite and my favorite spa service, the Mountain Bliss Package. You will receive a 90-minute massage, a facial, and a foot treatment. You will feel like a different person when you leave the spa."

"Trust me, I already feel like a different person."

Kelsey spent the next 30 minutes showing Sally her suite in more detail, the spa, the inn, and the grounds that were immaculate in every way.

∾

~SALLY'S JOURNAL~

Today has been one of the best days ever! It began with me waking up at Joseph's cabin, which I now call home, and having a wonderful visit with Margaret and her family. A quick visit with mom reassured me of the path I am on, which I needed more than I knew.

I then drove to this little piece of Heaven called Mary's, which I have dreamed of coming to for as long as I can remember. It is more spectacular than I dreamed possible, just like my life right now. I spent the afternoon walking the grounds, reading, and praying. There is the most perfect gazebo overlooking the valley, and I found myself more relaxed than I have ever felt in my life. I closed my eyes, leaned my head back, and fell asleep with the sun warming my skin.

I also began a new journal today. Margaret gave me a journal right before I left and encouraged me to dream and plan as I felt led. I am calling the journal my New Beginnings Journal. Now, I will cozy up in this bed fit for a queen and dream of what tomorrow might bring.

Chapter Forty-One

SALLY WOKE WITH THE SUNRISE, which was typical after more than a decade of getting up early on the farm and for the cafe. She grabbed her things and made her way to the terrace to watch the sun continue its ascent over the mountain ridge. She read through 2 Corinthians, feeling encouraged to live her life more fully in the truth that she is, indeed, a new creation.

As Sally finished her time in the Word, she felt her stomach rumble. She looked at the clock and realized the dining area should be open for the gourmet breakfast they provided. She made her way to the bathroom, which was bigger than her bedroom at her parents' house, and stepped into the luxurious shower. The aroma of vanilla and rosemary filled the air. "I could get used to this," she whispered as the warm water fell to the pebble floor.

Sally was the first to arrive at the dining area. The hostess was just as kind as Susie and Kelsey had been upon check-in. She escorted Sally to the veranda overlooking the valley and seated her at a table next to the fountain.

Breakfast was brought out in two courses, with delicious coffee and fresh-squeezed orange juice as accompaniments, but the best part of the morning was simply being quiet and still in such a beautiful setting. The dew slowly melted away, squirrels frolicked in a nearby tree, and two ladybugs casually walked along the arm of Sally's chair.

When Sally had eaten her delicious breakfast, she thanked her server and began the walk back to her suite. As she was stepping through the doors to go back into the inn, another guest bumped into her, spilling her coffee.

"Oh my gosh, I am so sorry," the young man jumped back, shielding his eyes from the sun that had limited his vision.

"It's okay, I should have noticed you. I'm sorry." Sally attempted to dab the warm coffee off her shirt.

"Let me go get something to clean that for you."

"It's okay, really. I can clean it better in my room. It's really not a big deal."

Sally looked up at the same time as the other guest.

"Austin?"

"Sally?"

"Oh, my gosh, what in the world are you doing here?" Sally felt her heart rate increase dramatically as her palms began to sweat.

"Sally, gosh, it's so good to see you. I'm here with my sister. Mom and Dad loved it here and Isabell and I needed a break after handling all the affairs after the crash, so she suggested we come here for a little getaway and to do some local hiking. What about you? Are you here with someone special?"

"No, I am alone. My time here is a gift from Margaret. I live in their second home, and her family was coming into town, so she was kind enough to treat me to a little break of my own."

"Wow, that's cool. I can't believe we ran into each other like this, and when I say ran into each other, I am being very literal."

Sally joined Austin's laughter as heat continued to rise in her face.

"Well, I would ask you to join me for breakfast as my sister is sleeping in, but it looks like you already ate."

"Yes, I just finished, but maybe I'll see you around. Enjoy your breakfast ... it's really nice to see you again."

"The pleasure is all mine," Austin replied as he took her hand and gave it a gentle squeeze.

Sally felt the warmth of his hand and felt a surge of heat rush through her body. She smiled and walked away, shaking her head in disbelief. As she passed the front desk, she paused. Susie noticed the hesitation in her demeanor.

"Can I help you with something, Sally?"

"Ummm, I was wondering if my room is still available for another night?"

"Let's see. Yes, it is. Shall I go ahead and reserve you for one more night?"

"Yes, please," Sally felt her face blush again.

"Wonderful. I know your friend will be thrilled; she was hoping you would take full advantage of the experience."

"Well, I think she just got her wish," Sally walked away with a spring in her step and a flutter in her belly.

ONCE BACK INSIDE HER SUITE, SALLY FOUND HERSELF out of sorts. She tried to read, but couldn't focus. She attempted to write in her New Beginnings Journal, but her mind felt scattered. She thought about texting Margaret, but she didn't want to interrupt their family time.

Sally sat on the edge of her bed watching Creation continue to wake beyond the tall windows, and her mind began to wander back to her high school boyfriend, Derek. Feelings of shame and regret surfaced as she stared at her reflection in the windows.

"You don't belong here ..."

She sat for several minutes staring at herself and the world beyond. Darkness crept in, and within moments, Sally felt tears rolling down her face.

Sally began wiping her face with her cheap, coffee-stained t-shirt.

She thought of Austin and his family and their wealth and their gorgeous farm and felt complete embarrassment for having any feelings for him.

"He is out of my league. Gosh, I must be stupid." Sally changed shirts, shaking her head in disbelief.

"I am such an idiot."

Sally grabbed her journal and, with her emotional baggage in tow, she headed for the gazebo.

~

~SALLY'S JOURNAL~

I thought I had worked through my issues with Derek, but I guess I was wrong. He broke down every part of me. I lost my confidence, abandoned my thoughts of college, ignored my responsibilities, and gave him all of me, well, almost all of me. When I withheld the final part of me, he ditched me after slapping me around because he said I led him on. What a jerk and a liar…

When he left me on the side of the road, in the middle of the night, miles from home, with my clothes ripped and my face bleeding, I literally wanted to die of shame.

It's a miracle that he didn't force himself on me that night because he was so angry. I think he was honestly too drunk to follow through, so he just slapped me around, yelled every horrible thing you can imagine, and then abandoned me. It took me almost two hours to walk home that night, but it took me years to forgive myself for being so stupid and for being such a coward.

Derek never apologized and made no effort to contact me after that night. He simply used me up and dumped me. He went away to college on a baseball scholarship, and his parents moved farther north, so thankfully, I never had to see him again. That summer changed the way I saw myself.

I haven't thought about Derek in a long time, but I also haven't felt romantic feelings toward anyone since then, until now.

God, please take away the feelings I have for Austin. I know it wouldn't work for a guy like him to be interested in a girl like me. I have nothing to offer him.

Chapter Forty-Two

SALLY SPENT most of the next day outside, trying to take her mind off the possibility of seeing Austin again. Her spa appointment was scheduled for 4:30 p.m. As the time approached, she took a book and sat on the bench that was nestled under a canopy of roses leading to the spa entrance. A tranquil fountain softly flowed while Sally read and reread the same page, finding it difficult to concentrate.

A lady walked toward Sally at 4:25 p.m., humming and smiling as she approached. She was an older, plump woman who smelled of lavender and peppermint.

"Well, hello, beautiful. You must be Sally."

"Yes, ma'am."

"Perfect. My name is Raquel. It is so wonderful to meet you." Raquel stretched out her round arms and pulled Sally in for a hug.

Sally felt warmth radiate from the friendly massage therapist, and her anxiety about the appointment subsided. Raquel led her through the spa, giving her a tour, which ended in the dimly lit massage room prepared especially for Sally.

"Okay, Miss Sally. I read on your intake form that you've never had a massage or a facial."

Sally lowered her eyes. "Yes, ma'am, this is my first time in a spa."

"Well, honey, you are in for a treat."

Raquel went on to explain the basic details and what to do and expect. Raquel left the room, and Sally followed the instructions and hurried under the warm blanket.

Relax, relax, relax, she thought as her body began to shake.

Raquel entered the room and noticed Sally shaking. Raquel turned down the lights and walked over to the massage table. She laid her hands on Sally's shoulders and began lightly kneading her tight muscles in rhythm with the gentle melody of the soft music that was playing.

"Miss Sally, I remember the first time I got a massage. I was so nervous, scared to death to be honest, but then the therapist began working her magic, and girl, my life was never the same." She chuckled, and Sally felt her body begin to relax.

"Miss Sally, I am going to start with the facial. If anything doesn't feel comfortable, you just let me know."

"Yes, ma'am," Sally whispered.

"Just call me Raquel, sweetie. You are making me feel 100 years old," Raquel chuckled again.

Steam filled the room, which mingled with the alluring scent of essential oils. With each stroke of Raquel's hands, Sally felt her body relax. Within minutes, her mind began to wander to Austin.

Sally began to think about the first time she'd seen Austin and how handsome he looked when he met them in the driveway, with his chiseled jaw and muscular build. She fondly remembered how confident he appeared when telling her and Margaret about his family. He had been such a gentleman, opening every door and catering to their every need.

She could picture his piercing, blue eyes when he was speaking, never once distracted by the outside world. And most of all, she could almost feel the soft yet calloused touch of his hand on hers earlier that morning.

Raquel finished the facial and began the foot treatment. Sally had never felt anything so wonderful. The smooth rhythmic motion began to unravel decades of stored pain, both physical and emotional. She lay with her eyes closed and felt her body continue to relax.

"Atta girl, let yourself go, Miss Sally, it's okay," Raquel whispered as her hands worked what felt like magic.

When Raquel had completed the foot treatment, Sally rolled over onto her stomach as instructed. With each deep stroke, Sally's emotions became more heightened. Tears fell loose from a deeper part of her soul. Sally sniffled as she tried to contain herself.

"Miss Sally, it's not unusual for a massage to bring out our deepest emotions. We women try to be so strong all the time. I think most of us have years of unresolved sadness just sitting in our souls. It's okay to cry, or yell, or whatever you may be feeling. I will work on releasing these tight muscles of yours, and you feel free to work on releasing some things that perhaps you needed to let go of a long time ago."

Sally began to cry even more. "How did you know?"

"Oh, honey, while our situations are all unique, we all hold onto lies from the world. But when we get quiet and still in our souls and our bodies, the truth begins to rise. The truth of who you really are beckons from the depths of your soul and pleads to be set free."

Sally lay still, allowing her tears to fall.

Raquel spent the next hour untangling the knots in Sally's muscles, and the Holy Spirit untangled the knots in her heart and soul. Scripture came to mind as she recalled her many times in the Word.

Remember not the former things, nor consider the things of old. Behold, I am doing a new thing ...

When the massage was over, Sally lay for several minutes as Raquel gave her time to get dressed. She felt as if she could float from the weight that she had shed. Raquel was waiting for her in the waiting area with a mug of warm tea.

Sally hugged Raquel. "I can't thank you enough. That was

truly one of the most incredible experiences of my life. Thank you."

"Miss Sally, I believe you are on the brink of something truly remarkable in your life, but honey, you've got to let go of the past before you can grab hold of the future."

Sally closed her eyes, feeling truth wash over her. She hugged Raquel again, unable to speak words that could convey the enormous amount of gratitude she felt.

"You've got this, beautiful girl. Now go live your life! Show up boldly and with full confidence that you are worthy of all that God has in store for you."

Raquel patted Sally on her shoulder and turned and walked away. Sally wrapped her hands around the warm mug, bowed her head, and thanked God for her life and for the opportunity to leave years' worth of baggage on the massage table.

SALLY WALKED BACK TO HER SUITE AND PLOPPED ON the bed, sending five of the ten lavish pillows to the floor. She laughed softly and grabbed her phone, pulling up Margaret's number to send her a text.

- I want to thank you and Mitch for treating me to this special time away. I just left the spa, and it was a spiritual experience to say the least! And, you will never believe who is here.

Margaret was working on the legacy book when her phone lit up. She responded immediately, excited to hear from Sally.

- I am so glad that you are enjoying yourself! The curiosity is killing me! Who is there?

- Austin McCain, from the interview we did at the farm.

- Oh, my gosh, what a surprise! What is he doing there?

- He and his sister came for a little getaway. Isn't that crazy?

Margaret laughed, amused at how God works in all of the details.

- I don't think crazy is the word I would use. Perhaps it's divine intervention.

Sally smiled and took a deep breath, breathing in possibility.

- Thanks again, Margaret, and please tell Mitch how much I appreciate him taking a chance on me.

- God orchestrated this, Sally, not us. We are just willing servants. Enjoy!

Sally sat up in the bed, gazed at the late afternoon sun, and fully accepted that it was time to let go of the self-doubt and worry that held her hostage. She grabbed her cutest outfit, freshened her hair and makeup, and headed to the main dining area in hopes of seeing Austin.

SALLY SPENT ALMOST TWO HOURS IN THE DINING AREA before giving up on the opportunity of seeing Austin. She had brought her journal along, so she made her way outside to the valley overlook and sat by the fire pit. The sun had already set behind the trees, which made it impossible to see the pages, so she lay her head back and listened to the sounds of the night instead.

Distant tree frogs sang in unison as fireflies created a light show that reminded Sally of being a little girl on her parents' farm. She and her mom would run around with mason jars, collecting lightning bugs and then releasing them. It was one of her favorite summertime memories.

The stars hung in the sky as an almost full moon lit the valley below. Sally began thinking about what Raquel had told her during her massage. *The truth of who you really are beckons from the depths of your soul and pleads to be set free.*

Sally had perhaps never heard a more beautiful way to say what she had felt for so long. While she hoped she would see Austin, she felt an overwhelming sense of peace. She closed her eyes, listening to the night, and was almost asleep when she heard footsteps from behind. Her eyes opened as she sat up in her chair.

"There you are, I have been looking for you everywhere." Austin pulled a chair next to hers.

"Well, I am glad you found me," Sally said just above a whisper.

"I am glad too, really glad." Sally felt a surge of adrenaline when Austin laid his hand on top of hers, giving it a squeeze.

Sally and Austin sat in the cool night air as the flames danced within the fire pit.

"Sally, why don't you tell me more about yourself. I have to admit, I have thought about you several times since we first met."

"Well, there isn't much to tell, up until I met Margaret. Working for her and Mitch has really changed my life."

"I have a feeling there is more to you than meets the eye."

Sally leaned forward, noticing his gentle smile.

"Well, let's just say I am working on that. I've spent most of my life just settling for what I thought my life was going to be. It's not that it was bad, but I guess I always knew that maybe God had more for me. That probably sounds really silly," Sally exhaled long and slow, amazed she had the courage to speak so candidly to someone she had only met briefly.

"I don't think it sounds silly at all. I think it's a really great example of how God works in our lives. I honestly felt the same thing when I started my own business."

"Really?"

"Yeah. Everyone just assumed I would work with my dad, and that would have been a good option, but I kept feeling like God wanted more from my life, too."

"Gosh, I would have never guessed that."

"I don't usually open up to people I don't know that well, but there is something about you that makes me feel really comfortable."

"I feel exactly the same way."

Austin and Sally spent the next three hours talking about life, love, and loss. They took a moonlight stroll, then had late-night hot cocoa by the fire. They laughed and they cried.

A little after midnight, Austin walked Sally back to her suite. As they said their goodbyes at the door, Austin held Sally's hand and then used his other hand to softly touch her face. Her heart quickened at his touch.

"Sally, I want you to know that I just had one of the best nights of my life. My mom and dad would have loved you."

"Thank you, Austin. It was a very special night," Sally squeezed his hand. "And that is a very sweet thing to say."

"Well, it's true, and what's not to love?"

Sally felt her face get hot again as Austin leaned in and kissed her lightly. Sally took a deep breath, breathing in the moment, breathing in life, and breathing in her future.

Austin leaned back, looking deep into her eyes. "My sister decided to go home tomorrow, but I thought I might stay the extra day, if that's okay with you?"

"That would be great."

"Perfect, I will see you in the morning. Just knock on my door when you are ready for breakfast. I am in the Treetop Suite." He pulled her in for a hug and turned and walked away. She watched him until he disappeared out of sight.

She walked into her suite, both excited and exhausted. She kicked off her shoes, climbed into bed, and began a text to Margaret.

Chapter Forty-Three

MARGARET TIPTOED down to the kitchen early the next morning. Luke and Matthew were sleeping soundly as she passed their rooms. She stopped long enough to watch them breathing in and out. "What a miracle," she whispered.

She poured herself a large glass of water and grabbed her journal. As she passed her phone, she realized she had a text message from Sally. The words stunned Margaret as she read the simple sentence multiple times.

- I think I am in love with Austin!

Margaret's fingers quickly typed a response.

- Oh, my goodness. What!?

Sally slept as Margaret paced the floor, wondering what God was up to now. Two hours later, Margaret got her answer while she was eating breakfast with her family overlooking the creek.

- I will tell you all about it when I get back to the cabin tomorrow, but in the meantime, I will say he is wonderful! We are spending the day together! You didn't set this up, did you?

Margaret laughed out loud.

- No, silly, I did not set this up. Enjoy every moment! I cannot wait to hear all about it!

Sally spent the rest of her day with Austin. Together, they explored the grounds, enjoyed lunch in a nearby grassy meadow, and ate dinner under the stars. The more Sally learned about Austin, the more she liked him, and thankfully, it seemed the feeling was mutual.

THE NEXT MORNING, AS THE SUN ROSE ABOVE THE mountains, Sally heard a soft knock at her door. She held her hands up to her chest and grinned as she asked, "Who's there?"

"It's me, Austin."

Sally's heart began to beat a little faster, and her smile broadened when she opened the door and saw his sleepy face.

"I hope it's not too early. I missed you." Austin extended his hands and took hold of hers. She felt heat rise through her body as he looked into her eyes.

"I missed you, too," she said softly.

"I thought maybe we could eat our breakfast by the fire this morning. There is a little chill in the air, and I wanted our last time together to be special."

Last time... thought Sally.

Was this just some quick weekend romance for him?

"Sure ..." Sally lowered her eyes, feeling her doubt rise.

The sunrise did not disappoint as Austin and Sally savored their breakfast and their time together. He was all smiles, while she was more reserved.

"Are you okay?" Austin laid down his coffee mug and leaned forward, locking eyes with Sally.

"I'm fine," Sally averted her eyes, feeling her palms sweat.

"Are you sure? You aren't saying much."

"I guess I'm just tired. I'm sorry."

He reached for her hand. "You don't have to apologize."

He took a deep breath and exhaled forcibly. "I want you to know that our time together has been wonderful, and just what I needed." He lifted Sally's hand to his face and gave it a soft kiss. "Thank you, Sally."

"It was a wonderful weekend," she replied, barely above a whisper.

He stood and gently pulled Sally to a standing position. He pulled her in close and wrapped his arms around her.

He released the embrace, gently kissed her, and headed toward the inn.

Sally felt as if the air had been pulled from her lungs. She watched him disappear through the trees while trying to hold back the tears.

"I knew I wasn't good enough for him," she proclaimed under her breath.

SALLY'S DRIVE BACK TO THE CABIN FELT LONG AND painful as she replayed her time with Austin over and over in her mind.

What did I do wrong?

Is it the way I look?

Is it because I'm not wealthy like him?

When she arrived, Margaret rushed out to meet her.

"Tell me all about it!"

Sally looked at Margaret, shaking her head, and allowed the tears to fall.

"Uh oh, what happened?" Margaret laid her hands on Sally's dropped shoulders.

"I don't know. I thought he liked me, but when he left this morning, he didn't even ask for my number, and he didn't say anything about us seeing each other again. I don't know what I did wrong."

"Oh, Sally, I'm sure you didn't do anything wrong. Maybe he just isn't ready for a relationship right now. You must remember that he has been through a lot recently, and he knows how to contact us, so maybe that's why he didn't get your number."

"I don't know, and right now, I don't want to think about it. I just want to focus on getting back to work and getting what you need from me done. I need to accept that it was a beautiful weekend and move on. I don't mean to sound ungrateful," Sally shrugged her shoulders while wiping the tears with her hand.

"I am so sorry, Margaret, please don't let what I just said take away from what a great gift it was to be away at such a beautiful place."

"Sally, that's life—great beauty among the ashes. Why don't we go inside, and I'll make us some lunch? Then we can head to the creek, you can tell me what happened, and we can go over the remaining few details of the book, if you feel like it."

"Thanks, Margaret. I don't really feel like talking about Austin. Let's talk about the book instead."

Chapter Forty-Four

MARGARET DECIDED to stay at the cabin until the legacy manuscript was complete and ready to hand off to Ernie. She spent her days in the loft editing and thinking of each individual and the legacy they had left behind. Her heart ached with grief as she pushed herself creatively to somehow capture the essence of each individual. She prayed for clarity and direction as her hand gracefully moved across the page.

Bill
Trudy
Miguel
Samantha
Penny
Stanley
Jeff, Joy, and Cheyenne
Chris

As Margaret looked over the list of names, she felt immense gratitude, "I still don't feel worthy of this assignment, but thank You, God, for choosing me to carry it out."

She ran her finger over the creamy page, and her mind began to wander onto a recurring thought she'd had since the day of the plane crash.

What about the other passengers on the plane? The ones who didn't get featured in a magazine, the ones who didn't contact Mitch. How did their stories end?

She reached for her journal, took a sip of her warm coffee, and began to write.

~

~*Margaret's Journal*~

I find myself once again wondering about the other passengers aboard Flight 7889. Many of the relatives and friends chose to remain private and anonymous, which is certainly understandable, but what about the others? Could it be that some individuals who perished did not leave a very desirable legacy?

We often live as if it doesn't matter what we say or do. As if we are a singular being that isn't impacting the world around us. But the truth is that a legacy is always left, the question becomes whether it shapes the world we leave in a positive or negative way.

And then there is the question of eternity. What about the passengers who had not put their trust in Jesus? What about their stories? I like to believe that in the final moments, the wonderful souls we have learned about were able to witness, pray, and share the love and saving grace of Jesus with others aboard.

This entire experience reminds me to live as if this moment could be my last. It reminds me to forgive easily and love boldly, to stay in alignment with God and His will for my life. It reminds me that I have a responsibility to live my life in a manner that impacts the world around me in a positive way and that life is fragile, yet God is still very good.

Chapter Forty-Five

MARGARET WAS in a deep sleep when her phone began to ring from across the room. She slowly made her way to the insistent ringing, her face lighting up when she realized it was Ernie.

"Hi, Ernie"

"Well, hello, young lady. How the heck are you?"

"I'm doing great. How are you?"

"I'm pretty good—feeling better now I've fully given up that retirement gig," Ernie chuckled.

"I'm glad you are doing so well. By the way, you will be happy to hear that I am almost done with the manuscript."

"That's my girl, I can't wait to get my hands on it. Just the sample pages you sent over have created quite a buzz around the publishing house."

"You should have been the one doing the interviews. It was life-changing, but so emotionally draining. I am telling you; I could have never done it without God's grace each day."

"I bet. You know me, I can't handle the emotional stuff, but the wifey insisted that I bring home the samples and we both sat and cried when we read about that first couple, ummm, Bill and Pam, I believe, were their names."

"Yes, Bill and Pam," Margaret fondly thought of Bill's grandsons climbing all over the massive treehouse.

"I feel certain you are being led by something bigger than yourself, young lady. This is a story for the ages, and I sure am glad we get to walk this path together."

"I completely agree. I was created to write this story and be a voice for these wonderful souls."

"I agree 100 percent. This is by far your most relatable work. Your words are going to change lives and set some people free. Hallelujah, praise the Lord!"

Margaret laughed as she nodded her head in agreement. "You have always been one of my biggest cheerleaders. Thank you, Ernie."

"Well, we are on the same team, so I gotta cheer big. We've got something big to celebrate, you know?"

"Yes, we do," Margaret nodded.

Margaret ended the call with Ernie and began looking for Sally. After searching the entire cabin, she walked onto the back deck to find Sally writing in her New Beginnings Journal.

Margaret quietly stepped to the edge of the deck, spotting a squirrel hopping from tree to tree. *It must be fun to be so free.*

Margaret's mind began spinning, trying to think of something fun for her and Sally to do. She continued to watch the squirrels, and then an idea came to her.

"Sally, I'm sorry to bother you, but I am wondering if you are up for a little adventure?"

"Of course, what do you have in mind?"

"There is a fantastic bookstore about 45 minutes from here. I've only been there once, but it has a cute little cafe, and lots of books and journals and other goodies that we would both love. I thought maybe we could use a break and take a day trip."

"That sounds like a great plan. Of course, I just had a break, but I'm game."

"Well, I think you need a little break from your break," Margaret winked and headed for the door.

~

ONE HOUR LATER, MARGARET AND SALLY HEADED down the mountain toward a faster pace of life. Christian music softly played as Margaret looked at each passing vehicle, thinking of the drivers, the passengers, and the legacy they were each creating in that very moment.

Do they understand how precious this day is? How valuable their lives are, and that it could all be gone in an instant?

Sally gazed out of the windows, seeing reminders of Austin everywhere she looked. The tall trees stretching up to Heaven and the white, puffy clouds that formed shapes just like the day she and Austin had lain on their backs in the soft, green grass, sharing stories of life and love.

As they approached the city, they were each grateful for new distractions. They found a cozy little table just outside the cafe and enjoyed the most perfect lattes and a nice lunch. The city was bustling with the sights and sounds of busy everyday life.

"I'm not sure how you feel about all this movement and noise, but this place helps me love the cabin even more," Margaret said as she watched two women argue about the parking spot closest to the cafe.

"Yeah, it's kind of fun to do something like this occasionally, but city life is not for me, which is yet another reason it wouldn't work with Austin. His parents may have had a farm, but he lives in the city now. That would not work. I would suffocate in the city. Not that I need a bigger reason than him not being interested in me, but you get the point."

"Sally, I think you are being rather hard on yourself. Give him a few days before you declare it hopeless. Men and women do not think alike. He is probably not pining away worrying about whether you realize how he feels about you, not because he doesn't care, but because he has a lot going on. You said he had a big meeting, and he is still dealing with his parents' will. Men tend to focus on one thing at a time."

"You're right, I am being hard on myself, and I'm complaining. I'm so sorry."

"Don't apologize, just realize that love is a process and it's complicated. Please, don't count him out yet," Margaret covered Sally's hand with her own. "You are a treasure, and he must realize that. And, if he doesn't, you deserve better, plain and simple."

"Okay," Sally sipped her coffee, remembering more of Raquel's words. *Miss Sally, I believe you are on the brink of something truly remarkable in your life, but honey, you've got to let go of the past before you can grab hold of the future.*

~

~SALLY'S JOURNAL~

Margaret and I went into the city today. We had lunch and browsed Christopher James Booksellers, which is the largest bookstore I have ever been to. It was great to get away from these never-ending thoughts about Austin.

While we were at the bookstore, Margaret purchased blank journals. She bought several so we can give them to others as we feel led, just like she did for me a few months ago.

When I journal, it quiets my busy mind and opens my heart. I have learned that I can't write about one thing while worrying about something else at the same time, and that is the beauty of journaling.

I realize it's not the journal that will hold the key to my new beginning, but, in many ways, it is the flame that often sets my heart ablaze.

I am finding forgiveness for the wounded parts of me, a genuine acceptance of God's unique plan for my life and hope for a brighter future.

Chapter Forty-Six

A SOFT RAIN was blowing against the cabin when Margaret woke from her deep sleep. *Wow, it's amazing how much better I sleep now that my life isn't a total wreck,* she thought as she pushed back the quilt.

She put on her cozy robe, sat on the edge of the bed, and opened her Bible. She read through the first chapter of Colossians, recalling a conversation she and Mitch had had about these verses a couple of days ago.

"And He is before all things, and in Him all things hold together ..."

"Thank You, Lord, for what You have done, are doing, and will do in my life. May I be like the apostles and never cease praying. May I be filled with the knowledge of Your spiritual wisdom and understanding. Help me to bear fruit in all that I do. Amen"

She laid her Bible on the bedside table and walked quietly through the cabin, grateful for the warm shelter from the rain. She filled the tea kettle and turned on the stove, watching the flames dance in the dark cabin.

With her mug in hand, Margaret sat at the kitchen table and opened her laptop. The previous night, she had read through the legacy book and felt as if she had it nailed down, except for the ending. Something about the ending just didn't read right.

Hoping for inspiration, Margaret scrolled through page after page of the manuscript.

"What am I missing? Why do I feel such a block when it comes to the ending?"

Margaret leaned back in her chair and sipped her tea. She was still sitting at the table when Sally came up the stairs. Margaret got up from the table and walked toward the kitchen.

"Good morning, I have good news," Margaret said as she rewarmed her mug. Sally's face brightened with excitement. "What?"

"Other than finding a better way to close out the book, I think *The Ripples We Create* is complete and ready to be handed off to Ernie. I worked late last night, and I got up extra early this morning, and I think we are set," Margaret breathed out a heavy sigh.

"Wow, that is so exciting, and I love the title. I'm glad you chose that one. I know you have been undecided."

"Thank you. I also really like the title, but at the end of the day, Ernie and the new publishing team may have other ideas."

"I hope not. I think you know what's best. It's your baby, after all."

Margaret smiled. "If only the publishing world were that easy," she laughed while putting her mug on the counter.

"Sally, thank you for everything you did to make this possible. I feel so extremely blessed to have you in my life." Margaret reached forward and gave Sally a hug.

Sally gently pulled away, looking Margaret in the eyes. "I feel like I am the blessed one. Helping with this book has been the most rewarding thing I have ever done."

Margaret stared back into Sally's eyes. "We have both been on the receiving end of countless blessings since we met." She patted Sally on the back and poured them both a cup of hot tea with a dash of cream.

Sally took the mug, sipping the warm, creamy liquid and feeling the steam rise. "So, what's next?"

"Well, after breakfast, I am going to head to the city. Ernie and Michelle are coming over for brunch tomorrow, and I want to get the sample manuscript printed before they arrive. I'm hoping to be inspired for a more memorable ending on the drive home, but overall, I am very pleased with our final product."

"I bet Ernie will love it. I've told my mom and dad all about the interviews, and they are both excited to read the book, which says a lot. Dad doesn't usually read anything unless it's about farming."

Sally grinned, thinking of her dad sitting in his old chair on the front porch, going through his agriculture magazines for hours.

"Well, rest assured, your sweet parents will get one of the first copies. You and I will have to autograph it for them," Margaret winked at Sally.

"Oh, my goodness, Mom will feel super special getting an autographed copy."

Sally began setting the table, shaking her head in disbelief, amazed at the wonder of her life. "You know, since I have been working with you, Mom has actually started going to the library and reading a little herself. She never took the time before, but she and Dad are both enjoying life more and more, it seems."

Margaret brought over the quiche she had prepared and smiled, "That's wonderful. It does seem like the more we live in our unique calling, the more those around can do the same."

MARGARET SET OFF ON HER DRIVE BACK TO THE CITY, and Sally began working outside the cabin. Sally took great pride in cleaning up the yard. For years, she had helped her parents around the farm, and her hard work ethic and knowledge of gardening were coming in handy. With each bush trimmed and annual pulled up, Sally felt a greater sense of belonging and usefulness. Joseph's cabin had been a place of refuge for Sally years ago, and it was still a beacon of light to her today.

Sally spent the next two hours listening to the birds sing to each other with the distant sound of the creek soothing her senses. As she pulled up the last of the dead sunflowers, her phone, which she had left on a nearby stump, began to ring.

Sally walked to her phone and didn't recognize the number on the screen. She waited a moment and then heard the voicemail alert.

"Sally, this is Kelsey from Mary's Inn and Spa. Can you please give me a call?"

That's strange. I wonder if I forgot something.

Sally hit call, hoping for a quick answer.

"Good afternoon, and thank you for calling Mary's Inn and Spa. This is Susie. How may I serve you today?"

"Hi, Susie. This is Sally. I stayed there for a few days last week, and I just received a phone call from Kelsey. I am returning her call."

"Oh, yes, dear. Please accept my apology in advance. I am so very sorry for the mix-up. Hang on, and I will let Kelsey know you are on the line. Again, please know we are all very sorry this happened."

What could she possibly be talking about? Do I owe them for something? Did I mess something up? What is going on?

Sally's heart began to race as her brows drew together.

"Sally?"

"Yes."

"This is Kelsey. I am sure you must be wondering what in the world is going on."

"Yes."

"Last week, when you were here, there was another guest who checked out on the same day as you, a Mr. McCain. You are familiar with Mr. McCain, correct?"

"Yes, if you are talking about Austin."

"Yes, Austin. When he was leaving that morning, he handed me an envelope and asked me to be sure that you received it upon check-out. Unfortunately, right after he left, I got a call from my mom explaining that my dad was being rushed to the hospital. I left in such a panic that I forgot all about the envelope. It was still in my work sweater when I got back today. Sally, I am so sorry. It was completely irresponsible of me."

"Oh, my goodness, is your dad okay?"

I need to sit down.

Sally threw off her gardening gloves and sat on the tree stump.

"Yes, Dad was released from the hospital yesterday, thank you for asking. You are so kind to ask, considering the circumstances."

"It's okay, Kelsey, I'm sure I would have done the same thing."

"So now, the question becomes how you would like to receive the envelope? We can certainly mail it through priority mail, or we can hold it for you. It is sealed, so it has remained private."

"Hmmm ... I think I will come get it, if you don't mind. I'm not that far from you. Is it okay if I head your way in about an hour?"

"That sounds great, and just let me check ... yes, Raquel just had some time open up at 5 p.m., how about we schedule you for a massage to compensate you for our mistake?"

"That's really not necessary, but I certainly appreciate the offer."

Sally stood, feeling the tension tighten in her neck and across her shoulders. "However, I would be a fool to pass up time with Raquel, if you are sure she wouldn't mind?"

"Great, then it's settled. We will see you soon. Thank you again for understanding."

"No problem," Sally answered as heat rushed through her body.

"Oh, and Sally? I am going to call Mr. McCain and let him know what happened. We feel it is incumbent on us to inform him of the situation."

"Sure, I understand."

Sally cleaned up the yard tools, took a quick shower, and dressed as her mind raced, wondering what was inside the envelope.

Chapter Forty-Seven

THIRTY MINUTES after the call from Mary's, Sally began making her way back to the place she had found love. The afternoon sun was dropping behind the trees as her favorite worship song seemed to urge her on.

Sally parked her car, took a deep breath, and walked in, spotting Kelsey by the fireplace speaking with other guests. Kelsey saw Sally and waved, gesturing with her hand that she would be with her soon.

Susie came out from behind the desk and greeted Sally. "I am so sorry this happened. I don't think we have ever had another guest leave an envelope for someone. I sure hope it wasn't a time-sensitive issue."

"I'm sure it's fine. I'm just glad Kelsey's dad is okay."

"You are such a sweet girl. I'm sorry you had to drive back, but I am glad we got to see you again so soon."

Susie patted Sally on her shoulder and smiled a deep smile. "Kelsey will be with you soon." She walked back to the desk, leaving Sally standing in the foyer with her palms sweaty and her heart thumping.

Kelsey was still speaking with the guests when Raquel came walking down the hall.

Raquel saw Sally and sped up to give her a big hug. "Good news, beautiful lady, I finished early. I can see you now."

Sally felt herself shrink back from the warm embrace, "Ummm, actually, I am waiting for Kelsey at the moment—she has something for me."

"Oh, okay, I will be in my room when you get done. It feels like you could use a little relaxation."

"More than you know."

Kelsey spent another five minutes conversing with the guests. The longer Sally waited, the faster her heart seemed to beat. Sweat began to bead on her forehead. She scanned the room, taking in the details and trying to distract herself from feeling the wave of nausea that surfaced.

Her mind raced.

She took a deep cleansing breath, coaching herself from within.

Calm down.

Kelsey began walking toward Sally, looking concerned.

"I am so sorry that took so long. Are you okay? You look really pale."

Sally swallowed hard. "I'm okay. I guess I am just a little anxious about what this is all about."

"Oh, Sally, I really am sorry. It's unlike me to be so irresponsible."

"It's okay, I promise. I am sorry to rush off, but I need to get going. Raquel is waiting on me. I probably should have passed on the massage," Sally bit her lip and tried to swallow the lump in her throat.

"Of course. Here you go," Kelsey handed the envelope to Sally. "Thank you for being so kind and understanding. Please enjoy the massage, it's the least we could do."

Sally walked out of the inn and toward the spa with the envelope clutched to her chest.

Should I read it now or wait? I don't know what I should do ...

"Miss Sally, come on over, I am ready," Raquel called out when she saw Sally from across the lawn.

I guess that's my answer.

Sally walked into the treatment room, carefully placed the envelope in her purse, and hesitatingly lowered herself onto the massage table. Raquel began the service with Sally lying on her stomach. Her eyes, which were open and alert, peeked through the massage table. Her heart was still racing when Raquel began rubbing her back.

"Sally, honey, are you okay? You feel like you are carrying the weight of the world in these tight muscles of yours."

Sally closed her eyes, trying to relax and ignoring the question at hand.

"Miss Sally? Did you hear me?"

Frustrated, Sally answered, "Yes, I heard you. I just don't feel like responding."

Raquel continued the rhythmic movements, "Okay, I'm sorry."

Sally felt tears escaping from her eyes, dropping through the hole in the massage table. "Can we please not talk?"

"Sure, honey, if that's what you need today. I won't say another word. You just lie there and try to relax. But first, do you need a tissue?"

"Yes, please ."

Sally had been scheduled for a complimentary 90-minute massage. At the 33-minute mark, when she was asked to flip onto her back, Sally sat up, pulling the sheet up as she spoke, "Raquel, I am really sorry for how I spoke to you. I drove back up here today because someone that I think I love left me an envelope the last time we were here. I didn't even know about the envelope until today. I assumed he wasn't interested in me this whole time because he so casually left on our last morning together."

Raquel hung on every word, reaching to turn down the soft music.

"Right before I walked in here, Kelsey gave me the envelope he left for me, and I have no idea what it says. Raquel, I have never felt this way about anyone ..." Sally pulled the sheet up to her face as tears soaked through the soft, white fabric.

"Oh, Sally, dear one. Where is the envelope now?"

"It's in my purse."

"Here is what we are going to do. I am going to step out and let you get dressed. You can either stay in here or go somewhere else, but Sally, you need to see what's in that envelope. I will tell the girls to comp you another massage for a day that is better for you."

"Okay, thank you so much."

"And Sally, if you need me, I will be in the spa's reception area. Everyone else has gone for the day, so you yell for me if you need me. Okay?"

"Okay, and Raquel?"

"Yes, lovey?"

"Thank you."

"Why, of course. Now, you take your time." Raquel closed the door behind her.

Sally pulled the sheet around her and hurried to her clothes.

She took the letter out of her purse and sat on the plush chair in the corner of the massage room. She held her breath as she cautiously peeled back the seal of the envelope. She closed her eyes as she unfolded the paper.

When she opened her eyes, she was met with pristine handwriting that seemed to flow onto the page. With a deep breath, she began to read.

Dear Sally,

I am writing to you today because I have been awake all night thinking of you, and I feel as if I might be a coward in the morning and pass on the opportunity to tell you how I feel.

When I first met you at my parents' farm, I felt broken in every way. I only did the interview because my sister asked me to, not because I wanted to. I put on a strong front because that's what I was taught to do, but truthfully, I was angry at God. I was angry that my parents' lives were cut short and even more angry that my baby sister is gone.

My anger began to diminish when I talked to Mitch about the interview. He heard me, he listened, and he cared. He began my healing process. And then, when you and Margaret showed up for the actual interview, I felt joy and peace for the first time in weeks. Margaret was so kind and loving, and you simply amazed me. Your gentleness, your humility, and your beauty—it all touched me in a way that I never knew was possible.

I thought of you every day after we met, but I didn't want to interrupt the process of you and Margaret writing the book. I was also worried that perhaps I fell for you because of my grief.

When I arrived here at Mary's, I felt my mom and dad everywhere I looked. I saw the many places they had sat over the years because the photos are scattered throughout their home. I felt their love, and I thought of you. I longed to see you, to call you, to hear your voice again.

And then, I opened the door and there you were. You were just as radiant as the day I met you. I literally thanked God on the spot when I saw you. I felt terrible when I was with my sister that day, because all I could think of was you.

The first evening we shared was the most vulnerable and honest I have ever been with anyone in my life. I showed you the real me. Our next day together confirmed my feelings for you even more.

This morning, I will tell you goodbye. I am not good at good-byes. I am not good at expressing how I feel, so this letter will serve as my goodbye. It will also serve as something more.

I have never met anyone in my entire life who makes me feel the way you make me feel. I realize we just met, but I love you, and I want you in my life.

If you aren't interested in a relationship, I understand. I will be moving back to my parents' farm in the next couple of weeks, so please feel free to call me if you are interested in seeing where this could lead. If I don't hear back from you, I will know that is your answer. Thank you for opening my heart and for giving me hope.

With all my love,

Austin

Sally held the letter in her hand, shaking from head to toe. She stood and reached for her phone. She paused as she began to dial Austin's number, which he had written at the bottom of the letter.

Wait, she heard her soul whisper.

"Wait? I don't want to wait," she said aloud in the quiet room, which was engulfed in the scent of lavender.

Her hesitation irritated her, but she urged herself to put her phone away. She picked up her purse and headed for the door.

Raquel was sitting quietly reading a magazine when Sally walked into the reception area.

"Raquel, thank you again."

"My pleasure. You're smiling, so I hope that's a good sign."

"He says he loves me too, but this letter is almost a week old, so I hope he hasn't changed his mind."

"I feel certain he's not changed his mind. Love has a way of waiting things out."

"Thanks, Raquel. I appreciate you so much."

They walked toward each other and embraced in a warm hug. Sally became enveloped in Raquel's plump arms and deep concern.

"Listen, honey, if he is romantic enough to leave you a love letter, he's a keeper. Now, you go get that man of yours, and next time, you tell me all about him."

Sally walked out of the spa and started walking toward her car, but she found herself drawn to the gazebo instead. She made her way to the built-in bench with her thoughts melting together. She opened the letter and re-read it several times. She hung on each word, feeling the weight of Austin's affection toward her. She felt a surge of warmth pass through her body as she reread the words *I love you and I want you in my life.*

As the sun began to descend behind the trees, Sally folded the letter and carefully put it back in her purse. She listened to the sound of the evening and closed her eyes, considering the miracle of it all.

I should call him now, while I am here in this perfect place.

Sally reached for her phone but stopped when she heard footsteps behind her. She sat motionless, hoping the person would see her and choose another spot. The steps got closer and closer, and then she heard his voice.

"Sally?"

Sally's heart skipped a beat.

Oh, my gosh, is that him?

Sally stood and turned around. "Austin, what are you doing here?"

"Kelsey called me and told me what happened. She also told me that you were driving back to get the letter, and I naively assumed that meant you cared enough about me to want to know what was inside that envelope. Am I right?"

"Yes ..."

"I honestly don't have any expectations of you, but I had to tell you in person that I think you are amazing." He stepped in closer, sweeping her hair away from her face.

"Sally, you have taught me how to love. And whether or not you love me back, I'm grateful that I now know what real love feels like. I am grateful that my anger is gone and that I get a chance to live a life my parents and sister would be proud of. And mostly, Sally, I am grateful that when you walked through my parents' door for the first time, you also walked into my heart."

Sally stood gazing into Austin's eyes. She wanted to think of something wonderful and poetic to say, but the words hung in her throat as she moved in even closer. "Austin McCain, I love you, too," Sally whispered as he wrapped his arms around her.

The sun dropped behind the trees as dusk settled onto the

land. A new beginning was erupting as the first stars of the night could be seen in the distance, and the beating hearts of new lovers echoed over the valley.

Love wins and waits, Sally thought as she breathed in her very own New Beginning.

Chapter Forty-Eight

ERNIE AND HIS WIFE, Michelle, let themselves in when they arrived at Mitch and Margaret's home in the city. Margaret rushed to greet them.

"Hope you don't mind that we didn't knock. You know Ernie —he thinks he's part of the family," Michelle said. She hugged Margaret while shaking her head and handing Margaret a bottle of champagne. "This is to celebrate the completion of your newest book and us being reunited."

"You guys are like family, so always feel free to come on in. And thank you for the lovely bottle of champagne."

Ernie wrapped his arms around Margaret, squeezing her tight. "So, how does it feel to have completed another masterpiece?"

"It feels great, but I have to admit, I still feel like I haven't found a great way to end the book. I can't quite put my finger on it."

"Well, if anyone can figure it out, you can." Ernie gave her a swift pat on the back.

Margaret smiled, feeling completely at home with Ernie and Michelle. "Mitch is out back with the boys. I just got a text from Sally before you walked in, so I need to make a really quick phone call, and then I will join you guys."

Margaret walked up to her bedroom to call Sally, who answered on the first ring.

"Hey Margaret, I'm sorry to bother you, but I had to call you. You are never going to believe what happened."

"You are never a bother. What's going on?"

"I got a call from Mary's Inn yesterday after you left. Austin had left me a letter the morning he checked out, and they accidentally forgot to give it to me. Kelsey at Mary's realized the mistake and called me, so I went back and got the letter. Margaret, you are never going to believe this. It was a letter telling me that he loves me. And to top it off, Mary's called Austin too, and he drove here to see me."

"Oh, my gosh, I knew it. I knew he had feelings for you!"

Sally stood looking over the valley from the gazebo at Mary's, watching an elderly couple walk hand in hand in the distance. She smiled, feeling grateful to be starting her own love story.

"I feel like I am living in some kind of real-life fairy tale. It was pretty late in the evening when we met up, so Austin checked, and they happened to have two suites available, so we stayed the night. We were up until 2 a.m. talking, then back up at 7 a.m. for breakfast and a hike. We are both leaving soon; he has a business meeting later this afternoon."

"Sally, this is beyond amazing. I have never known anyone who deserves happiness more than you."

"Thank you. All of the credit goes to you for giving me the opportunity to meet such a wonderful guy like Austin."

"You did all the work, Sally, not me. I simply shared lessons that I have learned along the way. I don't deserve any credit."

Margaret glanced out of the bedroom window, seeing her family and Ernie down below, and smiled, feeling complete peace wash over her body. She moved to her bed, leaning back into the plush pillows that held her healthy, happy body. "So, now what? How did you guys leave it?"

"We both agreed we should take it slow and see where it goes. Austin is actually in the process of moving back to his parents' house. He is going to take over the farm, run his business from there, and move out of the city. Can you believe it? It's like God is working out every detail."

"Yes, He is, Sally. Yes, He is."

Margaret and Sally ended the call as Ernie and Mitch walked back inside, filling the home with deep laughter. Margaret closed her eyes and offered a brief prayer of thanks.

Margaret made her way to the upstairs landing, excited to tell Mitch about Sally, but then paused, deciding it could wait.

Be in this moment, she thought to herself as she looked into the great room with her boys lounging on the sofa, Mitch and Ernie having a grand time in the kitchen, and Michelle making herself at home as she cut fruit.

Ernie noticed Margaret coming down the stairs. "Okay, young lady. Let me see it. You have made me wait long enough. Let's see that manuscript."

Margaret laughed, "Long enough, Ernie? Need I remind you that I just began this project a few weeks ago? If I recall, that is about six months faster than any other book I have ever completed, and this one involved me interviewing grieving families. Give a girl a break."

"Okay, okay, you know I am just eager to get the tear-fest going for the wifey," Ernie chuckled.

"Don't let him fool you. He is just as eager to get the tissues out for this story as I am," Michelle said, while giving her husband a little wink.

"Well, I am honored by your sincere interest," Margaret walked to her worn, leather satchel that Mitch had given her when she became an author. All eyes were on her as she pulled out *The Ripples We Create*.

"Here you go."

Ernie began thumbing through the manuscript. "Joking aside, I am really proud of you, Margaret. You have been through a lot. I feel truly honored to be helping you get this into the world. This may be your best work yet."

"Thanks, Ernie. I think you are right by saying it may be my best work yet. It felt like a divine assignment."

Ernie spent the day visiting with Margaret and her family while skim-reading the manuscript. His loud, joyful demeanor grew quieter as he read each story, in awe of the many facets of each legacy that were so eloquently portrayed. His eyes became fixed on the manuscript, and his senses elevated.

"This book you have written is going to change lives, young lady. A lot of lives."

Margaret was standing with a mug of hot tea in her hand, leaning against the back of Mitch's chair.

"Mom is always changing lives. That seems to be her special-ty." Luke stood to hug his mom. Matthew stood and joined in.

"Aw, you boys are the sweetest." Michelle looked at Ernie, who nodded his head in agreement.

Ernie smiled and laid the manuscript down. "Margaret, I have never read anything like this. You really outdid yourself."

"I just got out of the way and allowed God to lead. I embraced the pain and the heartache of each family as I sought to love mine more and more." She hugged her boys tight. "Perhaps it's my life that's changed the most ..."

Chapter Forty-Nine

THE SUN BROKE through the trees, spilling light into the cabin. As Sally said her morning prayers, her mind began to wander to Austin.

She walked to the loft to get a new journal. Since she and Margaret had placed the journals in the nook of the desk, she had been praying about who should be the first to receive one. Her quiet time that morning kept pulling her to Austin. His love letter to her had demonstrated his ability to express himself through writing. Perhaps a journal would be an excellent opportunity for him to further release his grief and move forward in his life after the untimely death of his family.

As she entered the loft, she noticed a single ray of sunshine illuminating the desk. She picked up a soft, tan leather-bound journal, took a pen, and inscribed what her soul was pouring forth:

For everything there is a season.
May this be your season to love.
Sally

Sally closed the journal and laid it back on the desk. She scanned the other books, noticing the old Bible. She touched the worn spine and ran her fingers over the words *Holy Bible.*

"Gosh, I can't believe I've never really looked at this," she whispered.

Sally picked up the tattered Bible, walked over to the chair, and sat, beginning to thumb through the aged pages cautiously. She flipped to her daddy's favorite passage, the 23rd Psalm, and was surprised to find an envelope placed between the pages. The envelope looked new in comparison to the Bible and had the words, *May this Bless your Life,* written in rather messy hand-writing.

"Hmmm, I wonder what this is?"

Sally went downstairs with the Bible carefully tucked under her arm and called Margaret.

"Hello."

"Hey, Margaret. You got a minute?"

"I'm actually with Ernie at the publishers, but we haven't gone in yet. What's up?"

"Okay, I'll be quick. I went into the loft to get a blank journal for Austin, and I noticed that old Bible. I knew it was there, but I've never actually looked at it. I can't explain it, but I felt drawn to it today. I know that sounds weird, but anyway, I opened it to get a better look, and there is a new-looking envelope in the Bible that says, *May this bless your Life.* I was just curious if you knew anything about it?"

"Hmmm, I don't know anything about the envelope. The Bible was there when we bought the cabin. The previous owner never mentioned it, but I have admired it since I first got to the cabin earlier this summer. I've never actually looked in it myself. Feel free to open the envelope. You can let me know what it says later."

"Are you sure you don't want me to wait on you to open it?"

"I'm sure. You have a much longer history with the cabin than I do, so go ahead, I really don't mind. I am excited to know what it says."

"Okay, thanks, Margaret. I'll let you know. Y'all have a great day."

Sally walked down the loft stairs and sat on the couch. She traced one finger along the edge of the envelope.

Something doesn't feel right about opening this in here ... her soul whispered.

She paused, unsure what her hesitation was about. She sat quietly, her anxiety growing.

"Hmmm ... how about outside?" she asked herself, wondering why this felt like such a big deal.

Peace washed over her, so she placed the mysterious envelope back inside the old Bible and headed for the creek. She breathed in the cool morning air as she descended the steps.

A fluffy-tailed chipmunk scurried past her, and songbirds sang their morning songs. She laid the Bible in the chair beside her and leaned back, allowing the rushing water to calm her senses further.

Sally noticed the hammock and thought of Mitch and Margaret lying there and the love they shared. She noticed a brilliant red cardinal with its mate on a nearby branch and thought of her parents, ever faithful to each other. She noticed the tall trees that swayed ever so slightly and thought of Austin and their time lying in the soft green grass under the trees at Mary's as they opened their hearts to one another.

After several moments, Sally sat up and opened the Bible. She ran her fingers under the flap of the envelope, which had been sealed. She took a deep breath and, very carefully unfolded the paper.

Chapter Fifty

To WHOMEVER HAS OPENED my dear Bible,

Thank you for opening this cherished treasure of mine. It may seem strange that I would type this letter to an unknown reader, but I felt a burden to do so, and I try to never ignore these spirit-filled promptings.

I want to tell you a little about myself, the cabin, and this Bible. First, my name is Joseph Porter, and as of today, I am 91 years old. I've lived a good, full life, which is why I am at peace knowing my time is running out.

I'm typing this letter during my last days. The doctors say that my heart is just about done pumping in this old body of mine, and they want to do surgery immediately, but I've decided against surgery. I honestly don't feel strong enough to withstand the invasive plan the doctors have proposed, and most likely, it would not end well. I have decided that a cold, dreary hospital is not where I want to take my last breath. I've spent the last 20 years of my life here in this town and in this cabin, and it's here I want to die.

I was married to the same beautiful woman for 49 years; we almost made it to 50 years, but my bride just couldn't hang on after years of poor health. I knew she was suffering, and I needed to let her go, but I have never stopped loving her or missing her. However, if you are reading this, it means that she and I have been reunited and all is well.

We had one son, who turned out to be a fine man with a heart of gold and a burning desire to lead other people to Jesus. He certainly has made me and his mother proud. He already knows my plan for this Bible, so don't feel like you need to find him. My desire is that this Bible would stay with the cabin.

Speaking of the cabin, I hope that the impact this special place has on your life is as meaningful as the impact it has had on my life. I built this cabin with the help of some of the local men 20 years ago. You will find some old pictures from across the years tucked away in the back of the Bible.

My bride and I moved here from Tennessee, where we both grew up and started our lives together. Shortly after we moved into the cabin, she became ill, and I spent the next decade caring for her and creating a place that she would enjoy waking up to each day. The past ten years, I continued caring for the cabin and the property, longing for the day that I could be reunited with my beautiful bride.

Now, about this Bible. My father was a preacher at a small church in East Tennessee. He and my mother were very poor as far as finances went, but they were the richest people I ever knew when it came to what really mattered. The Bible you found this letter in was my father's. His mother, my grandmother, gave it to him when he took on his first role as a young preacher. My father once told me that his mother used all their savings that year to purchase this Bible. It was undoubtedly the best investment she ever made.

My father used this Bible for over 50 years in every sermon he taught, every wedding and funeral he officiated, and every late-night visit to the homes of hurting people. But most of all, my father used this Bible to get to know Jesus.

When my father passed away, I received this Bible from my mother with instructions to carry on my dad's legacy of loving people and turning hearts to Jesus. Even though I was never a preacher, I took my mother's instructions very seriously and did the best I could to carry out my father's legacy of love and service to others.

I have been here on this Earth for nine decades and have seen many things change and many things come and go, but the Word of God remains the same and is a haven for all who dare to immerse themselves in it. I can wholeheartedly say that the Word of God is alive, it is true, and it will change your life.

In my 91 years, I have experienced a fair amount of heartache, but I have had even more reason to rejoice. Because of the promises and power of the words in this Bible, I have been able to live each season of my life with purpose as my friend and grace as my ally. Sure, I've had some doubts along the way, and I have made a lot of mistakes, but we all do; even the disciples who walked with Jesus struggled.

I have experienced God working miracles that you would not believe, and I have also experienced profound grace and peace when the miracles I prayed for did not occur. Life is this way, and so is our road to Heaven.

I invite you to open this daily or another Bible of your choosing. I would be pleased if this stayed in the cabin, but ultimately, the choice is yours. The tear-stained pages and the notes written throughout are a combination of mine and my father's. I often journal while reading my Bible, and those journals are now in the possession of our son. I often wrote out my prayers, and a few of those prayers are scribbled in the back. I pray they bless you.

My words matter not in comparison to the words within the pages of this great collection of books, which, combined, give us the Holy Word of God. Yet, I leave you with these final thoughts.

You are loved more than you will ever know by a God that is greater than you can ever imagine.

You need a Savior, and His name is Jesus. You need to trust that He died for you, was buried, and rose again, and that He is alive forever.

Your sins have been forgiven completely, and you do not need to carry shame or guilt if you accept Christ's forgiveness and make Him Lord of your life. In this same way, forgive others completely. Don't live your life shackled to bitterness and hate.

The devil is a liar, and so is fear.

Your life matters, and you have a purpose greater than you give yourself credit for. I urge you to love and serve others more than yourself.

Do not waste what you have been given. Use your talents, your gifts, and your wealth for things that have lasting value.

Live. Time moves too fast nowadays. Don't wait for life to get better to start living. Live now.

And, lastly, love. Love with everything that you have within you, and then love some more. After all, the greatest gift of them all is love.

In His unending grace,

Joseph

With tears running down her face, Sally leaned forward in her chair, laying the letter back into the Bible where she had found it. Through her tears, she noticed the underlined portions of the Psalm,

The Lord is my Shepherd
I shall not want.
He restores my soul.
I will fear no evil.
My cup overflows.
Surely goodness and mercy shall follow me all the days of my life.

Sally stood and gently laid the Bible in the chair. She kicked off her sandals and stepped her bare feet into the creek. She picked up a single pebble and dropped it into the water, watching a ripple emerge across the surface, radiating out as the pebble sank deeper. Sally smiled, excited to see how far-reaching the ripple in her own life would be.

As she stepped out of the water, she picked up her phone and sent a simple text to Margaret.

- I just found the perfect ending to the book.

THE END.

Or perhaps it's a New Beginning, the choice is yours.

Discussion Questions

1. At the beginning of the novel, we find Margaret at the end of her rope. Why do you think she finds herself in such a state of despair? Can you relate to these feelings?

2. When Margaret meets Sally at the cafe, Margaret temporarily dismisses her feelings of hopelessness. Why do you think that is? Have people in your life helped you see things in a brighter way?

3. When Margaret's family learns the truth about the contract, they become distant. Do you think it was fair of them to treat her this way?

4. The night before Margaret is scheduled to leave town, she experiences a moment of total surrender. This experience ultimately saves her life. Has there ever been a time in your life when you have surrendered? If so, what did you gain from surrendering?

5. When Margaret's family learns of the plane crash, they are overjoyed that she chooses to stay home and honor her commitment instead of going on the trip. Forgiveness isn't always that easy; however, it frees both the person who needs forgiving and the person

who is forgiving. Do you have stories of forgiveness in your life? Is there someone you need to forgive still today or ask forgiveness from?

6. When Sally is offered the opportunity to become Margaret's assistant and the caretaker of the cabin, she is filled with doubt and concern about whether she is capable or worthy of such an opportunity. Have you ever struggled with those same feelings?

7. Sally accepts the opportunity to become Margaret's assistant and caretaker of the cabin. Her doubts don't magically end. However, she continually pushes forward to glorify God with her life. Is there a time in your life that you have done the same? Perhaps there is an opportunity waiting on you right now.

8. The legacy stories are shining examples of how every life matters. Which of these stories do you most resonate with and why?

- Bill, the grandfather who was a dreamer, yet completely grounded.
- Penny, the mom, who was gracious and loving enough to stand for truth.
- Trudy, who showered her town with love, and her life led her husband to Jesus.
- Stanley, quiet wonderful Stanley, who lived a life of service and devotion to the Lord.
- Miguel, who demonstrated that your life can very well save the life of someone else.
- The McCain family, who lived bold, and fully awake .
- Samantha, who continued to shine brightly even in the trenches of life.
- Chris, who fought the good fight, even when facing death

9. Let's pretend for a moment that your life is a novel, and you are the main character. How are you showing up in your story?

10. There will come a time when all our lives on this earth will end. My prayer is that you will meet Jesus and He is able to say, "Well done, my good and faithful servant." When that happens, what do you want your legacy to be?

Quotes from your favorite characters

Bill Baker: "God, go before us." "Chase your dreams, but never forget who should be leading the way."

Penny Cartwright: "Remember who you are, and whose you are." "Go be the light that God has created you to be."

Miguel Martinez: "You are loved; God has a plan for your life."

Trudy Bailey: "It's okay, God knows your heart."

Jeff & Joy McCain: "Show up strong"

Cheyenne Heard McCain: "Smile, God loves you."

Stanley Reed: "Always remember God is good."

Samantha Cunningham: "YES, GOD can make me new!"

Chris Johnson: "You never know what people are going through, and sometimes the people with the biggest smiles are struggling the most, so be kind."

Joseph Porter: "Love with everything that you have within you and then love some more."

Ernie: "You need to write a new story for your life and then live it."

Raquel, massage therapist: "Now go live your life, show up boldly and with full confidence that you are worthy of all that God has in store for you."

A Letter from Margaret and Sally

As we worked on completing 'The Ripples we Create", we became increasingly aware of the power of love. Love is a place deep inside our souls. We are born to love and created out of the love God has for each of us. As a baby, we feel the warm embrace of our parents' love, and if we are fortunate that love continues throughout our life as our bodies grow and our lives evolve. We experience the love of our spouses, our extended family and our friends, as love takes on a deeper meaning with each year that passes.

Love can be found anywhere in which a person is willing to step out of their selves and see another person as God sees them, flawed, yet chosen. We have been told that love is an emotion, and sometimes it is, but more often love is a choice, an action.

Love is being there, even when it's hard. Love is staying when the fun has ended, yet the covenant remains. Love is often inconvenient and painful and devastating.

Love is a cross, a bloody, messy cross. But, love is also light bursting through an empty tomb with a risen Savior inviting you into His redemptive plan.

Love finds purpose, creates connection and can be felt in a

warm embrace and deep, meaningful intimacy. Love conquers all, believes in all and can, and will change your life.

Love when it's hard. Love when it's easy.

Love in the good times. Love in the bad times.

Love when it feels good. And love when it hurts.

Love until you laugh. Love until you cry.

Love because He first loved us.

Wishing you much love in your journey,

Margaret and Sally

Acknowledgments

To my husband, Tim who read and re-read the manuscript and helped tirelessly with edits. Your support and love helped me bring this labor-of-love to the finish line. I'm so grateful to be on this journey with you. I love you, always and forever.

To my son Nate, who has patiently supported my dream of becoming an author, while he was growing into a wonderful young man; I hope you feel my love in the pages of this book. Shine bright, my son, and keep your eyes on the Lord.

To our oldest son, Nick, and our grandsons, Christopher and James, I love you and I'm so grateful that God brought you into my life.

To, Breanna, my daughter-in-law, thank you for believing in me when I didn't believe in myself. Thank you for reminding me that this story mattered and that I was the person called to write it. Your early read of the novel and heartfelt reaction meant the world to me.

To my Mom and Dad, thank you for being a wonderful example of working hard and serving others. I hope this faith-filled, small-town story honors you. To my sisters, Teresa and Ann, thank you for loving me in every season of my life.

To the early readers, who I also call friends - Marie, Rebekah, Melanie, Sue, Kim, Amanda and many more who read a chapter here or there, thank you! Thank you for your honesty and your ongoing encouragement. I am so grateful for you.

To Tim and Nichelle Stewart, thank you for allowing me to share the story of your daughter, Cheyenne Heard, who was the inspiration for Cheyenne in the story. May her legacy live on in the pages of this book, as it does in the hearts of so many.

To Wendi Spain Johnson, thank you for allowing me to share the story of your husband, my friend, Chris Johnson, who was the inspiration for Chris in the story. I pray these words brings you a bit of joy and honors Chris and his legacy.

To my editor, Gill McDonald, and my cover designer, Hannah Linder, thank you for helping me make The Ripple the best it could be. Your patience and guidance were invaluable and appreciated more than you know.

To my new friend and fellow author, Hope Welborn, thank you for your direction and kindness. You are proof that the writing community is full of loving, generous people.

To The Ripple Launch Team, your encouragement and participation meant so much. What a blessing you have been in this final leg of the process. I appreciate you.

To every friend, client, and follower who has been an encouragement, thank you! Every kind word, prayer and generous gesture helped me keep going.

To Lucille's Mountaintop Inn and Spa in Santee Nacoochee, Georgia and the lovely owner, April, thank you for allowing me the opportunity to tour this beautiful destination, which became the inspiration for Mary's Inn & Spa.

To the many professionals in the publishing industry that have guided me to be my best. Rory and AJ Vaden and the team at Brand Builders, thank you for putting me in the room, so to speak, with others who weren't afraid to chase their dreams such as Kaylee, Shawna Marie, Lori, Leigh-Leigh and Peggy Sue, it's been a pleasure.

And lastly, but certainly not least, thank you to my Savior, Jesus Christ for rescuing me time and time again. I'll never understand on the side of heaven, why You chose me to write this lovely book. But, I can't deny the calling, so thank You for giving me the strength and the words to carry it out. May You be glorified in all that I do.

About the Author

Kathy Neighbors is known for her ability to seamlessly blend small-town fiction and faith to inspire and enlighten her readers. As a lifelong entrepreneur in the beauty and fitness industries, Kathy brings her love of encouraging and serving others to the keyboard, where she creates stories and blogs that touch the heart and nourish the soul.

Kathy spends her days giving back to her community and her free time writing, reading, hiking, and focusing on her family.

Join her on this beautiful journey @ kathyneighbors.com for free resources and extra portions of light and love.

Notes